A
WITCH
AND HER
DRAGON

A WITCH
AND HER
DRAGON

Cover Design: Enchanted Ink Publishing
Editing: Enchanted Ink Publishing
Book Design and Typesetting: Enchanted Ink Publishing

The text type was set in Garamond Premier Pro

ISBN: 978-1-7326782-7-9 (Paperback)

Thank you for your support of the author's rights.

Instagram: @emberlywyndham

THERE IS NO WORLD IN WHICH I'LL LET
ANYONE TAKE ALINA FROM ME.

I'D GIVE MY LAST SCALE TO SAVE HER.

EMBERLY WYNDHAM

A WITCH
AND HER
DRAGON

COVEN CREST ACADEMY

1

CHAPTER 1
ALINA

THE MAGNOLIA TREES ARE IN FULL BLOOM, their white-and-pink blossoms providing cheerful color to the garden. It was a long, cold winter, and spring has finally arrived. Which means I'm outdoors again, breathing in the flower-scented air and feeling my boots squish into the rain-soaked earth. Just last night, it poured, the droplets striking the windows in my chambers loudly enough to drown out the sound of the fires crackling in the hearths.

A crisp breeze twirls through the garden, sending a tendril of wavy hair dancing in front of my eyes. But my focus is beyond that, on the target one of the guards set up for me. Straw bursts from the holes in the human-shaped dummy, and a few pieces fall to the wet earth, only to be swept away with another burst of chill air.

I take a breath and lift my longbow, drawing the bowstring back until my thumb rests just near the corner of my mouth. The fletching tickles my skin as I breathe out slowly, adjusting my aim just slightly to account for the breeze still making the magnolia trees sway.

Then I release my arrow, letting the bowstring roll off my fingertips.

The arrow flies with a soft whistle and embeds itself into the dummy—right in the middle of the chest.

Lowering my longbow, I smile. At my feet, my spirit companion, Yuki, lets out an approving whine. I kneel to scratch the Arctic fox behind his ears.

"What do you think?" I ask.

He flicks his gaze to the dummy, which is now peppered with arrows. "Better. Your aim is improving." The breeze dances through his long white hair, making it ripple like an ocean tide.

"Your Highness," calls a voice from behind me.

I stand and turn to find my lady-in-waiting, Ms. Florence Fairhaven, moving toward me at a rapid pace. She holds her skirts up with one hand, keeping them clear of the mud, and in the other is an envelope.

It looks like a thick envelope. An important envelope.

My breath catches.

"Can you take this, please?" I say, holding my longbow out to the guard currently overseeing me. I don't know his name—the knights generally have very little to do with me apart from standing guard outside whatever room I'm in or accompanying me whenever I leave the castle, like statues with ever-watching eyes but very little to say. He steps forward and takes the bow from my hands with a sharp nod of his head, and once I'm free of it, I hurry to meet Ms. Fairhaven, Yuki trotting along beside me—though he's careful to avoid the muddy puddles.

"Is that . . . ?" I ask breathlessly as I come to stand before her.

"Correspondence from Coven Crest Academy," Ms. Fairhaven says. She holds the letter out to me, her lips pulling into a small smile, and I take the envelope with trembling fingers.

The purple wax seal—depicting the phases of the moon—is unbroken, and the envelope is thick. My heart pounds in my chest. Slowly, frost begins to creep from my fingertips, crawling across the parchment.

I'm letting my fear get the better of me.

Quickly, I banish the ice, then look up and meet Ms. Fairhaven's soft brown eyes.

"Go on, then," she says, clasping her hands before her and giving me an encouraging smile. "We'll not know until we know."

I bite my lip. Yuki presses himself against my calf, his presence an anchor of calm.

Then, though my hands still shake, I use my magic to create an ice blade at the tip of my finger and run it through the wax seal, slicing it open.

Inside is a carefully folded letter. I ease it from the envelope and unfold the parchment.

Dear Princess Alina Ravenscroft,

It is with the utmost delight and honor that we extend

to you this official letter of acceptance to Coven Crest Academy for the upcoming academic year. After careful consideration of your application, we are thrilled to welcome you as a member of our distinguished student body.

Your unique talents and dedication to the study of the arcane arts have impressed our faculty, and we have no doubt that you will bring a remarkable presence to our halls. It is our privilege to offer you a place among the finest young witches, warlocks, and magical scholars in the kingdom.

As a member of the Coven Crest community, you will have access to our renowned curriculum and the guidance of our esteemed professors. We are confident that your time here will not only further refine your magical abilities, but will also allow you to form lasting bonds with fellow students and contribute to the academy's rich legacy.

Additional information regarding your class schedule and roommate assignment will be forthcoming.

We eagerly anticipate the opportunity to welcome you to Coven Crest this fall. Should you have any questions before your arrival, please do not hesitate to reach out to our Admissions Office, and we will gladly assist you.

Warmest regards,
Headmistress Lysandra Moonhart
Coven Crest Academy

Before Ms. Fairhaven can ask me what it says, I scream and throw myself at her, wrapping her in my arms. Yuki yips in surprise.

"I got in! They accepted me!"

Laughing, she wiggles her arms free of my grasp to return the embrace. "Of course they did, Your Highness."

I pull back and arch a brow at her. "You think it's only because of Grandfather?"

Ms. Fairhaven shakes her head. The thin strands of gray in her upswept brown hair shine in the sun. "No, Your Highness. It's because you're an incredibly talented witch." She squeezes my arms. "They would be foolish not to accept you, regardless of your lineage."

Warmth swims in my chest, and I clutch the letter to my breast.

Then my stomach falls. Because I still haven't asked Grandfather if I can go. I didn't even tell him I applied. I figured it would be better to ask him if I could attend *after* getting accepted—more granddaughter leverage that way.

My gaze shifts upward, toward the soaring towers of Ravenscroft Castle, and homes in on Grandfather's study, at the very tip of the tallest spire. The purple flags atop the castle flutter in the wind, and the hundreds of windows reflect the spring sunlight.

"Well," I say, drawing myself up despite the anxious thrumming in my chest. "I suppose now I must meet with the king."

Ms. Fairhaven wishes for me to bathe before seeking an audience with my grandfather, but I don't bother to. I pass through the large solarium, my boots clipping across the sun-warmed stone underfoot, and barely hear the burbling fountains but for the thoughts racing through my mind.

What if Grandfather says no? What if his plans for me don't include furthering my magical education? What if he wishes for me to focus on politics instead?

Like Mother . . .

My chest pinches. If only Mother had been given the opportunity, she could likely rival the witches in Grandfather's personal coven, the Shadowfall Court. But many years ago, when she married my father, it was considered unbecoming for a woman of the royal family to pursue anything outside of having heirs and dancing in ballrooms.

But things are different now. Times have changed—thank the goddesses. And I refuse to become just a pretty thing hanging from a prince's arm.

No. I'm going to learn how to control my frost magic. I'm going to become the most powerful witch I can. And then I'm going to join the Shadowfall Court, like my mother always wished she could.

"Your Highness, the mud!" Ms. Fairhaven calls from behind me, snapping me out of my thoughts. "And you too, Yuki. Wipe your paws. They just polished the floors!"

Yuki lets out a snuffling laugh.

I quickly unlace my boots and tug them from my feet, then drop them beside the doors leading into the castle.

Now in only my stockings, I pull the doors open, surprising the guards on the other side.

"Your Highness," they say in tandem, bowing their armored heads.

I sweep past them, walking as fast as I can without breaking into a run. Yuki's paws whisper along beside me, his nails clicking. We'll need to trim them again—he hates it, though, so I'll have to woo him with cinnamon buns and strawberry tarts.

It's still early afternoon, so Grandfather will likely be in his study, where he prefers to spend his time when not seeing to his duties as the king of Elarwyn.

There are many, *many* stairs between here and Grandfather's study. But thanks to one of the air witches in his coven, there's a shortcut.

Feet thumping across the plush runner lining the long hallway, I move through the shafts of sunlight streaming through the high windows, then pause before the wind tunnel and turn to face Ms. Fairhaven. She's only just catching up, and one of the kitchen maids is right on her heels, moving toward me with a tea tray held in her hands.

Perfect.

Grandfather never misses his afternoon tea and cake. This might help me butter him up.

"I'm going to speak with Grandfather alone," I tell Ms. Fairhaven as she comes to stand before me, slightly winded from the jaunt down the halls. "And I'll take that."

The kitchen maid lets out a surprised breath when I place my letter upon the tray and then pluck it from her grasp.

"B-but that's for His Majesty, Your Highness."

"I'll take it to him. Thank you."

She blinks, then exchanges a glance with Ms. Fairhaven, who just sighs.

"Very well," my lady-in-waiting says. "I'll be in your chambers when you're finished."

I flick my gaze to Yuki. "Are you coming?"

His eyes scan the wind tunnel behind me warily. Then he sits and wraps his fluffy white tail around his paws. "I think not." His tone is only *slightly* affronted that I would even ask.

He's never liked the blast of air that sends you twirling up the many stories to the highest floor of the castle. But I've always felt free when I'm weightless like that, held aloft only by air.

I give the two women a smile, push the sliding gate to the wind tunnel open with my stockinged foot, and then step backward into the shaft. The gate closes, and I'm still smiling when a vortex of powerful wind wraps around me, lifting me from my feet, and shoots me up through the tunnel, all the way to Grandfather's study.

CHAPTER 2
RAELAN

I KNOCK SOFTLY ON THE KING'S STUDY DOOR while tugging my purple-and-gold-trimmed uniform back into place with the other.

I hate that damn wind tunnel. Always have. I'd usually take the stairs—all three hundred of them—but this might be urgent, and I wanted to get here as quickly as possible.

"Enter," comes the king's low voice.

The guards stationed on either side of the door give me looks as I grip the handle and push into the study. Their eyes are still following me as I close it firmly behind me.

I straighten up and clasp my hands behind my back. King Jorvick Ravenscroft stands at the window overlooking the gardens, a small smile on his face. He's wearing his leisure clothing: a fine long-sleeved tunic beneath a gilded vest, simple brown trousers, and a mantle trimmed in velvet. He doesn't look up at me, his pale eyes trained on something outside the window.

I clear my throat. "You sent for me, Your Majesty?"

I was in the training yard going through swordsmanship drills with some of the younger guards when His Majesty's messenger arrived with word the king needed to see me. I returned to the barracks promptly and cleaned myself up before making haste here. But now, seeing the king standing contentedly at the window, I'm wondering just how urgent it was.

"Yes," King Jorvick says. "And you're just in time. She'll be up here any minute now." He finally shifts his gaze to me.

My expression remains neutral as I ask, "She, Your Majesty?"

"Alina," he says, stepping away from the window and toward the large hearth burning along the back wall.

At the sound of her name, my stomach goes tight, my spine pulling me a bit more rigid.

Princess Alina Ravenscroft. The king's granddaughter, a talented but untrained frost witch, and—

"She just received her acceptance letter from Coven Crest," the king goes on to explain, "and she'll be up here soon, begging me to let her go." He chuckles and holds his hands out toward the crackling flames in the hearth. Despite the spring warmth outside, the castle remains chilly, and our fires still burn. "And if I'm to let her attend," the king continues, "I'll need you to go with her."

Me. Go with *her*?

My heart picks up its pace. I struggle to keep my face blank.

This cannot be happening.

"Am I the best candidate for the job, Your Majesty?" I ask, though I know I shouldn't, and I very nearly cringe as soon as the words leave my mouth. Who am I to question our king? But I can't just agree to this without at least trying to push back. I *can't* go with Her Highness to Coven Crest. I'd have to be near her, talk to her, *smell* her—

"I'd choose no one else," the king says, voice sharp. His eyes flick to mine, and he straightens up. "Are you questioning my judgment, Sir Ashvale?"

"No, Your Majesty. Never."

His expression turns curious. "Then what's the problem?"

I clench my teeth. I can't tell him what the real problem is. He might have me thrown out of the castle, or worse— have my head on a chopping block. But I can't let that happen. My family depends on me and on the king. They need me here.

And I'll do whatever I have to if it means keeping my family safe.

I'll even watch over Princess Alina Ravenscroft.

Fuck.

"There is no problem," I say firmly. "I would be honored to accompany Her Highness to Coven Crest. It would be a great privilege." Quickly, I bow my head, hoping the king doesn't see the tension in my jaw.

My head is still bowed when a light knock sounds on the door.

"Grandfather?" Alina calls out. "May I come in?"

My body goes warm at the sound of her voice.

He bids her enter. And as soon as she steps foot into the room, filling it with her sweet scent, my beast thrashes inside me. Because it wants her. It *needs* her. But I refuse to give in. For three years, ever since she turned fifteen and the magic between us came alive, I've been fighting my instincts, going against everything natural in order to keep the truth locked deep, deep inside.

The truth is that Alina Ravenscroft is my fated mate, the only woman my beast truly hungers for. She's the one I think of when I lie between other women's thighs, the one I dream of while asleep in my bed in the barracks.

She also has very little awareness that I even exist.

I didn't think I'd ever find my mate, so when the connection first flared to life, I thought I was dying, thought something was terribly wrong with me. When I told my mother of the symptoms I was having, she explained what it was—the mate bond—and warned me to keep it hidden lest the king discover the truth.

Somehow, I don't think he'd much like the idea of a dragon claiming his granddaughter. If I were in his position, I can't say I'd be too fond of the idea either.

Alina ignores me, like she always does. I could probably count the number of words we've exchanged on one hand. I'm a nobody to her, just another one of the palace guards, a knight who stands beside doorways and patrols hallways late at night.

No one.

The thought makes my heart twist, but I'm too busy fighting my dragon down to pay the hurt much attention.

If not for the chain of steel wrapped around my neck,

I'd be bursting out of my skin, filling this entire study with glossy black scales and tearing clean through the bricks and mortar that hold this tower aloft in the spring sky.

I have the king to thank for that. One of his witches imbued the links with binding magic to keep my dragon from escaping. As a boy, I lived in constant fear of transforming on accident, of hurting those around me. Like my father. But now I have nothing to fear; my dragon is locked inside, incapable of pushing past the magic's defenses.

Though that doesn't mean the pain isn't excruciating when it tries.

Usually, my dragon is quiet, used to being kept in chains. But when Alina comes around, everything changes.

Pain stabs through my chest, and I have to fight with everything I've got not to show the king and the princess how uncomfortable I am.

Stop! I snap at my beast. But it doesn't help. Never does.

The dragon is ferocious. And it's *livid* at being kept from her.

My fingers curl into fists at my sides. It's taking all my focus to remain standing and not double over in pain.

"I brought your tea and cake," Alina says. She moves toward the low table by the hearth, where King Jorvick is still standing. Every move she makes, every swish of her sky-blue hair, sends her scent swirling through the room. I've never been locked in so tight a space with her before, have never been subjected to torture such as this.

And if I have to accompany her to the academy, follow her around day and night . . .

I'm filled with dread at the very prospect.

But inside me, my dragon rejoices. It wants to be with her, wherever she is. It doesn't understand why I have to stay away from her.

I remain standing near the door as Alina pours two cups of tea—we guards aren't meant to be seen, aren't meant to be offered tea or cake or anything else—and hands one to the king. They make small talk for a moment, but I can tell Alina is antsy to get to the point. She's restless, fidgety. Her nails tap a rapid rhythm against the tea saucer in her hands. Finally, she's out with it.

"Grandfather, I have to tell you something . . ."

The king gives her a small smile. "What's that?"

Alina bites her lip. The small gesture makes heat curl through me, and I tear my eyes away, focusing my energy on anything else besides looking at her. Suddenly, the paintings hanging on the king's walls are *excessively* interesting. I start counting the clouds in a brush-stroked sky, the fluffy white sheep dotting the pasture.

One, two, three . . .

"I applied for Coven Crest Academy," she says slowly. "And I got in."

"Coven Crest? Is that so?" King Jorvick hums and sips his tea.

And Alina must notice something is off, because in my periphery—I'm still trying to count sheep—she narrows her blue eyes at him. "You . . . You already knew, didn't you?" She drops the innocent-granddaughter act and huffs out an annoyed puff of air. "Why didn't you tell me?"

"I should ask you the same question," he says. "I thought you knew you could always come to me."

Alina settles herself into an ornate chair before the fire and crosses her legs, her long skirts rustling.

I notice now that she's not wearing shoes, only stockings. My gaze makes it from her toes to her ankle before I pull myself together and resume staring at the pastoral painting hanging directly across the room from me.

I've lost count of the sheep, so I start again.

"Well, I wasn't sure how you'd take it," Alina says. "And I thought if I got accepted, I'd have more sway over your decision."

King Jorvick huffs out a laugh. "You've been paying attention during your persuasion lessons, it would seem."

Alina's light brown cheeks grow round as she smiles. "Always." She plates a slice of cake and takes a bite. "So," she says after swallowing, "can I go?"

King Jorvick lets out a long sigh. Then he looks at me.

And Alina's gaze follows, a furrow forming in her brow, like she's only just noticed me standing beside the door.

I'm drawn to look at her. And when her eyes meet mine, heat rolls from the base of my neck all the way down my spine. I clench my fists harder, digging my nails into my palms, seeking some point of focus so as not to become lost in the blue of her gaze.

"You may," the king says. "On one condition."

Alina's focus snaps to him, and the break in eye contact allows me to draw a breath.

One of her brows arches in the corner. "The condition being?"

King Jorvick gestures to me with his glistening teacup. "Sir Raelan Ashvale is to accompany you."

CHAPTER 3
ALINA

WHAT?" I SNAP. I CAN'T BELIEVE THE words that just came out of my grandfather's mouth. He wants to send me to the academy with a guard. A *babysitter*. "You cannot be serious."

Grandfather sips his tea, not bothered in the slightest by my outburst. "On the contrary, I'm perfectly serious. Raelan will accompany you, or you won't attend."

"B-but," I splutter, "what about the other students? They'll treat me like an outsider."

As the princess, I've been *other* all my life. And somehow, I convinced myself that this could be different, that I could get lost in the halls of Coven Crest, burdened with books and projects like all the other students, and I could become one of them, even if only for a few short years.

But if a knight is to follow me through the halls, I'll never fit in, will never come to know what it's like to just *be*. I'll still be Princess Alina Ravenscroft, the king's granddaughter, this fragile and untouchable woman that others have to be careful around at all times. Like I'm living in a bubble, or a glass cage.

"At first, they might," Grandfather says. "But in time, they'll come to know you for you." He moves to take a seat in the big crimson armchair across from mine, his blue eyes softening. "I've already had Mayleen assess the other first-year witches, and she's selected three who will be appropriate roommates for you."

Mayleen is one of my grandfather's witches, a powerful seeress. How many other people in the castle know I applied to the academy? I was certain it was a secret, but I see now I was mistaken. As usual, Grandfather was ten steps ahead of me. That's part of what makes him a great king.

"Those are my terms," Grandfather says simply.

I grip my cake fork tightly, my eyes cutting to the guard standing near the door to Grandfather's study. He has dark hair cut close to his head and intense dark eyes set off by light bronze skin. His jaw is sharp and clean-shaven, cheekbones pronounced. I've seen him around the castle many times, but I can't recall ever having exchanged more than a few words with him. And I'm not sure I've ever seen him smile.

"And how do you feel about this?" I ask. "Did you become a knight just so you could babysit a princess?"

I hope for him to react, to at least show *some* indication of being as annoyed by this as I am, but I'm disappointed.

All he does is stand slightly straighter, his eyes focused somewhere above my head. "It would be an honor to accompany Her Highness to the academy."

Pretty words in front of the king. I wonder what he'd say if I got him alone.

With a huff, I turn back around in my chair and stare at Grandfather, who's now perusing the cake options on the tea tray. He chooses a maple-cinnamon cake topped with thick buttercream frosting. That's one of Yuki's favorites. I'll snag him a slice before I leave.

In my hand, my fork goes icy, and I look down to see fractals spreading across the metal, creeping across the handle like ice forming on a lake in early winter.

This is why I need so badly to attend the academy. I feel so much magic inside me, wanting to come out, but I don't yet know how to control it, and the witches of Shadowfall Court are much too busy with their own coven duties to train me in the way I need.

Coven Crest Academy is my best option. It's where I need to be.

I just never imagined myself walking the grounds and halls with a shadow. Especially one so quiet and cold as Sir Raelan Ashvale.

Peeling my fingers from the frozen fork—and wincing in the process—I let out a sigh. Grandfather meets my eyes.

"All right," I say, leaning back in the armchair and letting out a resigned breath. "I don't like it, but I'll do it."

Grandfather smiles. "Wonderful."

CHAPTER 4
RAELAN

I HEAD HOME AT THE FIRST OPPORTUNITY. THESE days, it's not often I have much time off from my duties at the castle. But it's a beautiful spring day, warm enough for me to wear only a lightweight long-sleeved tunic, and it's the perfect opportunity to visit my family.

And to tell them of my new assignment.

I opt to walk into town rather than riding—I could use the movement and the fresh breeze. It's calming to me, helps chase some of the heat from my skin, and I need that.

Ever since being trapped in the king's study with Princess Alina, I've found myself—and my dragon—more restless than usual. At night, I see her face, imagine what it might feel like to push my hands through her long blue hair. Once, I dreamt of undressing her one layer at a time, then claiming her as my own.

When I woke, I was covered in sweat, and my dragon was raging at the chain around my neck, fighting to get free, to get to her. I was so bothered that I had to go practice my swordsmanship in the moonlit courtyard until the sun rose.

So, I'll walk. And I'll feel the cool air on my face. And I'll *not* think of Alina.

At least, I'll make an effort not to.

It's a short walk, and the cobblestone streets keep my boots from getting muddy. Everyone I pass smiles or lifts a hand in greeting.

After a long cold winter, it seems we're all grateful for the sun on our faces and the heat upon our backs.

When I arrive in Wysteria, I find the town bustling. Shopkeepers sweep their shopfronts, children chase hoops down the streets, and there's the sweet scent of baked goods in the air. I follow my nose to a little café called the Wandering Cup and open the door for a woman on her way out. She passes me with a grateful smile, and then I step into the building. Inside, the air smells of coffee and cocoa, with a slight hint of cinnamon sugar.

My mother loves this café, and I'm selfishly hoping that bringing her one of her favorite chocolate-strawberry croissants will soften the news I'm about to deliver.

The woman behind the counter takes my order with a smile, and I wait patiently as she begins gathering up the baked goods, enjoying the sunlight streaming through the big front window.

It's hard to believe I'll be headed to Coven Crest with Alina in a few short months. Classes at the academy start in late August, but because she's a first-year, she'll be expected early, to move into her dormitory and get settled on campus before the older students return. We'll be there until her winter break, at which time we'll return to Wysteria for Yuletide celebrations.

If I survive that long.

I reach up and touch the chain around my neck; it's warm to the touch, as it always is when I think of the princess.

"Here you are, love," the shopkeeper says, pulling my attention away from the window and my thoughts of the academy. Her brown eyes sparkle in the light coming through the front window, and she tucks a strand of short brown hair behind her ear as she leans forward with her arm outstretched. Behind her, in the kitchen, a young woman with pale lavender hair works on frosting cupcakes with focused intensity, not even glancing up at me. The women have the same light brown skin—mother and daughter, perhaps.

I take the paper bag from her hand and thank her before heading back out into the spring-warm streets.

My boots clip across the cobbles at a brisk pace. I turn onto Kingfisher Crescent and sidestep two children running down the road. They giggle as they pass me by. Then my strides slow without me meaning for them to. I clutch the paper bag tightly, though I'm careful not to crush the croissants and pastries inside.

I hope she takes this well . . .

The seamstress's shop where my mother works has the door propped open, and I pop my head through to say hello to Celia, the owner. She's with a customer, but she waves when she sees me, her hazel eyes crinkling in the corners.

21

Then I take a breath and head up the side stairs to the apartment above the shop, each step feeling heavier than the one before it.

Almost as soon as I knock, the door goes flying open, and my youngest sister, Gilda, squeals and launches herself into my arms, almost making me topple backward down the stairs. It's a miracle I save the pastries from being squashed by her.

"Who is it?" Mama calls from the back room.

"Raelan's home!" Gilda yells in return.

I pick her up with one arm, then step through the door and push it closed with my boot.

Inside, the air is pleasant, and one of the windows is opened wide, letting the fresh spring breeze twirl through, sending the drapes billowing.

Though small, this apartment is the nicest place my family has ever lived. When the king discovered my secret ten years ago, he made me a deal: He'd house my family in Wysteria—and help me control my magic—if I agreed to become his page and serve the kingdom of Elarwyn as part of his guard. At the time, my family and I were barely making ends meet, and my mother struggled to feed the four of us. My father was already gone by that time, and I was working as a delivery boy for a few shops in town, scraping together every eldertoken I could in an effort to help feed my two younger sisters.

The king's offer was a blessing. I wasted no time taking him up on it. And true to his word, he moved my family into this apartment as soon as I started my training as a page. My mother and sisters have lived here for ten years now—it's the only *true* home they've ever known.

And I will do whatever it takes to ensure it stays that way.

Mama steps out of the back room, where she and my sisters sleep. Her long dark hair is pulled back in a low bun, with a few tendrils hanging loose around her face. When she reaches up to push a strand behind her ear, her fingers brush the deep scars etched into her bronze cheek. The scars reach from her brow down to her chin, and she's blind in one eye because of them. They've been there since I was a child, yet I still take note of them every time I see her. The scars are a reminder of why the chain around my neck is so important, why I have to be careful with the beast that lurks inside me. Because if I'm not, if I lose control of myself for even a moment, I could hurt someone I love. Or worse.

"Raelan," Mama says, opening her arms wide. "Come here. It's been too long."

Still holding Gilda, I kick off my boots, then pad across the room to wrap Mama in my other arm. She smells of linen and rose, just as she always has. Breathing her in helps to calm the worry in my heart.

"Where's Clarice?" I ask as I straighten up, my gaze flicking to the bedroom in search of my other sister.

"I sent her on a few errands. She'll be home soon." Mama sniffs the air, and then she spots the bag in my hand. "You didn't!" she says happily.

"Of course I did." I hand her the bag, and when she opens it and a puff of sweet-smelling air comes out, she sighs.

Then her eyes—one dark brown, the other milky from the injury—snap toward me. "Wait a minute. Are you trying to butter me up for something?"

Ever since I was a boy, I've never been able to pull one over on my mother. Seems that'll never change.

I set Gilda down with a sigh, my smile falling. Then I nod once. "There's something I need to tell you."

MAMA'S CHOCOLATE-STRAWBERRY CROISSANT SITS ON a tiny porcelain dish, untouched. It has since lost the warmth it had when I left the bakery and no longer steams in the sunlight slipping through the window in the kitchen. Gilda, though, finished her blueberry-vanilla pastry within moments of me handing it to her. Now she's in the sitting room, a book open on the floor in front of her. She has her chin propped in her hands and kicks her bare feet while she reads, unaware of the seriousness of the conversation happening in the kitchen behind her.

"Can you refuse?" Mama asks, worry coloring her tone. "Perhaps the king will pick someone else."

I give a firm shake of my head. "I tried. But His Majesty picked me for this personally. It's set in stone. We leave in August."

Mama lifts a thumb to her lips and bites her thumbnail, her forehead furrowing. Her gaze darts to Gilda, then back to me. "I don't like this, Rae. You know you have to stay away from her. How are you going to control yourself when you're in such close proximity to her?"

My mother is the only person who knows of my mate connection to the princess. She knows how these work— she was, *is*, my father's mate. And she's one of the reasons I know I have to keep my dragon in control around Alina.

All it would take is one moment of weakness, and I could scar Alina the way my mother is scarred. I could kill her.

I barely know Alina, have only spoken a few words with her, yet my stomach twists at the idea of marring her beautiful face, of hurting her in any way.

The same goes for my mother and little sisters. Anyone close to me could be hurt if my dragon broke free for even a moment.

I reach up to touch the chain around my neck, hidden just beneath the collar of my tunic. The metal links are warm where they rest against my skin, heated from the inside out by the magic that dwells within them. If not for this chain, I don't know what would happen. I don't know who I'd hurt.

"I can do this," I tell my mother, catching the chain with my thumb and lifting it above my tunic so she can see it. "It's never failed me. The king's witches are powerful. I trust their magic."

"Even so," my mother says, dropping her hand from her face so she can reach across the table and place her palm atop my hand, "what of you? Even if your dragon is contained, *you* will still want her. No magic can change that." Her lips pull into a slight frown. Perhaps she's thinking of my father.

My whole young life, they were good together. They laughed and talked and danced at night after I had gone to bed. Papa was good to me. He taught me what I was.

But his most important lesson to me came on the day he snapped, the day he accidentally let his beast free and scarred my mother's face and half of her body, nearly killing her in the process. Then he left, choosing to abandon us rather than endanger us with his dragon. I know now that he didn't mean to harm her, but as a child, I couldn't comprehend why someone would hurt the person they love.

Now I understand. I know how it feels to unfurl my wings, to feel the earth crumble beneath my mighty claws. I know my power, an unthinkable, *unstoppable* power. And I know that without the magic wrapped around my neck, I'd be a slave to the beast inside me, unable to contain it, unable to control it.

My feelings are small in comparison.

Yes, being around Alina is painful—excruciatingly so—but I will bear that pain if it means my dragon stays contained and my mother and sisters get to continue living here, in this quaint little apartment over Celia's shop, drinking tea and eating croissants and watching the snow fall while knowing they're safe from the cold.

I will not make my mother worry for me. She does quite enough of that already.

I draw myself up at the table, filled with determination.

"I'll be fine," I tell my mother, placing my free hand atop hers. "It'll be no different from the past three years. She's a princess, and I'm her knight. I will do what needs to be done."

"Raelan—" Mama starts, but she's cut off when the apartment door opens to admit my middle sister, Clarice. Her dark brown hair has mostly escaped her long braid, and she has to blow it out of her eyes as she steps through the door, hands full with bags from whatever errands Mama sent her on.

My little sisters don't know of my dragon, nor do they know of Papa's. They were too young to understand why he left, and they didn't inherit the shifter gene. So, as far as they know, I'm just their big brother, a knight at the castle, the one who brings them croissants and pastries whenever I visit.

One day, when they're old enough to be trusted with my secret, I'll tell them the truth. Until then, it's safer for all of us that they don't know.

And with Clarice home, there will be no more talk of dragons and bonds and magic.

"Rae?" she says as she pushes the door closed. Her cheeks are flushed, and she's breathing hard from carrying all the bags up the stairs, but that doesn't stop her from sprinting the few steps to the kitchen and throwing her arms around my neck.

As I hug her back, I meet Mama's eyes.

And I just wish they didn't look so troubled.

CHAPTER 5
ALINA

THE TIME HAS FINALLY COME. I CAN'T REmember the last time I was this excited for something. My entire spring and summer were spent practicing my magic, poring over the pamphlets Coven Crest sent out to first-year students, and preparing to officially leave home for the first time.

And now we're finally on our way. The carriage is loaded up with my trunks, and Mother is seated on the plush velvet cushion across from me, watching me as I stare out the window at the verdant summer landscape rolling by. I'd hoped Father would be here to see me off, but he's on yet another political trip, this time to Dunmara, the kingdom to the south of Elarwyn. We had dinner together the night before he left, yet I still find myself wishing he were here today.

Coven Crest Academy is located northeast of Wysteria, near enough to be convenient but isolated enough that the students are further encouraged to focus on their studies instead of the bustling outside world. The castle is tucked away deep in the Mistwood, a forest warded by powerful magic to keep anyone who doesn't belong there out.

We're approaching the woods now. I scoot across my cushion and stick my head out the open carriage window to get a better look. A moment later, Yuki pops his head out beside me, mouth opening and tongue lolling out as the sweet-scented summer breeze plays through our hair.

A company of knights surrounds the carriage, each carrying the Ravenscroft banner—a raven against a deep purple background, threaded through with hints of gold. The flags flap merrily in the breeze, and the horses' hooves thump over the dirt as we draw nearer to the Mistwood.

I'm trying to peer ahead, to see if I can spot Coven Crest poking over the trees in the distance, but mostly I see the back of Raelan's head as he rides alongside the carriage. His horse is draped in purple and gold, and the armor he wears gleams in the afternoon sun. He sits perfectly straight, heels down, his banner carried high.

Somehow, he must know I'm looking at him, because he turns to look back at me, his eyes dark and narrow as they meet mine from beneath the visor of his helmet. His intense gaze sends a shock through me, and I sit back from the window immediately.

Every time he looks at me, I get the feeling he *really* doesn't like me, though I can't imagine why. I've never done anything to him. I've scarcely spoken to him.

But he's probably as excited about being my babysitter as I am about having a babysitter. That's to say, *not at all*.

"How are you feeling?" Mother asks, drawing my gaze away from the window—and Raelan right outside.

I meet her eyes—pale blue, like mine—and smile. I'm not going to let Grandfather's knight ruin this experience for me.

"Excited. Nervous." I lift a hand to touch the thin silver necklace hanging around my throat. Mother gave it to me as a going-away gift. It's imbued with her magic, and when I wrap my hand around the little songbird pendant, I can hear the burbling of the fountain in the solarium back in the castle and the chirping of the birds who frequent the garden in the warm months.

She gifted me a piece of home. And I'm going to carry it with me everywhere I go.

"I'm so grateful your grandfather allowed you this," Mother says as she opens her fan and begins fanning her face. Her brown cheeks and forehead gleam with light perspiration from the heat in the carriage despite the windows being open to allow the summer breeze to twirl through.

I'm suddenly thinking of Raelan again, of his dark eyes and cold stare. He's threaded through every thought I have of Coven Crest. When I imagine myself walking through the hallowed halls, I picture him trailing along behind me. When I wonder what it'll be like meeting my roommates and living away from home, I remember he'll be standing right outside the door.

I sigh and say, "If only he'd allow me to attend *without* a chaperone."

Mother's eyes flick to mine, her lips pinching. "You're fortunate you're even being given this opportunity, Alina. You're the first member of the royal family to ever be allowed to attend." Something like sadness drifts through her expression. "And of course your grandfather is sending you with a knight; your safety is of utmost importance."

My stomach pinches, and I drop my gaze. "I'm sorry, Mother." I reach out a hand and place it upon her knee, my skin brushing the soft material of her gown. "I'm incredibly grateful. I don't mean to sound otherwise."

My mother wanted dearly to attend the academy when she was my age, but she was not allowed—her duties as the princess came first. How spoiled I must sound to be complaining about having a knight to watch over me.

I lean back against the cushion and clench my fists in my lap. Beside me, Yuki nuzzles his head against my arm.

"We're about to go through the ward," Mother says, her voice lifting with excitement.

I look out the window, and as the carriage is swallowed up by the Mistwood, a slight shimmering veil falls over us. It's a touch cool, but not uncomfortably so, and it tastes sweet. It tastes like magic.

A thrill goes through me. After all these months of waiting and preparing and wondering what my roommates will be like, I'm almost there, almost at the academy.

Across from me, my mother sits up straighter, her blue eyes sparkling with her own anticipation.

And I tell myself that I'll not forget what a wonderful opportunity this is. I'll be grateful for my place at Coven Crest every day.

Even if Raelan Ashvale is there with me.

CHAPTER 6
RAELAN

AFTER PASSING THROUGH THE MIST-wood, we emerge in the sunlight on the other side of the forest. And standing tall against the blue sky is Coven Crest Academy.

The stone walls of the castle tower well over our heads, and purple flags embroidered with the academy's moon-phase crest billow atop the highest towers.

We pass through the barbican, experiencing a brief respite from the August heat, then ride into the courtyard on the other side. It's dotted with outbuildings and gardens, and I even spot an archery range. Carriages are cluttered about the space, with people unloading trunks and bags and hugging and crying.

But as we draw nearer, much of their attention turns to us.

I tense beneath my armor. Wherever the royal family goes, stares follow. I just hope that in short time, Alina will become a common-enough sight amongst the other students that they'll treat her as one of their own.

That would make my job a *little* bit easier.

Dragon aside.

I could feel her gaze on me as I rode alongside the carriage, and even now, I have the urge to turn and look for her. But I resist that urge. I have a feeling I'll be doing a lot of that now that I'm here.

Some of the carriages move to make way, and our procession rides up and stops right in front of the main castle. I don't dismount; rather, I scan the crowd, watching carefully for any signs of trouble. But mostly I see curiosity and awe, and my highly sensitive hearing picks up on the whispers of the gathered onlookers as the footman opens the door and offers his gloved hand to help Alina down.

They're whispering about the princess, wanting to get a look at her, wondering what classes she'll have and whether they'll have similar schedules. For now, it's all innocent enough. I take a breath, trying to relax my tight muscles.

Alina glides gracefully from the carriage, her long lilac gown whispering as it settles in the grass about her feet. A white fox jumps out behind her—her spirit companion, I know. Her pale blue hair is pulled back, revealing her light brown cheeks and startling blue eyes.

And when those eyes meet mine, my dragon responds with such sudden aggression that it makes me flinch and squeeze the reins. My mare tosses her head, upset with me for my mixed signals, and Alina arches a brow right before I tear my gaze away and reach down to pat Penelope's strong neck.

"Shh, girl," I whisper. "I'm sorry."

She snorts and gives me a side-eye—rightly so.

"Sir Ashvale," one of the young squires says, drawing my attention to where he's now standing beside my horse. "Would you like us to transport your belongings to your quarters?"

My stomach twists at the reminder.

Because I'm Alina's only assigned guard, the king wanted to ensure I would always be within close proximity of her, and he therefore made certain I would have a room right next to hers in the dormitory.

Part of me thinks the king is actually trying to kill me, to push me so hard my dragon has no choice but to rip me apart from the inside in its effort to get to the princess. Maybe this is a terrible test. If he knew the truth—that Alina is my fated mate—he'd probably not allow me within a square mile of his granddaughter.

I'm determined not to let him—or anyone else—find out.

"Yes," I say when the squire starts to squirm under the weight of my long silence.

He nods before departing, and I shake myself internally. I have a job to do here, and I have to do everything I can not to get distracted.

If only my dragon understood how dire the situation is.

Alina and her mother, Princess Rowena Ravenscroft, head up the stairs to the castle's entrance, accompanied by a number of guards and many squires carrying all of Alina's belongings. Two young squires strain beneath the weight of a mahogany trunk, their foreheads glinting with perspiration in the summer sun.

It's good for them. Builds character. And muscle.

A woman with long silver hair meets the princesses at the top of the stairs. I focus my hearing, homing in on her.

"Princess Rowena, Princess Alina." The woman dips her head in a show of respect. "Welcome to Coven Crest. I'm Headmistress Lysandra Moonhart. Please come this way. I'll show you to your dormitory."

Before stepping through the grand double doors, Alina glances back, and her eyes find mine again. A tingle rolls down my spine. But she's swept away so quickly that I can't even think to school my facial expression into professional disinterest, and when Alina is finally out of sight, my dragon calms down, disappointment flooding through me.

I let out a heavy sigh.

After swinging down from my horse, I remove my helmet and motion for a squire to assist me. "Take her to the stables," I say as I pass him the reins. "Brush her well, then turn her out with the herd. It won't do having her cooped up. Makes her grouchy."

Of course it does. My dragon knows how it feels to be caged. It'd drive anyone crazy.

"Yes, sir," he says, already starting away, Penelope's polished hooves clopping along behind him.

The whispers from the onlookers have died down some, but the staring still makes my skin prickle. I turn my back on the students and their parents and cast my gaze up at the towering double doors into the academy. And with a steadying breath, I force myself to climb the stairs and pass into the heart of Coven Crest Academy.

THE CASTLE IS A MAZE OF CORRIDORS AND CLASS-rooms and hallways with dead-ends. Portraits hang on the walls, plants reach for stained glass windows, and there's a comforting coolness to the air despite the summer heat outside.

After trying and failing to find my way around, I finally flag down a young witch and ask her to point me toward the north tower, where Alina is to live for the duration of her four-year stay at Coven Crest. I believe the other three dormitories—south, east, and west—are occupied by the older students.

The witch's cheeks flare pink, and she ducks her head as she says, "The castle can be hard to navigate. B-but I can show you the way, if you'd like. I'm here to help the first-years find their way around."

I give her a single nod, and she turns on her heel, her academy-appointed black robe fluttering about her calves. Despite her small stature, she moves at a quick pace, forcing me to stay focused on her and not get distracted by all the sights and sounds the castle has to offer. In time, I'll explore the castle fully, ensuring I know it well. It won't do to get myself—or Alina—lost in the twisting passageways.

Without meaning to, I picture Alina alone in a candlelit hallway, her blue hair fluttering around her cheeks, her lips pursed as she turns to look at me. And then I imagine what it might feel like to touch her skin, to draw my fingertips across her face.

My dragon flares to life again, eager and willing, and I flex my fingers and bite back a grunt.

"What's that?" the young witch asks, barely slowing her pace to glance over her shoulder at me.

I grind my teeth and force out, "Nothing."

Seeming startled by my brusque tone, she turns back around, and I have to remind myself that I'm going to be surrounded by students now, witches and warlocks here from all over Wysteria and its outlying villages and hamlets. I'll need to adjust my tone. These aren't knights and squires and pages, like I'm used to.

"Here it is," the young witch says, stopping at the bottom of a spiraling staircase. "The north tower. Would you like help finding the right room?"

"No, I can find my way from here," I say, gaze trained on the stairs. Other students' voices drift down the corridor, laced with excitement.

The witch's shoulders slump a bit as her gaze flicks toward the bottom of the staircase leading to the north tower.

"But I appreciate the offer," I tell her. My words come out softer this time, and I give her a small smile.

Her cheeks flush pink, and she squeaks out, "I-it was my pleasure. I'll be around if you need me. My name's Nella. I'm a second-year. I live in the south tower."

"Sir Ashvale." I bow my head to her. "And thank you for your help, Nella."

She gives me a quick nod, then scurries off back the way we came. When she's out of earshot, I shake my head and let out a sigh. Then I draw a breath and start up the stone stairs.

Dormitory doors flank the spiral staircase on one side, and arched stained glass windows are set at intervals into the exterior wall, allowing colorful summer sunlight to stream through and illuminate my way. I pause at one window, drawn by the vibrant red paint pigment used in the design. My eyes trace the form curling across the glass: a dragon, its wings outstretched, its eyes trained on the clear blue sky. Without meaning to, I reach out, and my fingers brush the dragon's wings.

In response, my back itches, like my own pair of wings want to burst through my skin and carry me up, up into the sky. But I can't. The magical chain around my neck makes sure of that.

It can only be removed by someone in the Ravenscroft bloodline, the intention being that I can't take it off or be forced to take it off by someone else, therefore endangering everyone I come into contact with. It's been too long since I last shifted into my dragon form, and the want—the instinctual need—to do so burns just beneath my skin, a fire that refuses to go out.

I should've asked the king for a night flight before embarking on this journey with Alina. Throughout the years, he's allowed me to occasionally shift and soar off—always at night so as not to be seen—and now I'm dreading having not asked him. At least then I would've been able to get some of my pent-up energy out. But I suppose it's too late for that now. I'm here, and I can't just fly away—even if I really wish I could.

The dormitory door to my right opens suddenly, and I steal my fingers away from the window and turn to regard the two young men who step from the room. They eye me and my heavy armor with wary curiosity, then hurry down the stairs, their boots thumping as they go.

My dragon does *not* like that male students live in the same tower. At least the rooms themselves are assigned by gender.

Flexing my fingers into fists, I continue up the staircase, searching for Alina's room number: NT33. Because all first-years will live in this tower, the staircase is bustling, and I have to keep stepping aside to allow students and their family members to pass by me, headed back down to the ground floor of the castle. Finally, I find room NT32, then climb the additional stairs to room NT33.

The door is already standing open, but I still knock loudly, my armored knuckles rapping against the wood, before stepping through the doorway. Not that anyone hears me. It's a madhouse in here, with squires and pages moving Alina's belongings about, along with a number of other people I don't recognize—probably friends and family members of the three other witches Alina will be living with.

My eyes quickly track the space.

It's surprisingly spacious and comforting despite being significantly smaller than anything the princess is likely familiar with. Near the doorway, a narrow spiral staircase leads up to a second-floor loft, where I imagine the beds are. Just past the staircase is a quaint living space with two purple couches, a large ornate rug, a few dark writing desks, and a brick fireplace, though it's empty right now—and good thing too, because it's warm in here even with the door to the cool hallway propped open and a breeze coming through the window.

Female voices drift down from the second floor: Alina's and a few others I don't recognize.

"Sir Ashvale," Princess Rowena says, drawing my gaze as she descends the last few stairs to the main floor. "I wondered where you were."

"Your Highness." I dip my head to her, hands clasped behind my back. "I am nearby. Always." I look up and meet her blue eyes, and she gives me a kind smile.

"I know you are." She reaches out and places a hand on my armored shoulder, though I'm not sure if she's trying to comfort me or herself. Then she draws away and says, "Have you seen your quarters? I believe they're just up the way." Gesturing to the open doorway behind me, she sweeps through it, and I follow her. She ascends the stairs, and a few of our squires part around us, pressing themselves along the curved outer wall and bowing their heads as we pass. "Ah, here it is. I've been told this room is typically used by older students, dormitory leaders, of sorts, but they've set it aside for you."

Princess Rowena stops just outside the doorway and waves a hand for me to go in front of her. So I do, and when I step into the room, I almost draw a breath.

I didn't expect much—a broom closet would've worked fine for me. But this is . . .

I draw myself up. "This is too much," I say aloud.

Behind me, Princess Rowena laughs. "Nonsense. You're here protecting my daughter. It's only right you have comfortable accommodations."

"A bed is comfortable, Your Highness." I take another step into the room. "This is . . ."

I don't quite have a word for what it is. But it's certainly more than I would ever have asked for.

The layout is similar to Alina's room, but much smaller, clearly for only one or two students as opposed to four. The main floor has a writing desk, two armchairs tucked close to a small side table, and a brick fireplace. I drift toward the staircase leading to the upper floor, and my sabbatons clink as I ascend each stair. When I step into the loft, I pause.

A bed stands against the far wall, flanked on either side by two empty bookcases. The squires already brought my trunk in, and it stands ready and waiting for me to unpack the few personal items I own.

"So," Princess Rowena calls from the main floor, voice lilting playfully, "will this be suitable, Sir Ashvale?"

Putting my hands on my hips, I cast one last look around my new home, and for perhaps the first time since the king called me into his study this past spring, I think this might actually work out, that maybe this will be okay.

Until Alina's familiar smell curls through the air from the hallway, sending my dragon writhing once more.

I'm reminded that no matter how comfortable my accommodations are, I'm still here to protect Alina, to be by her side, to guard her and watch over her.

And *that* is going to be anything but easy.

CHAPTER 7
ALINA

L ET'S SEE . . ." I HOLD UP THE PARCHMENT IN MY hand and trace my class schedule with a fingertip. "On Tuesdays and Thursdays, I have Introduction to Elemental Magic with Professor Stone."

"At one thirty?" asks one of my roommates, Lyra Wilder. She's seated on the rug in front of the couches, her legs crossed, one hand braced against the floor as she leans back and regards her class schedule. Her spirit companion, a pretty cinnamon-colored rat named Juniper, is fast asleep in her lap.

I take another look at my schedule and nod. "Yeah. Guess we have that class together."

The four of us are seated about our sitting room, schedules in hand, comparing our class lists. My other two roommates, Poppy Waverly and Maeve Vandermere, sit on the couch beside mine. Poppy adjusts her round glasses while Maeve fans herself with her schedule.

"You want to get out of here?" Maeve asks. She uses her free hand to lift her straight violet-black hair off her neck. Despite having our window open, our room is a touch warm today. "We can walk around the castle, find our classrooms."

"That would be great!" Poppy says. "I'd hate to be late on my first day . . ." She shivers a little. "I started having nightmares about that right after I got my acceptance letter."

"Why? Were you naked or something?" Lyra asks. The summer sunlight illuminates her curly red hair, which bursts out around her head like a halo, with tight ringlets hanging down past her shoulders.

Poppy blinks up at her, lavender eyes wide and light brown cheeks going a touch red. "What? No!"

"I don't get it." Lyra's crimson eyes narrow. "What were you having nightmares about, then?"

"About being *late*," Maeve clarifies, pushing to her feet and tapping Lyra on the head with her parchment. "Some of us actually care about being punctual, you know."

We've known each other for less than a week—we first-years moved in early, before the older students—but already, I'm coming to know these girls like close friends. Lyra was the last of us to arrive on move-in day, and since then, she's shown little regard for being *anywhere* on time, including our welcome ceremony a few days ago.

"Oh." Lyra smiles. "Yeah, that doesn't scare me."

I laugh and shake my head, then reach down and draw a hand over Yuki's soft ears. "What do you say?" I ask him. "Want to walk the castle with us?"

"Sure." He stands up and stretches, then yawns, showing off his sharp white teeth. "Maybe we can stop by the dining hall too? I wouldn't mind some more of those cinnamon buns..."

I smile. "That can probably be arranged."

I THINK IT'S DOWN HERE," LYRA SAYS. SHE'S HOLDING a map of the castle—it came in the welcome packet all the first-years received—and pointing down a corridor. She starts down the hallway, her loafers clipping along the stone as she goes. We follow behind her—*all* of us, including Raelan. I told him he didn't need to come, that he could have the day to himself, but in the cold manner I've come to expect from him, he declined.

Now he follows behind our group, so obviously *different* from all the other students drifting through the halls that he draws stares wherever we go. At least he's not wearing his gleaming metal armor today. He tried it our first full day at the academy, intending to wear it to the welcome ceremony, but I refused to go anywhere with him dressed like that. We're at an academy, for goodness' sake, not riding into battle. The fitted trousers and dark long-sleeved tunic he's wearing today are much more suitable for walking the academy's halls on this sunny August afternoon.

"Yup, this is it." Lyra reaches out to try the door handle, but it's locked. "Some help here, Juniper?"

The rat immediately scurries out of Lyra's pocket and runs down her arm, then uses her sharp little claws to descend the wooden door. She slips under the door, and a moment later, the lock on the other side clicks.

"Wait!" Poppy whispers. "What if someone sees us? We can't just break in like that!"

"Just blame it on me." Winking, Lyra pushes open the door to the classroom, then steps inside. She scoops Juniper up off the floor, then disappears into the room. Poppy glances both ways down the hall before following her, and the rest of us trail behind, Raelan bringing up the rear and closing the door behind us.

The classroom is lit with sunlight from the big windows. The golden beams illuminate the stacks of books in one corner and the plants crawling across the big desk at the front of the room. Shelves line the back wall, filled to the brim with all manner of items: crystals and rocks, jars of sand, twinkling bottles of mysterious liquids, and tall, slender candles of many colors. There are rows of desks and empty chairs, just waiting for the schoolyear to begin.

"This is where we'll be on Tuesday, Alina," Lyra says. Then she stops and turns sharply to look at me. "Or should we call you Princess Alina? Or Your Highness?"

I make a face and shake my head. "Alina is just fine."

Maeve boosts herself onto the edge of the professor's desk, swinging her long legs. "When I heard you'd be attending, I thought it was a rumor." She tucks a straight lock of silky hair behind her ear. "I never would've guessed I'd be rooming with you."

"Me either," Poppy says. She's lingering by the door, a few paces away from Raelan, looking uncertain about having snuck into the classroom.

"One of my grandfather's witches picked you," I say, taking a seat on the desk at the front of the classroom. Yuki sets off to sniff around, exploring the books and potted plants.

"What do you mean?" Maeve tilts her head and narrows her vivid purple eyes.

"She's a seeress. I don't know how her magic works, but she saw you three . . ." I glance around at the three girls, all so different and interesting in their own ways. "Hopefully that means we'll get along."

Lyra lets out a crisp laugh, but it's harmless. "We'll see." She looks out the window, then turns around and pops a hip, crimson-eyed gaze landing on Raelan. "And what about you, Sir Ashvale? How'd you end up here with the princess?"

My chest tightens up as my gaze slowly slides to Raelan. He's not spoken a word since we were up in the north tower. He's quiet as a shadow, though substantially more intimidating than one.

His dark eyes shift to Lyra. "His Majesty chose me for this duty. It's an honor to protect Her Highness."

Raelan's words make my stomach squeeze. "While we're here, you can just call me Alina," I tell him. "No need to be so proper."

Now Raelan's eyes are on me. His sudden eye contact sends a shiver up my spine. In this light, his skin glows with a hint of gold, and something around his neck flashes. Looking closer, I notice it's some sort of jewelry. A chain, maybe?

Odd.

None of the other knights wear any sort of adornment— as far as I know, that's not within dress code. I can't recall if

I've seen it on Raelan before or if he's just started wearing it as of late.

At first, I think Raelan is going to refuse, to insist upon calling me by my proper title. But then he gives me a barely perceptible nod and says, "Very well, Alina."

Another shiver goes down my back, accompanied by a single skip of my heart. He's never said my name before. And somehow, it sounds different on his lips. Prettier. Foreign, almost.

The girls give me varying looks, but Lyra's is by far the most obvious. Her crimson eyebrows are lifted, mouth turned into a sideways smile.

But before she can say anything, the door handle jiggles, and then the door swings open.

Poppy gasps and jumps out of the way so fast you'd think Maeve's spirit companion, Isis, had just tried to strike her. Not that Isis bites—according to Maeve, at least. I've not yet become quite used to looking for the red-bellied snake before sitting on the couches. Lyra almost sat on her just the other day, and she probably would have if Poppy hadn't pushed her swiftly out of the way.

A witch stands in the doorway, blinking at us in surprise. She's wearing a robe trimmed in yellow—I believe that designates her as a second-year, while our robes are all trimmed in blue. Her gaze flits between the four of us, then lands on Raelan, and her eyes widen.

"Wh-what are you doing in here?" she asks. "Classrooms are off-limits outside of class hours."

Poppy shrinks like she wishes she could disappear. Maeve just swings her legs some more, looking unbothered, and Lyra glances out the window into the sunlit garden like no one even said anything.

I open my mouth to reply, but Raelan shifts, turning so he's facing the witch.

"It's Nella, right?" he says. His voice is warm and soft, so unlike the tone he uses when he speaks with me.

Immediately, the girl's cheeks flush pink. She blinks up at him. "That's right. We met on move-in day." Her fingers grasp for the hem of her school robe. "I didn't think you'd remember, Sir Ashvale."

His smile is quick and easy. And it's so startling, I realize I've never seen it before. Every time we speak, he regards me with a neutral expression at best. Sometimes, though, I catch him watching me through narrowed eyes, his jaw tight, like he can't stand having to be here and watch over me, like every moment spent in my presence is a nuisance to him.

But that's between him and Grandfather. If he doesn't want to be here, he should've said something before we departed for Coven Crest.

"Of course I remember. Your help was much appreciated." He gives her another one of those smiles.

A kernel of heat flares to life in my stomach. Why is this *annoying* me so much?

"I was happy to help, but . . ." Her eyes scan the four of us again, then land on Yuki where he's seated beside a potted plant, soaking in the sunlight. "But what are you all doing in here?"

"Just finding their classrooms before the semester begins tomorrow. We didn't mean to intrude."

"Oh." Nella's gaze slides back to Raelan. Her cheeks flare again, and she glances away like she can feel their heat. "It's okay. I did the same thing my first year. But you'd better hurry up—the professors just got out of the faculty meeting, and they'll all be getting their classrooms set up for tomorrow. I'm sure Professor Stone is on his way here now. And he can be a bit . . . moody. But don't tell him I said that!"

Raelan's dark eyes sparkle. I clench my teeth.

"Thank you for the warning," he says. "Guess that means it's time to go." Raelan looks over at me, but as soon as his eyes meet mine, the smile he was giving to Nella vanishes.

What's his problem?

Poppy immediately scurries past him and Nella and into the hallway, mumbling a quick "excuse me" as she passes. Maeve pushes off the desk and walks from the room languidly. I stand just as Lyra steps in front of me. She sweeps her arm through mine, then leads me from the classroom.

"Thanks, Nella," she says as we pass by. "You're a lifesaver."

"Oh, sure." Nella's gaze lands on me. She quickly bows her head. "Your Highness."

My eyes flash to Raelan. Would she have known who I am if not for him?

Some people know what I look like, have seen me over the years, either at festivals and parades or just enjoying the shops and goods Wysteria has to offer. But Raelan is *obviously* not a student here—all it takes is one glance to know he's not a first-year wandering the maze-like halls. And as long as he's with me, everyone will know who I am.

The princess. The outsider.

For the second time today, I'm just glad he agreed to forego his armor for the foreseeable future.

After we've all exited the classroom, Nella steps into the doorway behind us.

"If students aren't allowed in classrooms yet, what are you doing here?" Lyra asks, her tone bordering on accusatory.

Nella shrugs. "I'm Professor Stone's student assistant." Her gaze flicks down the hall. "He's coming this way now."

Sure enough, voices drift down the corridor, and a few faculty members pause in the parallel hall, talking and laughing amongst themselves.

"Thank you, Nella," I say.

Her smile is quick. "Of course, Your Highness."

"Just Alina," I tell her. "Alina is fine."

I get the feeling I'm going to be saying that a *lot* in the coming days.

But here, in these halls, I just want to be me, not Grandfather's granddaughter, not the woman who may one day sit on Elarwyn's throne.

Just Alina. Just a witch trying to master her magic. Just a student, like everyone else.

Except for my bodyguard, who's now ushering me and my roommates down the hall and gesturing for Yuki to keep up.

"Bye, Sir Ashvale," Nella calls out from behind us. "S-see you around!"

I glance over my shoulder just quickly enough to see the smile he gives her. Then we're ducking around the faculty members and starting back down the wide hallway, as if we didn't just break into our elemental studies classroom.

Once we're out of earshot of the professors and Nella, Lyra skips over to Raelan and bumps him playfully. He arches a dark brow at her, stride not faltering.

Immediately, something in my stomach squeezes.

"Thanks for rescuing us, sir knight," she says, fluttering her eyelashes dramatically. "You're our hero."

Raelan doesn't respond. But his eyes find mine again.

And I don't quite understand the fire they light inside me.

CHAPTER 8
RAELAN

DURING MY MEETING WITH THE HEADMIS-tress the day after Alina moved into the north tower, I was told I'm to stand outside the room while class is in session. I pushed back, arguing that I'm to be near the princess at all times, but Headmistress Moonhart refused, stating I'd be too much of a distraction. She even said she'd take it up with His Majesty herself if she needed to, reminding me that Coven Crest is *her* domain and we're to follow *her* rules.

Begrudgingly, I complied.

And actually, it's a small miracle, one I didn't realize I'd be so grateful for. Being separated from Alina by a closed door helps give me a break from her, gives me and my dragon a moment to catch our breath.

These last few weeks have been excruciating. It's so much worse than I thought it was going to be. Alina's smell is around me all the time, and every time I see her, I have to fight my dragon's urge to break free and claim her, to wrap her in its claws and carry her off to some distant high tower where no one will ever find us again.

I absolutely *cannot* do that, no matter how vehemently my dragon is trying to convince me otherwise.

Far off, a clock tower chimes, its deep song reverberating through the castle corridors. It only takes about twenty seconds for the door to Alina's magical ethics class to fly open, and first-year students in blue-trimmed robes start pouring out. She's in the middle of the group, talking to two young men, her lips pulled into a big smile as she laughs.

My dragon coils.

As soon as she steps from the room, I'm at her side, and the smile that was on her lips moments ago flickers. I try not to take it *too* personally. She would likely react that way no matter which of the king's knights was standing here in my place. Still, it stings.

She carries on her conversation with the two other students, who eye me warily but say nothing to me. One of them invites her to the astronomy tower to study.

What they need to study so early in the schoolyear, I couldn't guess. He probably just wants to spend more time with her.

"I'd love to," she says.

A ripple of irritation goes through me. I tighten my jaw.

I've no right to be annoyed. Of course the male students are taking an interest in her.

But my dragon struggles to see reason.

The three of them start down the hall. I'm taller than most of the other students, and when they see me coming, they flit out of the way, creating an unimpeded path for Alina to walk down. Though most probably wouldn't realize it, I note the subtle tightening of her shoulders as the students make a path for her and then pause or turn to watch her walk by. But she plays it off smoothly, acting like she doesn't realize how the others stare.

I follow Alina and the two boys down twisting corridors filled with students and faculty and all manner of animal spirit companions. Then we come to a narrow arched door-way over which a glittering silver constellation has been etched into the stone. We pass through it to the staircase and start to climb. The steps ascend the tower in a tight spiral, and when we come upon other students on their way down, they have to press themselves against the cool stone walls to make room for us to pass.

Alina's smell fills the space around me, and my dragon encourages me to reach for her, to capture a strand of her hair and twist it about my finger. But I do no such thing. I take a breath and hold it, then busy myself with counting the stairs as my boots ascend each one.

By the time we've reached the top, I've counted to 310—making this tower slightly taller than the king's study back in Ravenscroft Castle.

We step out of the stairwell and into a tower with a big glass dome that provides an unhindered view of the early-September sky. Golden constellations glow upon the glass, depicting their locations in the sky despite the daylight making the stars impossible to see. Under foot, the floor is a tiled crystalline mosaic of celestial bodies. I lift a boot to find a star shooting across the sky.

Crescent-shaped couches hug the smooth rounded walls, and students lounge about, reading or studying or talking quietly with one another. Some gaze through telescopes trained on the open sky beyond the glass-dome ceiling.

That same sky calls to me, invites me to shed my human skin and unfurl my wings. The desire to do so makes my back itch, and I roll my shoulders in an effort to alleviate the discomfort.

Alina and her two companions find an open couch and drop their schoolbags alongside it before sitting down. I take up a position just to Alina's left, close enough to reach her should I need to but far enough away that I can turn my head just slightly in an effort not to be overwhelmed by her intoxicating smell.

As expected, the male students don't pull out books or notes of any kind. They just want to talk to her.

"So," one of them says. "Is he your bodyguard or something?"

Though my gaze is directed away, I can feel their eyes shift to me. My dragon gnashes its teeth, but I don't make any outward indication that I'm bothered or so much as interested in what they have to say about me.

"Yeah." In my periphery, Alina shifts, her blue hair slipping over one shoulder. "He's one of my grandfather's knights."

"And is he . . . always with you?" the other male asks.

Something about his tone sends me bristling, and my gaze slowly slides to him. I want to ask what business it is of his, but Alina responds before I get the chance to.

"Usually, yes." She opens her bag and pulls out a book, then sets it in her lap. Maybe she really *does* intend to study, even if the boys don't. For some reason, that comforts me.

Though it shouldn't.

"Isn't that a little bit . . . creepy?" the first boy asks. "Having someone follow you around all the time?"

"*So* creepy," his companion responds.

They laugh, and the sound is particularly cutting.

Alina tenses up—I can feel her energy in the air between us, palpable and impossible to ignore.

At my sides, my fingers curl into fists. Who are these boys, and why do they feel it's their right to question her this way? To tease her?

"Can you send him away?" one of the boys asks.

Now I turn fully to face them, and all three of them look up at me.

"No. But I can send *you* away," I say, voice low.

Alina's eyes widen. Then she quickly wipes the surprise away, replacing it with a thin smile. "Raelan," she says, trying to maintain her composure, though the tension beneath her words is obvious, at least to me. "Could you give us a bit of space, please?"

My response is immediate and unwavering. "Absolutely not."

Now her wide eyes narrow. "Excuse me?"

I'm still staring at the boys, who are starting to wriggle under the intensity of my glower. "I said *absolutely not*." To make my point, I take a step closer to the crescent couch they're all seated upon. "You"—I jut my chin toward one of the boys, whose thigh is a *bit* too close to Alina's—"move over. One foot."

His mouth pops open in a look of shock, and he throws a glance at his friend, then returns his gaze to me. His brow arches. "What if I say no?"

Good, a challenge.

Without hesitation, I reach down, grab him by the robe, and *physically* separate him and the princess, shoving him a foot down the blue velvet couch. "Then I will happily do it for you," I growl.

"Raelan!" Alina snaps, but I ignore her. My dragon would *very* much like to toss these boys from this tall, tall tower, and all its focus is on them.

"Man, get a grip," one of the boys says. "You're crazy." He quickly snatches up his bookbag and pushes to his feet. "I'm out of here."

"Me too," the other boy says. "See you around, Alina." He, at least, is smart enough to give me a wide berth as he stands. Then, without glancing back, they both stride across the tiled floor and pass through the doorway to the spiraling staircase, leaving everyone in the room staring at me—and the princess.

Her anger vibrates in the air around me, making my skin tingle with warmth.

"What the *stars* was that?" she asks, voice low and punctuated with venom. "What were you *thinking*?"

I draw myself up and adjust my long-sleeved tunic; it got rumpled when I manhandled the boy away from Alina. "They just wanted to get you alone," I say, and I somehow keep my voice level despite the anger singing through my veins.

"No, they wanted to get away from *you*, very much like I do right now."

Slowly, I draw my gaze away from the doorway—it doesn't look like the boys are coming back—and look down at Alina. She's clutching her schoolbook in her lap, and ice creeps from her fingers and across the book, turning it inch by inch into a block of ice. If she notices what she's doing, she makes no indication of it.

"It's my duty to protect you—that includes protecting you from other students who may have . . . ill intentions."

Alina's light brown cheeks turn a shade of red. "Ill intentions?" she growls. "Who are you, my *father*?" With a huff, she pushes to her feet, goes to throw her book into her bag, and realizes it's frozen solid. Dismay flashes quickly across her face, and I'm suddenly feeling a *touch* bad about making a scene.

Because everyone is *certainly* staring now.

So far as I'm aware, the princess is a powerful frost witch, but she lacks the ability to fully control her magic, hence her interest in attending the academy. But whatever her reason for being here, it's my job to protect her, even if that means keeping young men and their twisted thoughts away from her.

What about my twisted thoughts?

It's not lost on me that I'm the most dangerous thing here. As if reminding me of the power locked inside my veins, the chain around my neck burns, stinging my skin.

Cheeks still flushed, Alina shoves the frozen tome into her bag, then hefts the strap onto her shoulder. "I'm going to the library," she says. "You're dismissed for the day."

I don't miss a beat. "You can't dismiss me, Your Highness. I don't answer to you; I answer to His Majesty."

Her fingers curl into a white-knuckled grip around the strap of her shoulder bag. "Then I'll write to Grandfather, and *he* can tell you to back off."

"As you wish, Your Highness." I hold out a hand, gesturing to the staircase. My use of Alina's full title seems to further irritate her, if the sharp look she gives me is any indication. "Shall I escort you to the library now?"

"I told you to call me *Alina*." She lets out a frustrated huff, then stalks past me. And I realize for the first time how beautiful her anger is.

Even if it's directed at me.

Especially if it's directed at me.

You sick masochist, I think.

And then I follow her to the stairs, and we start back down from the astronomy tower.

CHAPTER 9
ALINA

ALL RIGHT, PAIR UP AND STAND UP. About three feet apart," Professor Stone instructs, waving his arm at us from where he stands at the front of the classroom. Thin gray light slips through the big windows, and candles flicker in sconces, sending shadows dancing across our desks.

I get to my feet and tuck in my chair, then turn to face my partner.

Lyra's crimson eyes are sharp and playful as she pushes her chair in and turns to look at me. She's wearing citrine earrings, which sway with every movement of her head.

"Now, we're going to practice an exercise that's all about energy flow, synchronization, and, of course, air—our element of breath, communication, and movement," Professor Stone says. "Take a moment to ground yourselves. Close your eyes if you need to. Feel your feet firmly planted on the floor. Imagine roots reaching deep into the earth, anchoring you, while your crown extends toward the sky, reaching up to connect with the limitless energy all around us."

Lyra's lips quirk up on one side, but she closes her eyes, and I do the same, taking a breath to ground myself. I quickly tap into my senses, focusing on what I can hear—papers rustling, students breathing, the tap of a boot against the stone floor—what I can smell—ink from our inkwells, the delicate scent of smoke from the candles burning in sconces along the walls, and something delectable floating up from the dining hall on the main floor—and what I can feel— my toes in my lightweight boots, my long robe tickling my stockinged calves, and something crawling up my—

I squint one eye open to see a rat clinging to my leg, trying to climb my stockings like a ladder. Without meaning to, I scream, making all the students around me jump and flinch.

"Miss Ravenscroft!" Professor Stone snaps, grasping his chest. "What in the name of—"

Before our professor can see what's happening, Lyra quickly pries Juniper off my leg and tucks her into a pocket on the inside of her robe. I narrow my eyes at her, but all she does is flash me a quick smirk before flicking her gaze to our professor.

"Sorry, Professor," she says, tipping her head and giving him an innocent smile. "It was just a spider."

Professor Stone comes to stand beside us, his brown eyes sharp, but before he can say another word, the classroom door swings open with such sudden violence that I start and whirl around, my heart leaping into my throat.

And it's Raelan standing there, his dark eyes looking murderous as they quickly find and home in on me. They burn with such intensity that I draw a small breath. Everyone else in the room turns to look at me as well.

It's been two weeks with Raelan following me around, but unlike my roommates, I still barely know him. It certainly doesn't help that he barely speaks to me. Or that on the rare occasions we *do* talk, it's usually just to argue.

I wrote Grandfather a letter after the argument with Raelan in the astronomy tower, but Grandfather brushed it off, choosing instead to ask about my classes and whether they're still serving apple potpies for dessert.

Yes, they are. Yuki loves them. But then again, Yuki has an incurable sweet tooth.

Grandfather scarcely even entertained my request for a new guard, so I suppose I'm stuck with Raelan. For now.

"All is well, Sir Ashvale," our professor says, letting loose a tired sigh. I think having one of the king's knights lurking in the halls puts the faculty on edge.

But Raelan doesn't even look at him. His stare holds me captive, sending warmth creeping across my face. Or maybe that's all the pointed stares from my classmates.

I give Raelan a curt nod, and only then does he finally step slowly back and close the door with a soft thump.

"Our very own knight," Professor Stone says without looking at me. He reaches up to adjust the bow tie around his neck, then returns to the front of the classroom. "How'd we get so very lucky?"

The other students laugh, and I bristle beneath my robes. Raelan seems incapable of *not* embarrassing me. I've yet to make any friends apart from my roommates, and the bitter part of me wants to blame it on him. Most of the students seem afraid of him—and after the show he put on in the astronomy tower, I understand why.

"Now," our professor continues, returning to the lesson, "begin to focus on your breath. Inhale deeply and exhale fully. Let your breath become your anchor. Notice the air as it moves in and out of your lungs. Feel how it travels through your body."

As the other students begin their breathing exercise, I whisper to Lyra, "Why is Juniper even *here*? You know we're not supposed to bring our companions into class."

Our companions can live in the castle with us, but having classrooms packed with students *and* animals would make things a touch crowded.

"She doesn't like being alone." Lyra shrugs, then pretends to be doing the exercise when Professor Stone looks our way. When he moves to the other side of the room, she continues, "I'm surprised you don't bring Yuki with you."

I try not to snort. "He's a white fox—not exactly inconspicuous. And he doesn't fit in my pocket." I arch a brow at her.

"Yeah, but you're the princess. Wouldn't they have to make an exception?"

"No exceptions," I say, tone clipped. "I don't want to be the princess here. Just another student."

"Are you sure?" Lyra whispers. "I mean, I wouldn't mind having a broody bodyguard standing outside the door. I'd take him off your hands if I could."

My cheeks flare with heat, and I choose not to respond, focusing on my breath as it travels into and out of my body.

"Good," Professor Stone continues. "Now we're going to add a bit more movement to the practice. Stay grounded as you breathe and push energy toward your partner. Control your air. This is *all* about control. When you exhale and push, feel your energy moving your partner back, even if just a little. Let them step or lean slightly as they respond. Keep this flow moving."

Lyra starts by pushing a gentle wind toward me. It sends my hair and robes fluttering, and the air is warm—perhaps from her fire magic. We're both elemental witches, which might be why we connected so quickly and formed such a sudden friendship.

"So, what's the deal with you and Raelan anyway?" Lyra asks. With all the students pushing air around the room, making papers rustle and robes snap, it's easier to speak without being overheard.

"There's no deal," I say, breathing out slowly and focusing on sending a gentle breeze toward Lyra. It brushes her hair back from her face and makes her take a step to steady herself. The citrine crystals dangling from her earlobes sway.

"Good, Miss Ravenscroft," Professor Stone says from across the room.

I look over and give him a smile.

"No deal? Really?" Lyra arches a crimson brow at me. She doesn't look convinced. "Are you sure?"

"I'm positive. He's my guard. A nuisance. That's it."

She pushes a gust back at me, and now I have to steady

myself. All around the room, students are adjusting their stances, bracing against their partners' air magic.

"In that case," Lyra says, her lips curling up on one side, "would you mind if I try him for myself? I mean, have you *seen* him?" She sighs dreamily. "And those *hands*. I love a man with big hands."

Suddenly, I'm picturing Raelan's hands on Lyra's waist, her lips against his, their bodies moving against each other in her bed in our loft.

Without intending to, I send such a powerful gust of wind toward her that she goes stumbling back and has to catch herself on the neighboring desk, spilling an inkwell in the process and startling the students standing there. From Lyra's robe pocket, Juniper lets out a squeak. Lyra's eyes widen in surprise.

"I-I'm so sorry," I say, quickly taking her by the hand and helping her up, then flicking an apologetic look toward the student whose inkwell was spilled. "I didn't mean to—" When I look up to meet Lyra's eyes, she's no longer regarding me with surprise, but with something notably more concerning. Like *suspicion*.

But I don't even know why I had such a strong reaction to the idea of her getting closer to Raelan. He might be my bodyguard, but that's it. We're not even friends. We barely know each other. I have no claim on him.

And I don't *want* a claim on him. I want him to go back to the castle and leave me be.

"And no, I wouldn't mind," I say quickly, just before Professor Stone sweeps over to instruct me on the merits of balance and the importance of controlling my magic.

"The purpose of this lesson is not *power*," he says to the class. "It's control. The elemental magics are incredibly potent and can be dangerous when wielded without caution. Now, continue." His brown eyes find me. "Carefully this time, Miss Ravenscroft."

I try to listen to him, try to focus during the rest of class, but all I can think about is Raelan standing outside the classroom, the concentrated wrinkle that always forms between his eyebrows when he's watching me from a distance, the sharp set of his jaw.

And I try very hard not to notice the tightening in my chest when I imagine him with any other woman.

Because Raelan Ashvale isn't mine.

And I'm certainly not his.

CHAPTER 10
RAELAN

ALINA IS THE LAST STUDENT OUT OF THE classroom. She says nothing as she breezes past me into the candlelit castle corridor. It's a gray day, and the sky has been darkening for the last hour as I've been standing outside Alina's elemental magic classroom. After Alina screamed, my dragon was so worked up that I had to focus all my attention on the clouds I could see through the windows in this corridor. I tracked their movement across the sky while taking steadying breaths, trying to calm my beast, to convince it that Alina was okay.

Now, though, as she stalks down the hallways ahead of me, her pale blue hair drifting behind her as she goes, I get the feeling she's not okay. Something must've upset her during class.

Or maybe *I'm* the one who upset her. Seems that's usually the case.

But I'm not going to ask. Every time Alina talks to me, my dragon gets riled up, and it's becoming physically *exhausting* having to fight my urges down, having to ignore the mate bond screaming through my veins for her.

So instead, I remain silent, my boots clipping along with hers as she navigates the busy corridor.

As we walk, the students eye me—some warily, others with unmasked interest—and Alina. But mostly, they keep their eyes away from Alina, as if they fear me lashing out simply because they expressed curiosity in their princess. And I know this bothers her. She wants to be treated like the other students, not like the king's granddaughter. That's not so easy to do when you've got a knight following you around.

At least I'm not in my armor. Alina absolutely forbade it after I tried to wear it to the welcome ceremony. Now I wear a crisp dark tunic beneath a sturdy cloak and trousers tucked into my polished boots. Simple and unassuming. It still doesn't stop the stares though.

We've only been here for a few weeks, but I've got Alina's class schedule perfectly memorized. She has half an hour before her next class, Magical Anatomy 101. It's her last class of the day, and when it's finished, she'll head back to her dormitory briefly to clean up and prepare for dinner in the dining hall.

Typically, Alina goes straight to class. She's one of those academic types who likes to be early so she has time to look over her notes and ask the professor questions before the other students arrive.

But today, instead of heading straight to class, she descends the spiral staircase into the grand hall, moves hastily across the marble floor to another hallway, and proceeds down it, heading in the complete wrong direction.

My eyes narrow at the back of her head. Still, I say nothing. I follow in silence.

And I'm still silent as Alina makes her way to the botany wing, where her Herbology and Potion Making 101 class is held on Mondays and Wednesdays.

Maybe she needs to speak with her professor?

Instead of stepping into the herbology classroom, she walks to the end of the hallway and pushes through one of the double doors into the side gardens, which hold numerous greenhouses and pots and raised beds overflowing with plants of all types.

I follow a few steps behind her, my boots clipping on the stone stairs. The air is crisp, bordering on cold, and the clouds overhead move swiftly across the sky, dark gray and heavy with the scent of rain. It'll start falling soon, bringing with it the first true days of autumn.

A few students rush past us, headed back into the castle, but once the door closes behind them, Alina and I are alone. She strides to the middle of the garden, then stops. I halt behind her, my gaze flicking around, assessing the greenhouses for any movement. Still, I see no students or faculty. Perhaps everyone feels the incoming storm and is seeking refuge inside the castle's sturdy walls.

Everyone except for us.

My eyes find Alina again. She's facing away from me, clenching the strap of the bookbag hanging over her shoulder. It looks incredibly heavy, bulging with the books she'll need for all four of her classes today. I've offered to carry it for her—multiple times—but she refuses. I've since stopped offering.

Thunder rumbles far off, pulling my focus. As I tip my face to the sky, the first few drops of rain start to fall. They're heavy and cold, the way early-autumn storms so often are. I relish the feel of them on my hot skin as they pelt my face and slip down my neck.

Being around Alina has become somewhat easier—I'm not in excruciating physical pain every time I see her—but I'm still in a constant state of heated agitation, to the point that I often wander the castle corridors at night, restlessly memorizing them in lieu of sleeping. And when I do sleep, it's Alina's face I see, her breath I feel as she whispers things I wish she could say in my waking hours.

The cold sensation against my skin helps chase some of the heat from my veins. I take a steadying breath.

Still, Alina says nothing. The rain pelts her blue-trimmed robe, turning the shoulders a slightly darker shade of black. I can tell she's cold based on the way she starts to hunch in on herself, and her long hair is snapping in the wind, along with her academy-issued skirt.

As the sky opens up above us, I strip quickly out of my cloak, then step up behind her and lift it above her head. I'm careful not to touch her, and I turn my face away when I get close, trying not to breathe her in.

Her scent is intoxicating, like fairy wine. Just one strong whiff sends my dragon roiling.

I'm not looking directly at her, but I see her in my periphery as she moves to quickly smack the cloak away.

"Stop, Raelan!" she snaps. When she looks up at me, her brow is furrowed, her eyes burning with blue fire.

And it does something to me. It makes me want to crush my mouth to hers, to run my tongue along her lips until they're no longer twisted into such an angry scowl. I want it so badly that I flinch from the desire singing through my veins.

I step back from her as my dragon rages, making the chain around my neck flare with heat.

"Stop what?" I finally force myself to say. To my credit, my voice doesn't tremble the way my insides are right now.

"Just . . . *stop*. You don't have to treat me like a child, don't have to come running for every little thing."

The rain falls around us, slowly soaking Alina's hair so it sticks to her flushed sandy-brown cheeks.

My eyes narrow slightly as rivulets of rain run down my cheeks and drip from my chin. "You screamed. Of course I came running."

"It was just Lyra's rat. She startled me is all." Alina waves a hand, then uses it to brush the wet hair from her cheeks.

"Protecting you is my duty," I say, clutching the cloak in my hand as the rain soaks us both. "It's the entire reason I'm here. *You* are the reason I'm here. And you constantly fighting that fact is doing neither of us any good."

"Yes, but—" Alina bites her lip, and I have to try very hard not to react to it. She has no idea what such a subtle gesture does to me. "But I want to be *normal* while I'm here." Some of the anger has gone from her voice, and she glances down toward her feet. "I've been the princess my

71

whole life. Here, I just want to be another student. And that's hard when I'm the only one being accompanied by a bodyguard."

Thunder rumbles again, closer this time. I need to get her out of the rain. She could catch a cold being out in the weather like this.

I draw in a deep breath, then let it out slowly.

"I understand," I say.

Alina's pale eyes flash up to meet mine. One of her sky-blue brows arches in the corner, like she doesn't really believe me. "You do?"

"Of course." I flex my jaw, trying not to show Alina how unhinged her close proximity makes me. Even now, my chain burns, biting into my flesh as it forces my dragon down. "But that doesn't change what I'm here to do. I still have to protect you, regardless of how either of us feels about it."

"Protect me? From what?" She lets out a short laugh, but it's not one of her real laughs; those sound like magic, while this one just sounds cold. "No one here wants to hurt me."

"You don't know that."

She narrows her eyes at me, then bites her lip again. I tear my gaze away, trying to distract myself. Instead of looking at her, I watch the plants in the raised beds thrash in the wind as it batters the garden.

"Fine," she concedes. "I don't *know* that. But I know I need some space. I can't have you breathing down my neck all the time; it's driving me crazy." She reaches up again, this time to wipe rainwater off her forehead. "Grandfather doesn't need to know exactly how many feet you stand from me at all times. If we're stuck together, a little distance might help us get through this." The anger in her eyes flickers and softens. "Please?"

At first, I think to tell her no, like I have every time she's asked in the past. But the look in her eyes stills the words on my tongue.

She wants to be normal for once in her life, and I get that.

I know how it feels to be the outcast, the odd one out. I know how it feels to lie awake at night wondering what it would be like to have a friend, even just one. My father taught me to stay away from the other children lest I accidentally shift and harm them. I thought he was being unnecessarily cautious and ruining my life with his incessant worries.

Until I saw what he did to my mother.

Giving Alina some space could be good for me too. I'd like to be able to sleep at night without dreaming of wrapping my claws around her and branding her with my mark, without wondering what it would feel like to rest my weight between her thighs and taste her mouth with mine.

Just the *thought* of it sends my cock hardening in my trousers, and I quickly shift the cloak in my hand to hide what's happening to me.

This is so unprofessional.

"Okay," I say slowly. And it's impossible not to see the joy it brings to Alina's eyes. I quickly add, "But I'll still be there at all times. I'll just try to . . . back off a bit."

Now her joy shifts into a smile. Meanwhile, I'm still trying to imagine anything *except* my teeth sinking into her flesh, marking her as mine. My cock is still hard.

Fuck.

"Thank you, Raelan. Truly."

And now she's using my name. Again. I really wish she'd stop doing that. It's more powerful than any spell she could cast over me.

I nod once, clenching my teeth so hard my jaw aches.

Alina takes a step closer to me, and I take a step back.

"Are you okay?" she asks, head tipping to one side. The movement sends her wet hair sliding, revealing her smooth throat. "You're . . . steaming."

Shit, she's right. I got so overheated thinking about the things I absolutely *cannot* do with her that the rain is now evaporating as soon as it hits my skin, turning to steam on contact. I'm lucky it doesn't sizzle like eggs on cast iron.

I clear my throat and take another step back. "I'm fine. I just run warm. Now, Your Highness, if you'd please." I use my free hand to gesture back toward the castle.

"For the *last* time, I told you to call me Alina," she says. But her voice isn't laced with anger this time, and it looks like she *almost* gives me a smile before finally heading for the double doors back into the castle.

This time I give her an extra few feet of space as I follow her into the candlelit corridor, where we both drip water onto the stone floor. And I think this will be good for both of us. Perhaps it's even necessary.

Because if I don't get control of myself soon, I don't know what the fuck's going to happen. And I absolutely *cannot* let anything happen. Because my family is depending on me to not mess this up. And I'm not going to fail them.

Even for my fated mate.

CHAPTER 11
ALINA

TRUE TO HIS WORD, RAELAN HAS BACKED off.

Kind of.

A little bit.

But it's something, at least. And I think he likes it better this way as well. He's still uptight, like all the guards I've ever known, but he doesn't look quite so rigid anymore—or maybe I'm just imagining it because *I* don't feel quite so rigid anymore. I didn't realize how crazy it was making me, being followed around so closely, feeling like my every move was being watched. And they were. They still are. But at least now I can almost pretend like he's not watching me. And for that, I'm incredibly grateful to Raelan.

So long as neither of us tells Grandfather, this arrangement should work out just fine.

"I don't *get* this," Lyra says, sitting back from the big table in the library with a sigh. Half of her bright red hair is pulled up into a curly bun on top of her head and is speared through with a hair stick.

Poppy looks up from her textbook on magical ethics and adjusts her round glasses. "Get what?"

"This rune translation. I've never needed to read a rune in my life. This is a waste of my talents." Lyra groans.

"It's not so difficult." Poppy shrugs one shoulder.

Lyra arches a brow at her. "Maybe not for you. Nothing's difficult for you."

"Well, I don't know about *that*," Poppy says, light brown cheeks starting to go red. "Would you like some help?"

"Yes. *Please.*"

I smile and turn the page in my textbook. This week in my potions class, we're learning a basic calming elixir, which I'm already thinking Lyra could use.

Just last week, she accidentally set fire to her bed curtains, and I was so startled that I didn't even get a chance to react with my frost magic before Maeve put out the fire with a pitcher of water, soaking Lyra in the process.

Only later did Raelan ask me why I smelled slightly of smoke—which was odd in and of itself, considering I thought I'd washed the smell from my hair.

I dip my quill into my inkwell and begin taking notes, trying to memorize all the ingredients needed for the calming elixir: lavender, chamomile, lemon balm, passionflower, ro—

"Maeve! Over here!"

I look up at Lyra's exclamation.

Maeve is crossing the library toward us, and the eyes of most of the guys in the library follow her, tracking her long-legged strides. But she doesn't even seem to notice. She walks right to our table, leans back against it, and arches an eyebrow at me while pushing her straight violet-black hair over her shoulder.

"Why's your knight standing in the hallway? Doesn't he usually want an eye on you at all times?"

"She convinced him to give her some space," Poppy says without looking up from Lyra's runes homework. "Remember?"

"Of course I remember." Maeve rolls her eyes, which are vivid purple, like the storm clouds she can summon at will. "But I didn't realize he was giving you *this* much space. He usually lurks whenever we study here." She pushes off the table and sinks into the chair next to mine, crossing her legs.

"I convinced him," I say, giving up on taking notes. We all have a break period on Fridays, and this is where we gather when the weather isn't nice enough to sit outside. Right now, another fall storm is brewing, tossing bright yellow and red leaves around the campus and striking the windows with vengeance.

"Not like it was hard," Lyra says.

My gaze snaps to her. "What do you mean?"

Even Poppy looks up from her book, and my three roommates exchange glances.

"What?" I cap my inkwell and arch a brow, then lean back in my chair and cross my arms over my chest. "Tell me."

"You could probably convince that man to breathe fire for you," Lyra mumbles, her voice a bit muffled as she opens her robe to pet Juniper, who's once again perched in the inside pocket.

"That's ridiculous," I say. "Raelan barely listens to me. I think the only reason he agreed is because it's easier for him too."

Poppy goes back to the rune translation, but Maeve cants her head at me. "Do you not see the way he looks at you?" she asks.

"Of course I do." With a huff, I put my inkwell and potions textbook away in my shoulder bag. "Like I'm a job. An irritant. A child to be monitored. I don't think he even wanted this job. But Grandfather forced him."

Lyra scoffs, and Maeve's plum lips quirk up on one side. Poppy is too invested in the runes she's translating to react at all.

"Alina, are you serious?" Lyra asks after tucking Juniper back into her robe pocket. "Or are you being blissfully ignorant?"

I narrow my eyes at her sharply. "Ignorant?"

Of all the girls, Lyra dropped the whole "princess" act the quickest, almost immediately regarding me as she would anyone else. And though she has a brashness I'm not quite accustomed to yet, I kind of enjoy it—I feel like I can depend on her to always tell me the truth, my lineage be damned.

Lyra holds up her hands. "I don't mean it in a bad way. I just mean . . . Well, it's so *obvious*. Isn't it obvious?" She looks at Maeve for affirmation, and she nods.

I'm losing interest in talking about this. For some reason, whenever the girls' conversations turn to Raelan, my skin starts to crawl. Ever since Lyra asked me if she could have him, I've felt odd, like maybe they'll all pay less attention to him if *I* pay less attention to him, pretend like he's not there.

Thus far, it's not been successful.

"I'm just saying, he watches you like he wants to eat you," Lyra says. She twists a curl around her finger. "I'm pretty jealous, to be honest."

Maeve lets out a short burst of laughter, which warrants a sharp look from the librarian nearby. Poppy's cheeks go red, and she puts a hand over her mouth to hide her smile.

"Now you're just being silly," I say dismissively, avoiding Lyra's eyes as I gather up the last of my belongings and stand from the table. "I'm a job to him. That's it."

Lyra gives me a sideways smile and tips her head at me. "If you say so."

"I do." I heft my bag onto my shoulder with a grunt, then push my hair back over my shoulder. "See you girls for dinner?"

They all nod and wave as I step back from the table and start across the library. My last class on Fridays is archery—by far my favorite class of the week. First-years only get to pick one elective, and when I came across archery in the Coven Crest class pamphlet, it was an easy choice.

But our range is outside, and with the way the wind is blowing, I have a feeling we might get rained on. I'll need to return to my dormitory and switch into my boots just in case.

The librarian smiles as I pass her by, and then I push through one of the big double doors and ease into the hallway. It's a bit drafty today, and the candles are struggling to battle the darkness from the thick cloud cover.

Raelan stands across the hall, dressed in black and draped in a thick cloak. His gaze is trained out the window, and he hasn't yet turned to look at me, so I'm given a rare moment to observe him without his awareness.

He's clean-shaven, like all the guards in the King's Royal Army, but there's a bit of a shadow along his cheeks and jaw, dark like his short hair and thick brows. His eyes are narrowed, focused. I wonder what he's looking for in the clouds. In these long moments of quiet, when all he does is stand around and wait for me, I wonder what he thinks about.

I still barely know him despite how much time we're now forced to spend together. But maybe that's a good thing—professional boundaries and all.

The library door opens behind me, another student passing through, and a draft sends my hair and robe fluttering. Raelan draws a breath, and his dark eyes snap toward me. As soon as he sees me, he straightens up, his typical cold demeanor and mask falling into place.

Looking at him now, I have no idea what Lyra and Maeve were going on about. He looks at me like I'm a slight annoyance, something to be withstood rather than enjoyed.

Enjoyed?

Is that what I want? For him to *enjoy* me? Enjoy my presence?

My chest tightens up a bit at the thought, and I quickly turn away, striding down the hallway along with the other students moving between classes or on their rest period.

Despite Raelan's size, he moves quietly, and I can scarcely hear his boots on the stone as he follows behind me, enough paces back now that I don't feel like he's breathing down my neck at every waking moment.

I reach the stairs to the north tower and start up them. A few students pass by me, smiling and nodding as they go, but soon, it's just me and Raelan on the stairs, climbing higher and higher as the wind outside taps on the stained glass windows.

I'm breathing hard by the time we make it to NT33—no matter how many times I climb this tower, I still get out of breath. Raelan doesn't even break a sweat.

I pull my key out of my robe pocket, force it into the heavy lock, and push the door open.

The scent of sage drifts out—Maeve lights a stick every morning before her daily meditation—immediately calming me. Yuki yips a hello from where he's sprawled on one of the couches in front of the fire. Behind me, Raelan pauses, his boots falling silent on the stone.

Whenever I'm in my dorm room, he waits out here in the hall—unless it's nighttime, then he retires to his room, which is just a short distance up the staircase from mine. He never comes inside, just stands here silently, waiting for me to go to my next class or to the dining hall. And he never complains, even if he often looks like he wants to.

"Would you . . . like to come in?" I ask, shocking even myself with the offer. "I could make us a cup of tea before archery. It'll probably be cold on the range today."

Surprise crosses briefly over his face, and his gaze flicks over my shoulder, to the room beyond. He draws a breath, and I think he's going to take me up on my offer. But then he gives a sharp shake of his head and steps back, putting another foot of distance between us.

"No. I'll wait for you here."

Though I don't understand why, his rejection feels like a slap to the face.

And I'm reminded that I'm just a job to him, a salary, a duty he does for his kingdom.

Foolishly, I let Maeve and Lyra get to me. But they're wrong. Just like I told them.

"Very well," I say, then step into the room and close the door without even glancing back. When it clicks closed, putting a physical barrier between us, I let my shoulders sag.

And I think, on the other side of the door, I hear Raelan sigh.

CHAPTER 12
ALINA

WHAT DO *YOU* THINK DIVINATION IS?" Professor Silvermoon asks the class. She walks slowly through our assembled desks, her long silver hair pulled back into a single braid.

A student at the right of the classroom speaks up. "I'm not totally sure, but I think it's using symbols or tools to understand what's going to happen in the future."

"Good," Professor Silvermoon says. "Anyone else?" Her dark blue eyes slide to my desk, where I'm seated beside Poppy. "Ms. Waverly? What does divination mean to you?"

Poppy sits up a bit straighter and pushes her round glasses farther up the bridge of her nose. "It's . . . It's a way to bring unconscious knowledge into conscious awareness," she says, her voice soft.

Professor Silvermoon makes a gentle humming sound as she moves toward the front of the classroom. A crystal ball sits on her desk, and a stick of incense smolders, sending a thin tendril of sage-scented smoke throughout the room. "Can you expand on that?" she asks.

Poppy clears her throat and adjusts in her seat. "Well . . . I think a lot of the time, we already know the answers we're looking for—we just don't *know* that we know them. Divination tools, like tarot or pendulums, help us access that inner knowing by giving it form through symbols or patterns. When we look at a card or symbol, it triggers something inside us—a memory, a feeling, a realization—that we might not have noticed otherwise. So, in a way, we're not predicting the future so much as uncovering hidden layers of the present or ourselves."

Professor Silvermoon tips her head. "Very good, Ms. Waverly. You have a dream-magic affinity, yes?"

Poppy's cheeks go a touch pink as all the students turn to look at her. She nods once. "That's right."

"It suits you." Professor Silvermoon gives Poppy a smile, then turns to regard the class. "Divination means many things to many different practitioners. But in this class, we treat divination as a reflective practice—a way to ask better questions, not just get easy answers. Whether you view it as a spiritual connection, a psychological mirror, or an art form, it's ultimately about empowering you to know yourself more deeply." She looks around the classroom. "Now, please pull out your tarot cards, and we'll get started with a daily pull and reflection."

When her eyes meet mine, a little tingle goes down my spine. Professor Silvermoon has a way of looking *into* you, like she can see right through all your layers and to the core of your soul.

I reach into my bookbag and pull out my satin card bag. It's a rich blue with little moons and stars embroidered on it with silver thread. Sliding the cards carefully from the bag, I set them on the desk in front of me.

Professor Silvermoon guides us through grounding ourselves, setting an intention, and asking a question. As Poppy gets to work beside me, pulling three cards for her reading, I close my eyes and focus on my question.

What's the potential lesson to be learned in the new opportunities I'm about to encounter?

I repeat the question as I skim my hands over the arc of glossy cards. A slight tingle in my fingertips draws my hand down, and I trust my gut as I pull a card and slowly flip it over to reveal it.

The card is reversed, which will affect my reading, and it depicts a moon suspended over a blue sky and deeper blue body of water, with a small island dotted with trees cradled within the moon's crescent.

I've not practiced much tarot or divination, so I reach for my tarot textbook and flip it open to the chapter on The Moon.

Slowly, I trace the paragraphs with one finger, brow furrowing as I read.

The Moon card reversed may indicate the possibility of self-deception, where you may be amplifying or distorting the reality of a situation. It's a reminder to examine whether you're caught in an emotional, dramatic retelling of events instead of sticking to clear facts.

*While it's natural to get swept up in emotional or intu-
itive waves, doing so won't bring you the clarity or stability
you need in times of uncertainty. It's important to anchor
yourself and seek truth, even if it means confronting discomfort or illusions.*

I sit back from the desk and stare at the words a while
longer, then back at the upside-down card.

Self-deception? Amplifying or distorting a situation?

At first, I have the desire the slide the card back into
the deck and pick another—hopefully one that's easier to
interpret. I glance at Poppy. She's smiling a bit to herself,
using her quill and ink to jot notes into a small brown notebook. Professor Silvermoon is drifting through the room,
long skirt swishing across the stone floor. She stops to help a
student with their interpretation.

I think to raise my hand and ask for her help.

But then Raelan's face flashes into my mind. I briefly
recall our argument in the astronomy tower, then all
those that followed. I remember how he held his cloak
over my head in the gardens, trying to protect me from
the rain. Then I see his sharp cheekbones, his dark eyes,
the gleam of the chain that hides beneath his tunics, only
visible every so often when he shifts and the light hits it
just right.

And in my belly, a little ember of heat flares to life. This
is the same flicker of heat I've been trying to ignore, to shove
down and douse with ice. But no matter what I do, it always
flares back to life.

Slowly, my gaze slides toward the classroom door. I know Raelan is standing right on the other side, waiting for me.

The ember burns a bit hotter.

Until someone steps directly into my line of sight, impeding my view of the door.

It's a boy with a mop of brown hair and sparkling brown eyes. He smiles easily and holds his card up to me. "You having any luck?" he asks. "I'm kind of confused about mine."

I blink, trying to wipe thoughts of Raelan from my mind, then give the boy a smile. "I'm struggling a bit too," I say, because surely I'm not self-deceiving in regard to Raelan. There must be another interpretation I'm missing. I flick my gaze to Poppy. "Hey, Poppy, think you might be able to give us some tips?"

She looks up from her notebook, glances between me and the boy, and nods. "Yeah, sure. Which card did you pull?"

The boy places his card down on the table: the Nine of Wands. I have no idea what it means, but Poppy scrunches her nose a bit.

"I'm Tristan, by the way," he says.

"I'm Alina. This is my roommate, Poppy."

"Nice to meet you both." He smiles quickly and easily, then pulls up an empty chair and sits at our desk with us. "So, what do you think?" He regards Poppy with a tilt of his head. "Does it foretell my untimely death?"

Though it was clearly a joke, Poppy doesn't seem to take it as one. She gives a sharp shake of her head, then points at the card and begins explaining the different elements to us:

the man holding a wand; the bandages covering the man's obvious injuries; eight other wands standing behind him.

The boy, Tristan, nods along, listening intently while Poppy explains the card to him. Meanwhile, my gaze slides to the door again.

And though I'd like to convince myself otherwise, I get the feeling I *did* read my card right. Now I just have to figure out what to do about it.

CHAPTER 13
RAELAN

AUTUMN HAS FULLY DESCENDED ON Coven Crest Academy. The heat of summer has gone, and in its place are cold mornings, falling leaves, and rain that never ceases. The sky has been dark all day, and my skin feels alive with the electricity in the air. It makes me antsy, irritable.

And like usual, Alina isn't helping.

Ever since she invited me into her dorm room, I've been unsettled. I don't understand her, can't quite read the expressions she makes and the words she says.

It's a small miracle we've been able to make this work. I've given her a bit more space these past few weeks, and thanks to that, I've even been able to sleep at night—mostly, though when my dragon is particularly agitated, like it is now, I still find myself wandering the corridors in the evenings, scaring the students who've crept out of their dorms to kiss each other in the darkened hallways.

I can already tell tonight will be a sleepless night. My dragon coils beneath my skin, hot and angry. It wants to spread its wings and fly, to taste the rain and dive through the lightning, to tumble with the thunder while it races across the clouds.

But no. There will be no freedom for it tonight, nor any other night so long as I'm here with Alina.

There will be a holiday vacation in December, for Yule, and when I return home to the castle with Alina, I will tell the king I need a brief respite from my duties. He'll understand. Since he took me in, there have been a number of occasions when I've needed to get away, to cut through the clouds and feel the cold air on my scales, to release all the pent-up aggression inside me.

Usually, I don't feel so strong an urge to let my beast free. But Alina changes all of that.

Right now, she's seated at the end of a long dining table, surrounded by her three roommates. She smiles and laughs easily with them, seeming comfortable in their presence. The dining room is lit by chandeliers laden with flickering candles, and heavy aromas drift through the air: fresh-baked bread, spices and herbs, stews and pottages and roasted vegetables.

I typically eat when Alina does. But tonight I feel on edge, and I have very little appetite.

For food, anyway.

My eyes track Alina's hand as she butters a thin slice of bread and lifts it to her lips. Her movements are graceful, elegant. She takes a bite of the bread, and a small dab of butter gathers in the slight depression above her top lip.

I imagine licking it off for her, claiming her lips with mine. I imagine the taste of her tongue, wonder what it might feel like gliding across my skin.

And in response, the chain around my neck burns, the magic battling my dragon down, keeping it contained. I flex my jaw and try not to react to the pain.

Alina looks up at me then, as if she can feel my eyes on her. Despite all the students lingering around the dining hall, she finds me easily, and she holds my gaze. Her blue eyes narrow slightly, lips drawing together.

I should look away. I always do.

But this time, I don't.

This time, my dragon meets her eyes and refuses to glance away.

And every second she holds my gaze feels like an eternity. In my periphery, everything else falls away, until all that's left is her.

Alina Ravenscroft. The princess of Elarwyn. A blue-haired frost witch. My fated mate.

Pain ricochets through me, making me clench my hands into fists and grind my teeth. A few students walking past take notice and step subtly away, giving me a wide berth while their eyes flick my way nervously.

The pain of holding myself back from her hasn't been as bad these last few weeks, but today is a different story. I've been fighting my instincts all day, and it's becoming difficult to stand for the aching thrumming through me.

We aren't supposed to resist our mates like this. It goes against nature, against our instincts. And yet I must resist.

Because no matter the torture, she is not mine to claim. She'll never be mine to claim.

My dragon just refuses to accept that truth.

A few students carrying dining trays pass in front of me, breaking my gaze with Alina. For a brief moment, I catch my breath, saved from the power of Alina's stare. But then I find her again, and she's no longer looking at me.

She's looking up at another student who's stopped at the end of the table to speak with her.

A *male* student.

My dragon roils as I watch them talk. Alina lifts a hand to tuck a strand of hair behind her ear, and I swear I can pick up her scent swirling through the room despite the hundreds of other smells drifting through this crowded space.

The other student shifts closer, bracing his hand on the table, so near to Alina's that he could touch her fingers if he wanted to.

Mine, my dragon growls. *Not his. Mine.*

I clench my hands harder, digging my nails into my palms, trying to use the pain to focus myself.

But it's not working. The edges of my vision are starting to go dark in an effort to help me home in on the one thing—the *only* thing—that matters.

Alina. Always Alina.

And before I can stop myself, before I even realize what I'm doing, my feet start to move, carrying me through the throngs of students, across the candlelit dining hall, and right up to Alina's table.

Everyone stops talking to focus on me.

"R-Raelan?" Alina says when I stop behind the male student.

He turns and has to look up at me. And I barely resist the urge to snarl.

"What is it?" Alina asks.

Still looking at him, wondering how far I could throw him across this dining hall without killing him, I say, "Urgent matter, Your Highness. Please come with me."

The male takes a step back, though not as quickly as I'd like. "I'll see you in class tomorrow, Alina," he says.

And hearing her name on his lips makes me bristle, sends a wave of angry heat from my head to my toes. He has no right to say her name so casually.

Alina's sky-blue brows crinkle as the male student steps away, and she stands slowly, still looking at me. "What's happening?"

"We're leaving," I say in way of answer. "Now."

Alina's roommates all stare as I take her by the arm and *gently* escort her from the dining hall. She doesn't resist, but she keeps asking, "What's wrong? What happened?"

I should stop. I should tell her I made a mistake and apologize for interrupting her dinner.

But I can't. All I can do is stalk down the candlelit corridor while rain hits the windows and slides down the glass in never-ending rivulets.

I don't even know where I'm going. All I know is that I needed to get Alina away from that boy—though I haven't yet determined if it's because I felt he's a threat or because my dragon can't stand the sight of another male so close to her, so casually comfortable with her, like those two I chased away from her in the astronomy tower. Right now, it doesn't matter. Because my hand is wrapped around Alina's upper arm, and she's stumbling alongside me, her hair falling around her shoulders and tickling my wrist where my long-sleeved tunic is pushed up.

A few students give her confused or troubled looks, and a silver-haired professor asks, "Miss Ravenscroft, is everything all right?"

"Just fine, Professor Silvermoon!" she says, waving the woman off.

We turn down another hallway. This one is quieter. And once we're alone, Alina plants her feet and rips her arm from my grasp with surprising strength.

"That's quite enough," she says, refusing to take another step. "Tell me what's going on. *Now.*"

I turn slowly to look at her.

We're standing in a narrow corridor, the din from the dining hall having faded into the distance. Overhead, stained glass windows run with rainwater, casting dim colors down across Alina's hair and face. Her eyes are wide, her lips parted as she breathes heavily.

"Well?" she snaps. "Is it Grandfather? Has something happened? Tell me!"

But I can't. I can't tell her what I am, and I certainly can't tell her she's my mate. I'd lose this position in the guard in a heartbeat, and my mother and sisters would lose their home.

No. I can't. So I just clench my teeth and hiss, "I felt a threat from that student. I wanted you away from him."

The worry in Alina's wide eyes slowly shifts, turning to the blue fire that sets my veins alight, that makes me yearn for her in the darkness when I'm alone with my hand and my thoughts.

"A threat?" Alina bites out, her fingers curling into fists at her sides. "Tristan is my *friend*, Raelan. He was just speaking with me about an assignment in divination class."

"How do you know?" I growl. "How do you know he's not just trying to get close to you so he can use you? You're the princess—you have to be more careful."

It sounds ridiculous, even to my ears. I'm grasping, trying to come up with some explanation for my erratic behavior. But there's only one explanation that makes sense, and it's the one I'll never speak aloud.

I expect Alina to yell at me, tell me I'm being a fool, threaten to tell her grandfather that I've failed in my duties and need to be replaced. So she surprises me when she crosses her arms and narrows her eyes, head tipping just far enough to one side that it makes her look catlike, perhaps even dangerous.

My dragon likes it.

Shit.

"You're lying," she says.

My skin prickles.

She has no idea how much I'm lying about. She doesn't even know I'm not human. But I don't say a word. I just clench my jaw and try not to breathe too deeply lest her smell overwhelm my senses.

"First those boys in the tower, now Tristan. What's actually going on?" Her voice is a bit quieter now, coaxing, like she thinks she can pull the truth out of me if only her words lilt just right.

And she could if not for the chain around my neck. It was already hot back in the dining hall, but it's growing hotter as it works to force my dragon into submission. But it's never had to work this hard.

A door opens down the hall, and a moment later, a student passes by us, mumbling, "Pardon me," as she goes. Alina takes a step toward me to make room. I step away. But it's a narrow hall, and my back is already brushing the stone wall. There's nowhere else for me to go.

The student disappears down another hallway, but Alina remains where she's at, arms still crossed, gaze unblinking as she glares at me.

"Raelan," she says.

My cock twitches when she says my name, and I'm grateful the corridor is only dimly lit.

Fuck.

"Don't, Your Highness," I bite out. She has no idea what her proximity is doing to me. I'm breaking out in a sweat just trying to fight the pain and desire warring through my body. If she takes another step closer—

"Don't what?" She arches a brow. "And I've told you a hundred times to call me Alina."

"Don't—" I swallow hard. "Come any closer."

My chest rises and falls rapidly, my heart racing, creating a sound like waves in my ears. I think I might pass out. I can't keep doing this. I can't—

A strange look comes over Alina's eyes, like a mixture of want and fear.

Then she does something incredibly stupid.

She takes one more step toward me, presses onto her toes, and brushes her lips against mine.

And I fucking lose it.

CHAPTER 14
ALINA

ALL I CAN HEAR ARE LYRA'S WORDS RINGing in my ears.

Would you mind if I try him for myself? she asked in class, and without meaning to, I almost threw her across the room with a burst of air magic. Then, in the library, *He watches you like he wants to eat you.*

The thought that Raelan Ashvale might want to eat me makes heat pulse between my thighs.

I'm not sure I've ever been so confused about someone—about *anything*—in my life. He barely speaks to me, seems to avoid touching me or being alone with me whenever possible, and gives me curt one-word answers when I ask him questions, yet he scared my male acquaintances away and dragged me from the dining hall because he thinks Tristan is a *threat*? He makes no sense. And maybe *I* make no sense. Maybe he's just as confused about me as I am about him.

But I have to know. I can't spend the rest of this school-year wondering if his glances mean something or if I'm just imagining the heat in his stare. And after that tarot reading in my divination class the other day, I haven't been able to get this silly idea out of my head.

The idea that I need to see if there's something actually here, something brewing between us, or if I've just deceived myself all along.

The hallway is dark and quiet. No one is here to see us. A voice inside tells me, *It's now or never.*

So in a moment of foolish recklessness, I close the distance between us and press my lips to his.

I brace myself, prepared for him to push me away, to tell me how inappropriate it is for a guard to be kissing the princess he's sworn to protect. And at first, Raelan goes tense, his lips hard beneath mine.

And I think I've made a mistake. A horribly embarrassing mistake.

But between one breath and the next, everything changes.

His hands come around my waist to grasp me in a firm hold, and he whirls me around, making me gasp as he presses my back against the cool brick wall in the dimly lit corridor. On mine, his mouth softens, working my lips like he's done this a thousand times.

Maybe he has, I realize. Maybe he's had a hundred women, has lain between so many thighs that he can't even remember the faces that go along with them. Maybe I pale in comparison, being so young and naive and inexperienced.

The growl he lets out as he presses his hard body against mine makes me hope I'm wrong.

I've kissed boys before—in the gardens back home, in quiet drawing rooms after escaping from stuffy waltzes—but no boy has ever kissed me like this. Raelan kisses me like a man. And I feel myself melting for him, becoming soft in his hands, pliable and easily molded.

His mouth ceases its ravishment of mine, and I catch my breath as he tips my head back and moves his lips to my throat. My heart gallops in my chest as his tongue glides across my skin, making me tingle in places I've only ever touched myself.

But now I want Raelan to touch me there too.

I know now I've been lying to myself over these past few weeks. The first time I saw Raelan in Grandfather's study, with his dark eyes and cold stare, I thought he'd just be yet another emotionless guard, someone to hold doors and scan courtyards before I passed through them. He was handsome, but it meant nothing.

Then he started appearing in my dreams, and then in my waking thoughts.

And I'm wondering now if he thinks about me as often as I think about him.

With heated abandon, I grab Raelan's hand and move it to the junction of my thighs. He doesn't resist. His hand cups my mound through my school skirt, and I let out a gasp.

Please, yes, I think, tipping my head back against the wall.

I *want* this. I'm not confused anymore. I know for sure.

Around me, the hallway falls away until all I can think about is him, his touch, his hand between my legs and his mouth exploring my neck. I start to open my thighs for him, seeking more of his touch, wishing for him to discover me, to teach me what to do.

But then Raelan recoils from me as if I slapped him, as if I drove a dagger through his chest. In the semidarkness of the corridor, his dark eyes look almost black, and I think it must be a trick of the light when his pupils contract, thinning into slits so narrow I can scarcely see them. They're almost . . . reptilian.

It sends my heart skipping a beat. *What the . . . ?*

He's breathing hard, gasping for breath, his skin glistening with perspiration. He winces and squeezes his eyes closed, doubling over in pain.

Something's wrong. I know this even before he turns and stumbles down the hallway, headed back the way we came.

"Raelan!" I yell after him, but he doesn't respond.

What's going on?

I chase him into the grand hall, arriving just in time to see him throw open one of the massive double doors and fling himself outside into the storm. My shoes tap across the marble floor as I follow after him. I step into the open doorway, a small gasp slipping from me as icy wind and rain lash my face.

The storm is intensifying, the sky overhead darkening with clouds and distant thunder. Fog rolls through the courtyard, thick and almost impenetrable.

And collapsed upon his knees in the grass is Raelan, a dark form hunched beneath the weight of the rain.

I run to him, ignoring the cold rain as it strikes my face and causes my vision to blur.

"Raelan!" I yell over another roll of thunder. My robe snaps wildly behind me, and the wind tears at my hair.

He doesn't turn as I approach.

On his knees, he bends low, fingers digging into the soft grass and soil, forehead pressed to the earth. His body is shaking.

"What's wrong?" I ask, sinking down next to him. But when I reach out to touch his shoulder, he flinches away, acting like my touch is scalding fire.

His body puts off steam in the cold air, drying the rain so fast that he's barely even damp. At the same time, the chain he wears around his neck starts to glow with strange white-blue light. Like magic.

Raelan screams, and I start, my stomach twisting violently.

I want to help him, want to fix this. But I have no idea what *this* even is. Is he sick? Hurt? Is the chain doing something to him?

My eyes cut toward the castle, but the fog is so thick now that I can't even see the stairs leading to the entryway. The towers that usually look down upon the grounds are lost in the clouds above. It's just us out here.

Breathing heavily, heart racing, I turn back to Raelan.

As his muscles strain, the chain shifts on his neck, revealing what look like burns etched into his skin.

Maybe that's the problem—the chain is hurting him, though I've no idea why or what it is. Could it be cursed?

Raelan screams again. I can't believe no one else has yet come to see what's happening. Perhaps they can't hear us over the wind and thunder and lashing rain.

No one else is coming. I have to help him. I know if it were the other way around, he'd help me.

So I push to my feet, coat my hands in a thin layer of frost to prevent any burns, and reach for him. He's too distracted by his pain to pull away from me this time. My fingers close around the clasp holding the chain taut, and with one movement, I have it open. The heavy metal links come away easily in my hands, slipping from Raelan's neck and into my palms.

The chain stops glowing. Raelan ceases screaming.

Pride goes through me. I helped him. I took his pain away. I—

Raelan's body starts to contort, moving in ways that look anything but natural. His back twists, his arms straining like they're about to be wrenched from their sockets.

Chain still gripped in my hand, I take one step back, eyes widening while nausea roils in my stomach.

Something is *very* wrong.

As thunder rumbles and the rain intensifies, casting more mist and fog across the courtyard, Raelan . . . *changes*.

His body writhes, his bones breaking, and I don't know how I remain standing as he becomes something I've only ever heard whispers of, something that is said to be so rare it might as well not exist at all. Something from a time long past.

The creature rises up, rain pelting its onyx scales, and its eyes—dark as pitch and flecked with shimmering gold—meet mine.

Terror shoots through me. It tells me to *run*.

But the grass is wet from the rain, and when I turn to flee toward the castle, I slip, falling hard. The chain snakes from my hand and coils onto the rain-soaked earth, no longer aglow. My hair sticks to my face, impeding my vision of the creature looming over me. I whip around and use a muddy hand to push the hair from my face. And when I do, my breath freezes in my lungs.

Because the dragon is gigantic, the single largest living thing I've ever seen. It's taller than the outbuildings dotted through the courtyard, and when it spreads its glossy wings, they block out the dim light from the stormy gray sky, leaving me trembling in deep dark shadow.

Its black-gold eyes home in on me, and its lips pull back into a snarl, exposing lines of glistening white fangs.

I know I should run, should try to escape, but I can't move. My body is frozen there on the wet earth, my knees coated in mud and grass from falling.

The dragon extends its head toward me, its neck long and sinuous in its movements. A single ridiculous thought goes through my head: *Lyra was right.* It exhales a steady stream of smoke, dousing my body in heat. I'm shaking so hard now that the songbird pendant my mother gave me is thumping against my chest with the sharp movements.

Just when I think the dragon is going to shred me with its razor-sharp teeth and swallow my ragged body whole, it rips itself away from me and gives a powerful downstroke of its wings, then another. The wind it creates buffets me, making me hold up a hand to shield my eyes from the rain and dirt and grass tearing through the air.

And then the dragon lifts from the ground, fog swirling around it, and with another few strokes of its wings, it rises into the misty gray sky and is swallowed up by the clouds, vanishing from existence almost as quickly as it appeared.

For a moment, I can still hear its wings beating the air over the sound of the howling wind, but after a short while, even that fades into nothing.

Now I'm in the courtyard alone, soaking wet and covered in mud. The rain continues to fall, only intensifying.

My whole body trembles fiercely, shaking so hard my teeth clack together.

What . . . was that?

It was Raelan.

Then it was a dragon.

A *dragon.*

Raelan is a . . . a . . .

Beside me, the chain I removed from Raelan's neck lies in the grass. My hands quiver as I reach for it, take it into my mud-smeared fingers.

"Alina!"

I clench the chain and cast my gaze to the stormy sky as two sets of feet pound toward me, splashing through the puddles and the mud. Then Lyra and Maeve are kneeling on either side of me, their faces scrunched in concern as they reach for my arms.

"What happened?" Lyra asks, raising her voice to be heard over the storm. Her red curls are already turning a deeper shade from being soaked by the rain. She glances around, forehead furrowing. "And where's Raelan?"

They pull me to my feet, but my knees can scarcely hold my weight, and I stumble. They catch me, but just barely.

"I . . ." I whisper, searching the sky again. "He . . ."

But the dragon—Raelan—is gone, vanished into the storm above.

My gaze flicks to the ruined clothes and boots scattered across the courtyard, then to the chain grasped tightly in my shaking hand, and I realize that I may have just made a terrible, *terrible* mistake.

"Come on, we have to get you inside," Maeve says. Rainwater runs down her forehead and cheeks, causing her long dark eyelashes to clump together.

She and Lyra help me through the mud and grass and back up the stairs to the castle, where Poppy is waiting for us, holding the door open. We all stumble into the grand hall, dripping rain onto the marble floor, and Poppy shoves the door closed with a heavy thump.

"You're freezing," Lyra says. She rubs her hands together, creating a tiny flame, then gently blows on the flickering ember, sending heat washing over me. It feels amazing.

But my body is still shaking—just not from the cold, like Lyra thinks.

All I can see is the way Raelan moved, the gold in his eyes, the sheen of his glossy black scales.

"You should sit down." Maeve helps guide me to a comfortable couch in the corner of the entrance hall. She sinks down beside me while Poppy and Lyra sit on the couch opposite us.

Finally, I start to get my wits about me.

"H-how'd you know where to find me?" I ask. "The fog . . ." It was so thick, I could scarcely see ten feet through it.

"I had a dream," Poppy says softly. "Last night, I dreamt we'd find you in the courtyard after dinner." She clasps her hands in her lap and regards me with a worried expression. "And we did."

Her dream magic. That makes sense.

But what still doesn't make sense is what I saw. Is what Raelan became.

There's a stained glass window behind Lyra and Poppy, depicting a witch in a long blue robe. Rainwater runs down the glass, making it look like she's weeping.

"Did you dream of anything else?" I ask, still staring at the witch in the glass.

What if she knows about Raelan? Will she say anything? Should *I* say anything? Something tells me no, to keep this secret until I have a chance to talk to him.

Assuming he even comes back.

Poppy cants her head and twists her lips to one side. "In the dream . . . there was a figure watching you. But I couldn't see their face. They were just a shadow."

"Uh, that's super creepy," Lyra says beside her. She wrinkles her nose and leans her weight onto the curved armrest. "Are your dreams always accurate? Because I didn't see anyone."

"Not always, no." Poppy reaches up to fiddle with a strand of her hair. "But they always mean something." Her eyes meet mine, and a tingle goes down my back. "I'm just not sure what to make of that one yet."

As long as she didn't dream of a dragon, I don't mind mysterious figures in the fog.

I flick my gaze back up to the stained glass, trying to see past the witch and into the sky beyond, but all I can make out is diffuse gray light.

Yet I know that up above the clouds somewhere, soaring through the storm, there's a dragon.

And I'm the one who released it.

CHAPTER 15
RAELAN

I. Am. Free.

My wings beat the air, carrying my body higher, higher. Thunder rumbles, and lightning strikes in the distance. But even this force of nature pales in comparison to me, to the power thrumming through my veins.

I burst through the dense cloud cover, and sunlight strikes my face, warms my scaled body as it cuts through the thin cold air.

It's quiet up here, above the clouds, where only sunlight can touch. All I hear is the wind and the sound of my wings beating against the currents.

But here I am. Free.

Joy spirals inside me, and I twist through the sky, feeling the kiss of the air on every inch of my body and every glistening scale, spreading my talons and twining my neck, finally free of the bite of metal and magic. I can't remember when last I soared above the clouds, but the human memory lurking inside my body tells me it's been much too long.

In this form, in my true form, I feel that I can breathe at last, like I've been holding my breath underwater, trying desperately to claw and fight my way to the surface. And now that I'm here, I never want to go back. I want to fly for miles, for days, for years. I never want to touch foot to the earth again.

Until *her* face flashes in my memory.

Blue hair. Brown cheeks. Eyes that burn.

Alina. *My* Alina.

When she looked up at me from where she lay sprawled in the grass, I *almost* took her, almost wrapped my talons around her and carried her into the sky. Only the terror on her face stayed my claws.

She reminds me of who—and what—I am.

I am Raelan Ashvale. And I will never leave her behind. So I must return, even if my very cells reject the idea of being forced once more into our human form, into what can feel like a too-small cage squeezing my body into a cramped, contorted shape.

My body yearns for her, my blood burns for her. She's mine.

Mine.

Mine.

And I have to have her. My heart whispers her name with every pump of blood through my veins, with every flap of my inky wings.

But not like that. Not when her face is etched with fear and her body is shaking with terror. I won't claim her against her will, won't sink my fangs into her throat unless she agrees with her whole being to be my mate, to bind herself to me forever.

And that will never happen. I know it as surely as I feel the autumn sun upon my scales. And the grief makes me scream to the sky, blasting fire into the endless blue.

So, I fly. I fly as high as I can, until the air gets so thin I can scarcely breathe. Then I tilt my wings and send my body into a downward spiral, plummeting back toward the clouds below.

And I relish this moment, this freedom, knowing that soon, very soon, I will have to abandon it once more. And abandon it I will. But I won't do it for myself.

I'll do it for her.

Always for her.

Even if she'll never be mine.

I FLY UNTIL THE SUN SETS OVER THE DISTANT HORIzon, painting the world in hues of coral and gold, then in swaths of glittering purple and black. I don't know how many hundreds of miles I must've covered, but I know it's time to return—to her.

I descend through the clouds and land in a clearing hugged on all sides by trees, though most of their leaves have turned shades of red and orange and fallen to blanket the rich soil beneath my claws. Because I can't chance being seen by anyone—especially after how badly I fucked up at the academy—I'll need to walk back in my human form.

My very *naked* human form.

It takes some battling of my own nature to force myself back into my small human bones, my wingless body, my earthbound feet. But I do it for Alina.

And when the cold air hits my skin, I gasp in a breath.

I'm on my knees in the leaves and dirt, my fingers digging into the soft wet soil. All around me, the air smells of rain and mineral and forest decay. But it smells nothing like it does when I'm in my true body. In comparison, my scent and sight are so limited it's almost disorienting, and I take a few minutes just to breathe and reestablish myself in this form.

And when I'm finally sturdy enough to stand, I turn my feet in the direction of Coven Crest Academy and start to walk. It's a long way back to the campus, and with no boots or clothes, I have to be more careful as I move through the forest, stepping gently and mindfully. My eyes, even in their human form, can see well despite the darkness, and I make my way back to the outskirts of the academy grounds with little difficulty.

But one problem still remains: I can't go walking onto campus fully naked. At the very least, I'd draw significant unwanted attention, and at the worst, Headmistress Moonhart would probably ban me from ever stepping foot onto academy grounds again, and that simply can't happen.

I skirt the campus, eyes sweeping the darkened outbuildings. Perhaps a student left a cloak lying around, or maybe I can sneak into one of the buildings and find a blanket or a tablecloth or *anything* to cover myself. I just need to make it back to my room, and then I can start to deal with the fallout of my transformation.

Suddenly, I'm hit with a barrage of my human memories from early this evening: kissing Alina in the hallway, the heat on my skin as she grabbed my hand and brought it to that perfect place between her thighs, then the excruciating pain that racked my body, Alina's concern as she knelt beside me in the rain, the chain searing my skin as the magic tried to hold my beast at bay.

With a jolt, I reach up to touch my neck and realize the chain is gone.

Alina removed it. As a Ravenscroft, she's the only one here who has the power to do so. Even I can't remove it on my own—a maddening but necessary component of the charmed chain.

And I *need* it back. Without it, I won't be able to do my job, likely won't even be able to stand in the same room as Alina without my dragon instincts taking over and trying to force my transition.

Fuck!

I did this. I allowed myself to get carried away by my want for her. And I may have just ruined everything. If the king finds out about this . . .

Maybe he already knows. Maybe Alina sent a messenger as soon as I flew away. The fear on her face when she looked up at me, rain soaked and trembling, makes my stomach twist uncomfortably. She was terrified of me. And for good reason.

But now she knows the truth, and there will be no taking that back. I need to find some damn clothes, get back to my room, and figure out how the fuck I'm going to fix this.

Continuing along the outskirts of the academy, sticking to the darkness of the trees, I come across a small thatched hut standing just inside the forest line. Potted flowers and herbs hug the walls of the hut, and large gardening gloves lie on a low bench cluttered with tools. Smoke puffs from the chimney, filling the forest with the scent of woodsmoke, and nearby, fluttering gently on a clothesline, are two pairs of trousers, a few earth-toned tunics, and a collection of woolen socks.

My gaze snaps to the side window of the hut. There's movement inside, a horned shadow gliding along the wall. Perhaps this is the groundskeeper I've heard about, the reclusive minotaur seldom seen but often whispered about.

Hopefully he won't mind me borrowing some clothes.

I wait another moment, but no one appears in the window. So with one swift movement, I sidle up to the clothesline and remove a tunic and one pair of trousers, then melt back into the shadows without a sound.

When I pull the trousers on and yank the tunic over my head, I realize that these *must* belong to the minotaur, for I'm no small man, yet I'm drowning in these clothes. But at least I'm dressed now, even if I may draw odd looks from anyone who sees me. At this point, though, that's the least of my worries.

I cast my gaze upward, to the north tower. The storm and fog have cleared, and candlelight dances through some of the dormitory windows. I wonder what Alina's doing right now, wonder if she's looking into the darkness as I'm looking back at her.

And I wonder what she's going to say about this.

About my dragon.

About the beast she unknowingly set free.

CHAPTER 16
ALINA

I TOLD THE GIRLS THAT I DON'T KNOW WHERE Raelan went, that he ran outside after we had an argument and I slipped on the grass chasing after him.

But I'm not sure they believe me. In fact, I'm almost certain they don't. But I can't tell them the truth. It's not my secret to tell.

It's Raelan's. And he has some explaining to do.

Assuming he even comes back . . .

"Thank you," I whisper to Lyra as she straightens up and eases Juniper into her pocket. Her rat was able to slip under Raelan's door, scurry up the wooden doorframe, and flip the heavy lock. At my feet, Yuki huffs out a disapproving sigh and gives me a sharp side-eye. He's not a big fan of such antics. Maybe Grandfather should've assigned *him* as my bodyguard.

"Are you going to tell me what's *actually* going on?" Lyra asks. She leans against the stone wall, her wild red hair pulled up into a messy bun, two smears of purple face cream swept under her eyes. She was getting ready for bed when I made the impulsive decision to wait for Raelan in his room.

I'm very suddenly reminded of our kiss in the darkened corridor, the heat of his mouth and hands on me, and I clench my fingers into fists.

"Not yet," I tell Lyra, and she pouts. "But I'll tell you what I can, when I can. I promise."

I step forward and pull her into a hug, careful not to squish Juniper between us.

"Fine, fine." Lyra pulls away and yawns. "Just be careful, all right?" Her crimson-eyed gaze flicks to Raelan's closed door, and a strange worried look crosses her face. "He seemed . . . off today. Grumpier than usual."

So, I wasn't the only one who noticed. Even before the commotion in the dining hall, Raelan seemed more uptight than he typically is—fidgety, like he wanted to crawl out of his skin. And I realize now that he probably did.

I almost gulp when I remember the way his body contorted, becoming something else. Something powerful and terrifying and . . . even beautiful.

"It was Tristan," I tell her, which isn't completely a lie. "I think he was uncomfortable with him being so close to me." Shrugging, I glance away, letting my eyes trace the facets in the stained glass window to my left. It lets a bit of silver moonlight in, illuminating the gryphon depicted on the glass.

"I told you he has it bad for you." Lyra's worried look morphs into one of her crooked-mouth smiles. "It's *so* obvious."

I shake my head, then reach for the door handle. "Thanks again." My gaze flicks to Yuki, who's sitting at my feet, his fluffy white tail wrapped around his paws. "You should go back with Lyra," I tell him.

His eyes narrow. "You want me to leave you alone with him? I'm not sure about this . . ."

With a sigh, I crouch down, then stroke a hand over Yuki's soft fur. "This is Raelan we're talking about. He's not going to hurt me. He'd *never* hurt me."

My body tingles with the memory of the dragon peering down at me, the flecks of gold in its eyes, the fangs as long as my forearms. It could've swallowed me in one bite. But it didn't. *He* didn't.

I'm safe with him. In my heart, I'm sure of it.

I shake myself back to reality and focus on Yuki. "We just have some things to discuss, that's all."

Yuki holds my stare for a long moment, then lets out a sigh. "Very well." He stands and yawns, showing off his sharp teeth, then turns to pad back down the stairs to our room. "But if you need anything—"

"I won't. But I know you're there if I do."

Lyra squeezes my hand and tosses one last smile over her shoulder at me, then heads back down the winding stairs with Yuki a few steps ahead of her. I stand in the moonlit corridor until I hear our door close, and then I turn to Raelan's room. And I step inside.

The room is dark and cold, and I shiver as I ease through the doorway and push the heavy wooden door closed behind me. Clearly, Raelan has still not been back since I last saw him early this evening.

Since he turned into a *dragon* and flew away.

My heart pounds just thinking about it.

He's a shifter. He has to be. But dragon shifters are so rare, they're almost considered nonexistent these days. I never would've guessed Raelan could be one . . .

And he never told me. But why?

Maybe he doesn't trust me. I *did* try to get him replaced with another guard, and that certainly doesn't build a sense of confidence and loyalty.

The thought makes my stomach turn.

I cross the dark room, being careful not to bump into any furniture as my eyes slowly adjust to the darkness. I grab a few logs of firewood from the stand tucked into the corner, then arrange them in the cold hearth, careful not to let the sleeves of my robe sweep through the ashes. As a frost witch, I've always found fire magic difficult, so I opt to start a fire the manual way: with the flint and steel from atop the mantel. It takes me a few tries—I don't often start my own fires—but when I finally get a spark to catch, a feeling of pride comes over me.

Such a small task, and yet I almost always have someone else to do it for me.

This is one of the reasons I wanted so badly to attend Coven Crest—not only to master my magic, but to get out of the castle and away from my life as a princess, to experience things the way others do, to learn who I am and what I can achieve when I put my mind to it.

And I suppose starting a fire is one of those small achievements.

As the tiny flame grows, creeping up the sides of the wood I so carefully stacked in the hearth, I push to my feet and turn to regard the room.

Raelan has never let me in here before, so it feels intimate being here now, especially without him.

The room is smaller than the dorm I share with Lyra, Maeve, and Poppy, but it's no less comfortable. There's a writing desk along the wall, and two armchairs hug a small side table, upon which sits a book and an empty teacup. A dark staircase leads to the loft, where I imagine Raelan's bed is.

Heat floods my face and neck at the thought of Raelan lying in bed, eyes closed, chest rising and falling softly with each breath. Does he sleep shirtless, long arms and legs draped across the mattress? What does he dream of?

Does he ever dream of me?

I don't know when exactly I started seeing Raelan differently, let alone wanting to press my mouth to his and feel his hand between my legs. At first, he was just a nuisance, an embarrassing burden I had to bear while trying to *pretend* I'm just another normal student here. Perhaps it was after our conversation in the garden that day, when Raelan agreed to give me more space. Once I no longer felt suffocated by him, I started being able to see him clearly—like rising above a forest to see how far it extends in each direction.

My gaze flicks to the single window, over which a drape has been drawn. I move toward it, my slippers quiet on the stone floor, and push the drape aside to look out.

The storm has passed, leaving the sky beautifully clear but for a few thin, wispy clouds. The moon—a waxing gibbous, I believe, if I'm remembering my astronomy lessons correctly—is bright and beautiful, glowing cheerfully in the nighttime sky.

I scan the horizon for a shadow, for a dragon soaring in the far distance, but I see nothing. And slowly, worry starts to creep up on me.

Does Grandfather know about this? Was the chain around Raelan's neck meant to control him, force him into subservience? Did I unknowingly release Raelan from servitude? And if so, will he even come back? Maybe he's gone for good. Maybe he's halfway across the continent by now. Maybe I'll never—

The door clicks behind me, and I whirl around with a startled breath.

A figure stands in the doorway, shoulders limned in silver moonlight slipping in from the hallway.

And Raelan's dark eyes meet mine from across the room.

CHAPTER 17

ALINA

RAELAN PAUSES IN THE OPEN DOORWAY, LOOK-ing equal parts surprised and wary to see me standing there. He's holding his torn clothing and boots in one arm, and the key to his room is clutched in his free hand, the metal glinting in the light. But he says nothing, offers nothing.

I suppose I'll need to take the helm, then. Not like that's atypical when it comes to having conversations with Raelan.

"H-hello," I say, then feel immediately foolish for stumbling over such a simple word.

"Your Highness," he says smoothly, seeming to remember himself as he straightens up and adjusts the bundle of fabric held in his arm. "What are you doing here?"

"I came to talk."

He regards me coolly, betraying nothing.

"About what happened," I clarify, as if I even need to explain.

Why is he making me so nervous all of a sudden? Apart from anger and frustration, I've never been uncomfortable around him, have never stumbled over my words or had to ask myself if I've actually forgotten how to breathe whenever his gaze lands on me.

I swallow hard and force myself to stand straighter. "But if you'd prefer I leave, I'll—"

He closes the door with a resounding click.

And now we're alone. In his room. With the door closed.

My eyes trace Raelan in the warm firelight. He's wearing an odd pair of clothes that are clearly much too big on him, the tunic so wide and baggy it very nearly slips off one of his broad shoulders. I didn't want to draw the girls' attention to Raelan's ruined clothing lying scattered about the courtyard when they found me in the rain, so I just left everything there, hoping someone else would clean them up and only briefly consider why they were there in the first place. I see now there was no need for concern; Raelan took care of it, the way he typically does.

He deposits his armful of clothing and boots onto the floor, then crosses his arms over his chest, gaze sharp as he regards me.

I quickly tear my gaze away and say, "Would you like some tea? I can make some while you get changed."

A thick silence stretches between us, broken only by the crackling of the flames in the hearth. I start to wonder if he's going to ask me to leave.

At long last, Raelan says, "The tea is there." He points to the mantel, which is home to a few glass jars filled with various herbs, then pads up the stairs to the loft, bare feet quiet on each step.

With him momentarily out of sight, I try to catch my breath, mentally scolding myself for my silliness while fetching the kettle and filling it with water from the pitcher in the corner. I hang it on a hook over the flames, then busy myself with preparing two teacups. Raelan has a few options for tea: lemon balm, chamomile, and peppermint.

"Which flavor do you want?" I call up to him.

"Peppermint," he replies, voice muffled, like he's pulling a tunic over his head.

My gaze flicks briefly to the loft overhead, but all I see is a subtle movement of shadow, and I tear my eyes quickly away.

I fill two cotton sachets with peppermint leaves, then toss them into a couple mismatched teacups and pour the hot water over the top. The minty scent swirls around me, reminding me of the gardens back home, where the peppermint plants grow so wild that our gardeners have to fight to tame them each year.

Raelan's feet thump softly down the stairs, and I steady myself before turning to face him, one cup held in each hand.

Now he's dressed in comfortable attire I've never seen on him before: a loose-fitting tunic and soft cotton pants, no armor or uniform in sight. Looking at him makes my cheeks warm. I only hope the firelight will hide the blush coloring my skin.

"Peppermint, as requested," I say, holding out his teacup.

He crosses the room slowly, perhaps even hesitantly, and when he takes the cup from my hand, I notice how careful he is not to touch my fingers.

But why?

A small burst of irritation goes through me. But it's good. It reminds me why I'm here, helps pull my head out of the clouds.

I settle myself into one of the armchairs near the fire, gesturing with my free hand for Raelan to do the same. He does so, but I note the tension in his shoulders, the stiffness in the way he's holding himself, like he's as unsure around me as I now am around him.

Best to be out with it, then.

"What was that?" I ask. "What happened?"

Raelan doesn't meet my gaze. Instead, he stares into the flames, the dancing fire reflected in his glassy dark eyes. A muscle in his jaw goes taut, and then he sighs.

"That was my dragon. It was released when you removed my chain."

His chain.

The reminder has me reaching into the pocket of my robe, fingers wrapping around the heavy metal, which is warm to the touch from being nestled alongside my body. I hold it up, the links clinking together, and Raelan's eyes find it.

"Who put this on you?" I ask. "Why do you wear it?"

Worry turns in my stomach. I can't imagine Grandfather would enslave someone this way. It makes me sick just thinking about.

I hope I'm wrong. If I'm not . . .

"The magic in the chain keeps my beast from emerging. Without it, I could transform at any time." Raelan stares at it while he speaks, but I can't quite read the expression on his face, don't know if he's looking at it with disgust or with longing—or perhaps a bit of both.

"Where'd you get it?" I ask, running my thumb over the smooth links. It's beautifully made, so I imagine it was crafted by an expert metalworker.

"His Majesty gave it to me," Raelan says, turning away from me to stare into the fire once more.

Simmering heat shoots through me. "Grandfather forces you to wear this? How could he—"

Raelan holds up a hand, halting me midsentence. "He forces me to do nothing. I choose to wear it."

I narrow my eyes at him. "Why?"

Without looking at me, he says, "It's meant to keep everyone around me safe. In exchange, I have to give up some of my freedom—the freedom to transform at will, to give in to my animal instincts." He swallows hard, and his eyes finally find mine. "Only a Ravenscroft can remove it. One of the Shadowfall witches imbued it with a powerful charm. Once it's clasped about my neck, I have no power to take it off. Had you not removed it today, you would not have learned the truth."

The truth: That he's a shifter. A *dragon* shifter. The rarest kind there is.

"And Grandfather has known this whole time?"

Raelan softens into his armchair and takes his first sip of tea. "Yes. He's known since I was a boy. I met him when I was eleven. And we have an agreement: He ensures my mother and sisters have a comfortable place to live, and in exchange, I serve him. The chain is the only way I can do that. Without it, I could hurt anyone at any time. Your grandfather—His Majesty—gave me my life back. He gave me the freedom to exist in this world without fearing I could lose control at any moment. And I'll be forever grateful to him for that. He's a good king. A good man. But if he finds out about this . . ." Raelan clenches his jaw.

If Grandfather finds out about this, he may very well replace Raelan as my personal guard. He might send someone else to watch over me, knowing the danger Raelan poses to me if I'm to remove his chain.

Like I did earlier this evening.

He may even remove Raelan from the guard entirely, which would put his family at risk.

No wonder Raelan has kept his distance from me. Because the moment I got close to him, this is what happened. And it could've been so much worse.

My heart twists at the idea of Raelan being gone. And the realization—that I *want* him here despite previously asking Grandfather to send some other knight to watch over me—hits me hard.

"Alina," he says, the word soft and warm in the semidarkness, sending butterflies through my stomach, "I'm sorry. I didn't mean to frighten you."

I think of lying, of telling him I wasn't afraid, but it would do no good. He must've seen my face, must've known how absolutely terrified I was as he towered over me, his eyes black as onyx and slitted like those of a snake. And his size—I've never seen something so enormous before, something rippling with so much power that it made my body freeze on sight.

Clenching the chain in my fist, I whisper, "You need not apologize. This is my fault. I saw the chain burning you, and I . . ." I swallow. "I didn't like seeing you in pain."

"Pain?" Raelan makes a small sound, like a laugh, and when I glance up at him, his mouth is pulled into a sideways smile. Such an expression is so rare for him that the image nestles itself into my mind for safekeeping. "You've no idea," he whispers, but he offers no further elaboration.

I set my teacup on the side table, careful not to slosh any onto Raelan's book, then stand and take a hesitant step toward him. His eyes flick up to meet mine as I hold the chain in my hands.

"You may have frightened me," I say softly, "but you . . ." I have to catch my breath before continuing. Goose bumps dance across my skin. "You're magnificent, Raelan. I'm not sure I've ever seen something so beautiful."

"Beautiful?" His eyes narrow slightly, and he pushes to his feet, setting his teacup beside mine. With him standing over me like this, I have to tip my head back to hold his stare. He's got that tiny smile on his lips again. "If you say so."

His minty breath makes the thin strands of hair around my face flutter. A delicate shiver goes down my spine at his proximity.

"Do you mind . . . ?" He gestures to the chain still held in my hands, then lowers his head a bit so I can reach him.

With fingers trembling, I ease the chain back onto his neck, fumbling a bit with the heavy clasp and the nervous beating of my heart from being so close to him. Raelan's skin is scabbed, burned from the magic earlier today, but he doesn't so much as flinch as the metal settles into place. The links glow with a dim blue light, then go dark once again, the charm having activated.

Raelan lets out a long breath, then straightens up and rolls his shoulders, like he's acclimating himself to the sudden added weight of heavy armor. "Thank you."

I nod once. My eyes trace his firm jaw, the shadow of stubble he'll most certainly shave off come morning. And without deciding to, I lift my hand, hold it toward him.

For a moment, my hand hangs there in the space between us. The fire flickers and crackles, the scent of woodsmoke and peppermint drifting around the warm room.

Raelan holds my stare, as if taking this moment to decide what he wants to do. Then he shifts just a bit, allowing me to place my fingers along his face, brush them across the ridge of his sharp cheekbone. My skin tingles at the gentle contact.

"Why were you in so much pain?" I whisper. "Why did it burn you like that?"

His eyes meet mine, dark and glittering in the firelight. "I think you know why."

The kiss. The touch. The heat burning between us in the dark.

It's the same heat building inside me now, swirling through my veins as I touch Raelan's hot skin.

"Will it hurt you again?" I ask. "If we . . . ?"

I want so badly to kiss him, but I don't want to hurt him. The desire and fear war inside me.

"I can withstand pain," he says, his voice low and heavy in the darkness.

My fingers drift down his cheek, across his throat. Beneath my touch, he shivers.

"Seeing you like that . . ." I recall his scream, the trembling of his body as the magic seared his skin. "It made me sick. I don't want to hurt you."

He lets out a low laugh, then puts a hand over mine, presses it against his chest until I can feel the heavy beating of his heart. "What *do* you want?" he asks.

To kiss him. To touch him. To taste him.

His eyes burn in the darkness.

And for the second time today, I give in. Once more, I allow myself to abandon reason and propriety.

My fingers curl, gripping the soft fabric of his tunic. Between one breath and the next, I close the distance between us.

And then my mouth is on his. And I drown in him.

CHAPTER 18

RAELAN

I'M A FOOL, A MASOCHIST. BUT I CAN'T HELP myself. And though I feel my control slipping, I can't bring myself to care. As long as I have this chain around my neck, and as long as Alina doesn't take it off again, I know I won't hurt her.

I, on the other hand, have become familiar with pain.

The pain of yearning for her while knowing I can't have her. The anguish of not telling her the truth, of not claiming her as my own.

If I have to feel pain in the name of tasting her lips one more time, of sharing her breath even for a moment, so be it.

This time, I won't give in.

She lets out a breath as I wrap my fingers around her waist. My dragon, previously curled quietly inside me, at ease after our long flight, starts to uncoil, drawn out by Alina and the urge I have to make her mine.

My fingers slip inside her open robe to touch the thin fabric of her nightdress. It's silky against my skin, a delicate little thing. I could tear clean through it, rip it from her body and leave it in tatters.

But I don't. I resist.

Alina presses her body close to mine, her hands coming up to wrap around my neck. I tense up feeling her fingers along the chain, but she whispers, "I won't do it again. I promise."

Her breath is minty as it drifts along my lips.

My fingers slide down her waist to cup her ass, and then I'm lifting her up, causing her to gasp as she wraps her legs around me. Her slippers fall to the floor with a soft patter, and the nightdress she's wearing glides up with the movement, bunching around her upper thighs and waist. My cock throbs as I crush her to me. Her mouth finds mine again as I take a few steps through the sitting area and press her back against the wall between the hearth and the small window, through which silver moonlight gleams.

Her long blue hair is loose around her shoulders, and I release one hand from beneath her to push my fingers through the silky strands. They slip between my fingers like water, so soft I feel they must be charmed with magic.

I fist her hair in my grasp and turn her head to one side, finding her throat with my mouth, picking back up where we left off in the hall before my dragon sent me running into the storm. She whimpers softly, such a breakable little thing, and my cock jumps. There's only a thin layer of fabric between us, and as I push my hips against her, I can feel how wet she is through my trousers.

I have the urge to sink my teeth into her neck, her wrists, her breasts, to claim her fully and feel my magic pulse through her veins, to make her *mine*. I want to tear her thin panties aside and bury myself inside her, to make her arch her back and claw my skin with only my name on her lips. She'd be better than any woman I've ever had, like a cask of precious fairy wine before a roaring fire, like strawberries dipped in a sinuous river of dark chocolate. She'd be everything and more.

"Raelan," she whispers in the firelit darkness. It's more a breath than a word, and I capture her mouth again before she can even draw a gasp.

Fully awake now, my dragon thrashes inside me, fighting once more to be free. But this time it doesn't wish to fly away; it wishes to stay here, to hoard the treasure that is Alina Ravenscroft, to curl about her and never let her free.

I could do it. If she were to remove my chain, I could claim her, fuck her, *have her*. No one would be able to best me, to wrest me away from her. I could—

No, I tell myself, abruptly cutting off that intoxicating train of thought. *This is Alina. The princess. My duty and charge.*

And I realize suddenly that I have her pressed against a wall, my dick straining for her, grinding along the wet slit between her legs.

What the fuck am I doing?

I need to get my head straight. Alina's very presence casts a spell over me, muddles my brain until I can't remember up from down, can scarcely remember my own name and place in this world.

And though my instincts rage against it, the truth is that my place is not inside her; it's beside her, guarding her, protecting her. I'm not the one who'll get to lie alongside her each night, to taste the heat between her thighs, to fill her with my seed and watch as it spills out of her.

Because if I do that and someone finds out—if the king or any member of the royal family were to discover what I've done—I'd be banished from the castle and perhaps even the kingdom. Then I wouldn't get to see her again, wouldn't get to catch her scent on the air or watch the way her pale eyes shine when she smiles. And that may very well kill me. It would be a slow death of the most tortured variety.

It takes every ounce of willpower I have to break our kiss and ease Alina slowly back onto her feet. When her toes are touching the cold floor, I plant my hands on either side of her head, curling my fingers into the stone as my arms shake with the fight raging inside me.

"Are you okay?" she whispers. Her eyes flick to the chain about my neck.

The magic is burning my skin again, but I scarcely feel the pain. Beneath me, with her head tipped back against the wall and her lips swollen and red, she's the most enchanting woman I've ever seen. And I have to get away from her before I do something that can't be undone.

Before I fuck up again like I did earlier this evening.

"I'm fine," I growl out. Pushing off the wall, I take a few wide steps back from her, putting enough space between us that I couldn't touch her even if I were to reach out. My dragon doesn't like it, but there's not a damn thing it can do about it, and neither can I.

Alina lifts a hand to her mouth, fingertips touching her lips. Then she smiles, and a small laugh drifts from her, a melodic sound accompanied by the crackling of the fire.

"What's funny?" I ask her.

She shakes her head, sending the blue strands I was just grasping drifting around her cheeks. "Not funny. I've just . . . never been kissed like that."

I think that's a good thing, but I hadn't realized she'd *ever* been kissed, and an ember of envy flares to life inside my chest. Who the hell has she been kissing? Who would dare put their mouth on *my*—

I stop myself again.

But no matter how many times I remind myself that I can't have her, my dragon refuses to acquiesce. And I realize that as long as I'm in her vicinity, this battle will never end. Yet I'd rather spend my whole life fighting than to be parted from her.

And I must therefore tread very carefully. Everything is balancing on this, on my being able to do my duty and not overstep, not fall from this delicate tightrope I'm walking with her.

"We should get you back to your room," I say, adopting the formal tone I typically use with her—and every member of the royal family.

Alina's smile slips. For a moment, I think she looks hurt, but then she straightens up, adjusts her nightdress and robe, and says, "We should."

She finds her slippers and eases her toes into them, then runs a hand over her hair, smoothing the wild strands. I open the door for her and hold my breath as she walks by, even though I know my whole room smells of her now—and even worse, it smells like our desire, like *her* desire.

Dammit.

136

This will be yet another sleepless night.

We descend the stairs to her room, me following a few steps behind. When Alina gets to her door, she pauses and turns to face me.

"So . . . you're okay?" she whispers, voice soft.

At her question, I'm reminded of the burn marks on my neck, the way the metal chain rests uncomfortably against them.

I give her a firm nod. "I'm fine, Your Highness. Please don't worry about me."

Her eyes narrow slightly, brow wrinkling. Then she lets out a breath, rights her shoulders, and grips the door handle.

"Well, good night, then."

"Good night," I whisper.

And then she's gone, the door opening and closing softly behind her, and I'm left standing in the hallway alone.

CHAPTER 19
ALINA

AS SOON AS I GOT BACK INTO MY ROOM last night, the girls were all over me, asking me what happened with Raelan. But I just put on my best neutral smile and told them it was nothing; we simply spoke and made amends, and he returned me to my room.

They didn't believe me.

And neither did Yuki.

But I want to keep this secret—*our* secret—to myself, if just because I don't even know how to feel about it yet. When Raelan kissed me in the hallway, then again in his room last night, I felt his hunger, his desire. While I was pinned against his wall, my legs wrapped around his waist, I could feel how hard he was through his thin trousers, and it just made me want him more.

In a moment, though, he went back to the cold, professional Raelan I know, the one who treats me like a princess rather than a person, like I'm his duty and not his desire.

And I don't know what to think. The only thing I do know is that last night after I crawled into bed and drew the drapes around the mattress for privacy, my hand slipping between my legs to relieve the pressure that had been building all evening, the only face in my mind was Raelan's. Even now, as I lounge about the dorm room with a cup of tea, still wearing my nightdress and a thin satin robe, he's all I can think about.

He's probably standing outside our door right now, in his usual spot beside the stained glass window, his jaw held firm and his eyes narrowed slightly in concentration. It's his typical look, the one I've come to know from him. But it's not the one he was giving me yesterday, when his eyes burned with black and gold and his pupils tightened into thin slashes, like a beast was lurking just beneath his skin, waiting to burst free.

And burst free it did. Because of me.

I move to the window and push the drapes aside, then peer down from the tall north tower. But I can't see the courtyard from here, can't tell if anyone has noticed that something strange took place there amidst the storm and the torrential rain.

"Good morning," Maeve says from behind me, startling me enough that I almost spill my cup of chamomile tea. I turn from the window and lean against it, letting the sun warm my back and shoulders.

"Morning," I say. "Water's hot if you want tea."

Maeve and Poppy descend from the loft and into the main living space. They each pour a cup of tea, and then Maeve sinks down onto one of the couches, tucking her long legs beneath her, while Poppy goes to stand before the hearth, where a small fire is burning.

"Lyra still sleeping?" I ask.

"Of course she is," Maeve says, her voice a bit husky with sleep. "Snoring like a wildebeest."

Poppy giggles. Her short light lavender hair is pulled up halfway, and her big round glasses glint in the sunlight coming through the window behind me. She looks soft, like spun sugar at a summer festival.

"I was thinking maybe we could go into Wysteria today," she says, voice small, timid. It's taken her a while to start warming up to us. "My mom owns a café. We could get scones, walk around a bit."

"Your mom owns a café?" Maeve asks, perking up. Her dark purple hair looks glossy as ink, falling over her shoulders and down her chest in a sleek sheet. I'm not sure I've ever seen it tangled or rumpled. "Why didn't you tell us before?"

Poppy's cheeks go a tinge pink. "Oh, I don't know. It just never came up, I suppose."

"What's it called?" I ask her. "The café, I mean."

Poppy's lavender eyes light up. She lifts her teacup with a small smile. "The Wandering Cup."

I'VE NOT BEEN BACK IN THE CITY SINCE I LEFT FOR Coven Crest, and it feels oddly comforting to be walking the familiar cobblestone streets. Some people recognize me and bow their heads or offer friendly greetings as I pass, but I mostly blend in with my group of friends—if not for Raelan walking a few strides behind us, we'd hardly draw any attention at all.

I can feel his eyes on my back, and his gaze warms me more than the bright autumn sunlight shining down from the cloudless blue sky. When I told him earlier that we planned to walk into the city today, he seemed unsure, jaw feathering, but he voiced no complaints. Now here we are, sharing laughter and banter as we head toward Poppy's mom's café.

When we arrive, the door to the quaint little shop is already propped open, and the smell of chocolate and baked goods drifts out, making my mouth water. The other girls enter first, and I follow behind them, Raelan a few steps behind me.

The café is warm and welcoming, with glass display cases at the back and plants taking up all the sunny spots near the front windows. A cat lounges in a patch of sunlight, sleeping all stretched out, soft belly pointing to the ceiling. A few other patrons are just finishing up at the counter, and when they step away and Poppy's mom sees her, they both squeal, and Poppy's mom comes around the counter to sweep her daughter into a hug.

Maeve, Lyra, and I exchange quick smiles. Lyra still looks a bit sleepy; we had to drag her out of bed this morning. Only the promise of sweets got her feet into her boots and her boots out the door. She leans against me and yawns.

Poppy makes introductions swiftly, then gestures to Raelan over my shoulder.

"And this is Raelan," she tells her mother.

The woman, Layla Waverly, widens her eyes at Raelan. "Well, it's good to see you. I wondered why you hadn't been around lately."

We all turn to look at Raelan. He offers Layla a small smile. "Got any of those chocolate-strawberry croissants today?"

Layla grins. "Of course. And what would you girls like? I've got fresh blueberry scones, cinnamon rolls, and strawberry shortcake."

"Ooh, shortcake for me!" Lyra says, suddenly perking up out of her stupor and making the rest of us smile.

While we put in our order, I keep glancing back at Raelan, but he won't meet my eyes.

He knows this place, then. He must come here often for Layla to know his order by heart.

Suddenly, I feel as though I don't know him at all. And in a way, I suppose I still don't. He's barely told me anything about himself. I didn't even know he had sisters until he mentioned them last night. What else about himself does he keep buried inside?

We take a seat at a small round table, and Poppy carries two more chairs over, offering one to Raelan with a shy smile. He looks hesitant, like he'd rather stand over my shoulder, but in so casual a setting, that would surely be odd. Finally, he steps forward, thanking Poppy and making her cheeks flush a deep shade of scarlet.

The five of us cram ourselves around the table, bumping elbows and knees like we've been friends for a lifetime. Raelan sits next to me, but he's careful not to let his leg touch mine beneath the table, and it sends a little twinge of hurt through me.

But then I remind myself of his scream yesterday, the way his body shook beneath the pouring rain, the burns from his chain—which I can still see now, in the golden sunlight streaming through the polished front windows.

He's already withstood such pain because of me. It feels selfish to hope for more, to want more, and yet deep inside, I can't help myself.

His cheeks and jaw are clean-shaven today, like I expected they'd be. I wonder how his skin would feel if I were to brush my fingertips across it. I liked the shadowed stubble on his face yesterday, rough beneath my hands, but now I want to touch him again, to know him in all his forms.

What do his scales feel like? I wonder briefly.

Raelan's dark eyes flick in my direction, catching me staring. A bit of warmth rushes into my cheeks, and I look quickly away.

"So, do you come here a lot?" Poppy asks Raelan, her voice timid.

Before today, I'm not sure I've ever heard her speak to Raelan directly.

"Often, yes. My mother and sisters like the croissants and pastries. I bring them some whenever I have leave from the castle."

A ghost of a smile pulls on his lips, then is gone just as quickly. It makes me want to know more about his family, about his sisters and the woman who raised him. He's such a mystery to me, like a book I've only just opened to the first chapter. And I'm desperate to read more.

But Layla sweeps up to the table a moment later, a gleaming silver platter balanced expertly on one hand.

"Here you are, dears," she says, and I have to clamp my mouth shut to keep it from watering as she slides tiny colorful plates onto the table: strawberry shortcake for Lyra, a cheese Danish with black coffee for Maeve, a cinnamon roll for Poppy, coffee cake for me, and a chocolate-strawberry croissant for Raelan. The plates barely fit on the table, and it's comedic trying to eat with our shoulders brushing and elbows bumping.

Lyra almost causes Maeve to spill her coffee, which causes a short and lighthearted argument, and Poppy smiles as she licks vanilla frosting from her fingers. I eat my coffee cake with my hands, appreciating the freedom I have away from the castle, to experience some of what life must be like for people who don't grow up as a Ravenscroft. It makes my shoulders feel light with buoyancy.

Beside me, Raelan regards his croissant with hesitation, not yet having taken a bite.

Poppy pushes her glasses up with a knuckle and says softly, "Is everything okay? Would you like something else?"

He glances up at her question, then gives a sharp shake of his head. "No. Everything's fine." He finally lifts the croissant and takes a bite. I watch the muscles in his jaw work as he chews, then the bob of his throat as he swallows, and it makes me warmer than it probably should.

"Anyone going to the runeball game today?" Lyra asks. Since it's a weekend, we're not wearing our school uniforms, and Lyra is instead dressed in a billowy tunic and trousers, and she pulls one knee into her chest as she takes another bite of strawberry shortcake. Her curly red flyaways look almost copper in the light.

"I am," Maeve says, but she doesn't sound excited about it. "My brother's playing. I told him I'd go and watch."

That's right—Maeve mentioned early on that her step-brother attends Coven Crest as well, though he's a year older than us. I've not yet had the opportunity to meet him.

"I'll go with you," Poppy says.

And that draws all of our eyes to her. She flushes.

"I thought you hated sports," Lyra says.

"I'm trying to branch out." Poppy shrugs. "It might be fun."

"Highly doubt it," Maeve grumbles, but Lyra lights up.

"We'll all go!" she says. "Alina, are you in?"

I don't have anything else to do this weekend, except studying for an upcoming exam in my magical anatomy class. After swallowing my last bite of coffee cake, I nod. "Sure."

"Yes!" Lyra pumps her fist in the air, making us all roll our eyes.

The conversation drifts leisurely between classes and exams and the upcoming Samhain festival, but I'm distracted. I keep glancing at Raelan from the corner of my eye, watching him pick at his croissant. Is he thinking about his family? Wishing he could visit them?

Well . . . why couldn't he?

I push up from the table amidst another argument between Lyra and Maeve, this one regarding the merits of cream in coffee, and feel Raelan's gaze on me as I walk to the counter.

Layla is just finishing icing a batch of cupcakes and looks up with a smile. "Can I get you something else?" she asks.

With a lowered voice, I say, "Can I get what Raelan typically orders? For his family, I mean." I reach into the inside pocket of the cloak I'm wearing to pull out my coin purse. I don't carry much currency—Grandfather thinks it's dangerous for me—but I do have some eldertokens, and it's more than enough to purchase a few croissants.

Layla gives me a knowing smile as I covertly slide a coin across the counter. "Of course, Your Highness. I'll have them ready in a moment."

I give her a small smile, then return to the table.

"You order something else?" Poppy asks.

"No." I wave a hand. "Just thanking your mother. She's quite gifted. Maybe she should teach a baking class at the academy."

"Ooh, I'd take that," Lyra says. She picks up her last bite of strawberry shortcake and reaches into the top of her tunic, where Juniper's head suddenly appears. She nibbles the shortcake, then licks Lyra's fingers clean.

I swear, she takes that rat *everywhere*.

This morning, I invited Yuki to come along with us, but he had *plans* today—something about meeting up with a red fox he was recently acquainted with—so he turned down my offer. I'll have to ask him how it went when we get back.

"A baking class?" Poppy smiles and wipes the last bit of vanilla frosting from her plate, then puts her finger into her mouth. "I'm not sure about that. I think she'd miss the café too much. It's home, you know?"

We all nod and make sounds of agreement. Then we gather up our plates and deposit them in the bin at the back of the café. At the same time, Layla holds up a small paper bag and says, "Here you go, Your Highness."

Everyone watches me as I step forward and take the bag, offering Layla a smile and a thank-you. Then I turn to Raelan. A touch of nervousness twirls through my stomach. "These are for your mother and sisters. I thought we could visit them while we're in town."

His mask slips for a moment, eyebrows lifting and eyes widening in surprise. He opens his mouth to say something, then closes it again, seeming unsure.

Have I made a mistake? Does he not want me to accompany him?

Maybe our kisses yesterday meant a lot less to him than they meant to me.

"I mean, you can take them alone," I say quickly, already hating the waver in my voice. "I'll just head back to the academy with the girls, and—"

"No." Raelan's voice is firm. He glances at the bag, then back at me. "We'll go together."

Poppy, Lyra, and Maeve all give me varying looks, ranging from mischievous (Lyra, of course) to mildly curious (Maeve) to shy (Poppy). Beneath my breast, my heart thumps hard.

Because I'm going to meet Raelan's family.

CHAPTER 20
RAELAN

I SHOULD'VE SAID NO. I *WANTED* TO SAY NO. BUT when Alina's eyes hit mine and she held up the crinkly paper bag filled with treats for my mother and sisters, how could I?

Now we're walking down Kingfisher Crescent, Alina a stride ahead of me. Every time the breeze catches her hair and dress, it sends her scent—mixed with chocolate and strawberry and sugar—swirling around me. I keep turning my head slightly away, trying to avoid the intoxicating aroma, but no matter what I do, it surrounds me, beckons to me, tempts me to grab hold of her and drag her down a narrow street just to press my lips to hers.

But I don't.

"What are your mother's and sisters' names?" Alina asks, twisting slightly to look up at me over her shoulder. The sun turns her eyes an even paler shade of blue, like an icy lake at the height of winter.

"My mother is Soraya," I say, finally finding the power within myself to tear my gaze away. "My sisters are Gilda and Clarice. Gilda's the youngest." I think for a moment, then add, "She's probably going to act . . . enamored around you. I apologize ahead of time."

Alina's smile is quick and warm. "No need. I've always thought it would be lovely to have a younger sister." She reaches up to tuck a long strand of hair behind her ear, and I hold my breath.

A few more paces down the cobblestone walkway, I gesture to the seamstress's shop coming up on our right. "It's here," I say.

Alina pauses, stepping aside for me to go ahead, and it's a relief when I can no longer smell her. My dragon coils inside me, hot and frustrated at being kept from her.

But it's nothing compared to yesterday—both in the courtyard just before Alina removed the chain from my neck and later in the evening, when I very nearly let myself lose control with her. In comparison, this is nothing.

We climb the stairs to the apartment above the shop, Alina's steps quiet behind mine. At the top, I knock firmly. On the other side of the door, there's a scurrying of curious feet, followed by my mother's voice.

Then the door swings open, and my young sisters blink up at me in surprise. But that only lasts for a second before their gazes flick to Alina, and their faces do something akin to setting aflame.

"Y-Your Highness!" Clarice squeaks. She drops into a clumsy curtsy, pulling Gilda down alongside her.

"What's that?" Mama says from the back room.

"The princess is here!" Gilda squeals.

"*What?*"

"Oh, and Raelan too!"

Compared to Alina, I'm the afterthought. And I'm completely content with that.

My mother comes out of the back room holding a bolt of fabric, a thimble on one thumb, her long dark hair pulled up atop her head and stuck through with some type of stick. When she sees me, then Alina, her eyes go wide.

"Hello," Alina says behind me, her voice gentle. She makes no indication of being startled by my mother's scars. "We were at the café, and Raelan mentioned you like the croissants." She holds up the crinkly paper bag. "I wanted to bring you some. I hope I'm not intruding."

"Come in!" Gilda says, grabbing for Alina's arm. But Clarice quickly intercepts, pulling my youngest sister back.

"You can't grab her like that!" she snaps. "She's the princess! Mind your manners."

"Oops." Gilda's cheeks go pink. "Sorry."

"Come in, please," Mama says. "Let me just put some things away. Raelan, will you get the table?" Mama gestures to the kitchen table, which is currently buried under piles of clothing, bolts of fabric, and what looks like a grocery list.

Alina glances up at me, a small smile pulling at her mouth, and somehow, it makes me smile too.

I'M NOT SURE WHAT I EXPECTED OF ALINA, BUT SHE wholly surprises me. She takes quickly to my young sisters, even going so far as to let them show her around the tiny one-bedroom apartment, as if there's anything of interest to look at. But Alina plays along, nodding and smiling as Gilda shows her the doll I purchased for her last year.

"She's beautiful," Alina says, holding up the doll, which has certainly seen better days. It was pristine when I bought it, but now its fabric is slightly worn, and it looks to be missing a small patch of hair. "Your brother got this for you?"

"Yes. That's why she's my favorite."

At Gilda's words, Alina's gaze flicks to mine from across the small space. I return her stare and am thankful when she breaks eye contact first.

Mama clears her throat as Gilda drags Alina away again, though to show her what, I've no idea.

"She's . . . special," Mama says, voice low so as to avoid anyone overhearing.

My gaze finds hers. "Yes."

This is the first time my mother has met the princess; she met the king ten years ago, when he first took me in, and she was present in the throne room at my knighting ceremony, but Alina has only ever been a distant figure, someone you know of but don't truly know. Yet here she is, in our tiny apartment, entertaining my sisters as if it's the most natural thing in the world.

"Come," Mama says, pushing up from the table. She leads me to the front door, and we step out onto the landing at the top of the narrow stairs. Once the door has closed firmly behind us, she turns to look up at me. "I'm worried about you, Raelan."

I reach up to scratch the back of my head and realize my hair has grown out a bit. I'll need to have it cut again soon. "Why?"

My mother's gaze flicks to my neck, where I'm sure she can see my burns. "This isn't good for you." She lifts a hand as if to reach out and touch me, but I capture her fingers with mine and lower them, squeezing affectionately.

"I'm fine. I knew it would be a challenge, but I'm persevering."

Her eyes narrow, lips puckering into a displeased pout. And then she says something that sends my head spinning. "Perhaps you should tell her the truth."

It takes me a moment to get my thoughts straight. Finally, I whisper, "What are you saying? You know what could happen. If His Majesty finds out, he might never allow me within a hundred miles of her. He could have me removed from the guard."

"He could," Mama says, tipping her head, "or perhaps he'd understand."

"You'd risk it? You'd risk our *home* on that?" I almost can't believe what I'm hearing.

She chews her lip, gaze darting away to watch a few customers leaving the shop below us. "You've already sacrificed so much for us, Raelan. This family is not your responsibility. It's *mine*. And I don't want you suffering like this for our benefit."

Heat rises inside me, messy and confused.

"I *want* to protect you," I say, voice low and sharp. "What would you—"

The door swings open to reveal Gilda standing there, Alina and Clarice standing a few steps back. Alina meets my eyes, and then her gaze flicks to my mother, and a brief look of confusion crosses her face before Gilda says, "Raelan, will you come play dolls with us?"

With my youngest sister gazing up at me like that, and Clarice and Alina smiling over her shoulder, I feel my shock and anger at my mother's words draining away.

"We'll talk later," Mama says, smiling like we weren't just having such an important conversation. "You've got dolls to play with."

CHAPTER 21
ALINA

RAELAN COMES ALIVE AROUND HIS FAMILY IN a way he's never come alive around me. It takes him a while, but he eventually softens, as if each moment spent here helps to pry one armored plate from his shoulders and chest, until it's just Raelan—beautiful, beaming Raelan.

He plays dolls without embarrassment, then carries Gilda around on his back, making her squeal with delight. Clarice, who seems to be in her early teenage years, watches with a look that tells me she *wants* to play but is perhaps too shy in my company to do so.

"Your hair is beautiful," I tell her as I help her put the last few dolls into a wooden toybox. "I'm quite jealous."

Her hair is as dark as her mother's, and it's thick and beautifully wavy. At the compliment, she reaches up to tuck a wave behind her ear, cheeks reddening. "Th-thank you. I like yours too. It's blue because you're a witch, right?"

I nod once, then hold out a hand. Clarice watches as frost dances across my palm, and then I send a few snowflakes drifting through the warm autumn air. Her hazel eyes gleam, following a flake until it settles upon the windowsill and melts into nothing.

"Wow. You're amazing."

I laugh as I push to my feet. "My professors may disagree with you."

Clarice's lips quirk up on one side. "How could they? You're the princess."

"Well," I say as we rejoin the rest of Raelan's family in the main room, "even princesses have to go to school, and we're not good at everything, despite what the fairy tales might say."

Gilda is still giggling as Raelan slings her off his back and sets her on her feet. He musses her hair lovingly, then says, "All right, little one. I think it's about time I get the princess back to the academy. She probably has a paper to write."

He withstands a barrage of begging and whining but doesn't give in.

Over Gilda's voice, I say, "Perhaps I can come visit you again."

All four of the Ashvales turn to look at me. My skin prickles under the weight of their stares.

"That is, if Raelan is okay with it," I add quickly.

"Of course he is!" Gilda exclaims. "And you can do anything you want, right? So, you'll come back tomorrow?"

Raelan and Soraya open their mouths to intervene, but I

say quickly, "Maybe not tomorrow, but very soon. I'll bring you another dessert, and we can play dolls again."

This seems to placate her for now, at least enough for me and Raelan to slip out the door, waving goodbye all the while. Soraya steps out behind us, closing the door. The air has a bit more of a chill now, as clouds have started creeping across the sky, hiding the sun from view.

"Thank you for visiting us," Soraya says. "It was quite a treat, Your Highness." She dips her head to me, then looks to her son. "And it wasn't so bad seeing you either." She pulls him in for a hug and plants a kiss on his cheek, then steps back.

"The pleasure was mine," I say. "And I do hope to visit again."

"You're welcome anytime." Her eyes—one milky, one brown—flick to Raelan, and something unspoken passes between them, though I can't say what it is. Perhaps something having to do with their whispered conversation this afternoon. I'd like to know what it was, but it's none of my business—and besides, I probably couldn't pull it from Raelan even if I tried.

We bid goodbye to his mother, then descend the steps from the apartment back to the cobbled walkway below. Our boots clip along the stone, accompanied by the light sounds of conversation as we move through Wysteria. A breeze sends a few colorful leaves skittering across the road, and I draw my arms around myself to ward off the chill.

"Thank you," I say as we start back in the direction of the academy. "For letting me meet them."

Raelan makes a small sound in his throat but otherwise doesn't respond.

My eyes flick to him, and I find that he's wearing his mask again, a slight furrow in his brow.

Treading carefully, my curiosity getting the better of me, I ask, "Your mother . . . What happened?"

I noticed right away the scars running down the length of her face, right over her milky-white eye.

A moment of quiet passes between us. I'm not so sure he's going to respond—and I'd understand. This really is none of my business.

Eventually, Raelan lets out a small breath. "My father did it. On accident. It was years ago, and he left right afterward. I think he was afraid to hurt us." His dark eyes meet mine. His gaze is sharp. "It's why I wear this chain. Why I have to be careful."

I picture the beast that burst from his skin, bigger than any living creature I've ever seen. It—*he*—could have swallowed me in one gulp or shredded me into thin ribbons with his glistening fangs.

I should be afraid—it's the most logical response to something so intimidatingly powerful. But when I trace Raelan's face with my eyes, take in the wounds still marring his neck, I can't bring myself to fear him.

Perhaps something is the matter with me.

"I'm sorry. I didn't mean to pry."

He looks away again, leaving me to ponder his words.

I suppose I never stopped to wonder which of his parents was the dragon shifter, who gave him the magic that runs through his veins.

"What of your sisters? Do they have . . . ?"

"No." The word is clipped. "Thank the deities." At his sides, his fingers curl into fists. His brow crinkles further.

"Are you . . . upset?" I ask.

My hope is that he'll quickly deny it, but he doesn't. Instead, he takes a deep breath through his nose, then lets it out in a sigh.

"You're making this difficult, Alina."

His use of my name makes my heart patter pleasantly. Despite me having asked him to use it instead of my title, he rarely does. "What do you mean?"

When his eyes meet mine, they're dark. "You know what I mean. This"—he gestures between us with one quick movement—"can't happen. We both know it. Why make things harder than they need to be?"

The pleasant thrumming of my heart shifts abruptly, turning hot with anger. "Why can't it happen?" I ask, halting on the sidewalk. The people walking behind us have to shift to flow around. Raelan takes me gently by the elbow and escorts me into the mouth of a narrow alleyway, out of the way of passersby. He glances around before replying.

"You know why."

His cold tone has me gripping the edge of my cloak, clinging to it to keep grounded. I remind myself of his scream, the way his body trembled. His *pain*.

But then we kissed last night. So why, now, is he acting so distant again? He's making me dizzy.

"Please elaborate," I say, trying to keep my anger and hurt at bay.

Raelan's jaw flexes, his eyes sharpening as he looks down at me. "Because you're the princess, and I'm just your guard. In no world are we allowed to be together. Wishing for it will do no good. It'll hurt us both."

I cross my arms. "That's ridiculous. My grandfather—"

"Is the king," Raelan says, cutting me off. "What do you think he'd say if you told him about us? About what we've done?"

"Well, he . . ." I trail off.

In truth, I'm not sure what Grandfather would do. He's always told me that he wants me to carve my own path, to marry for love rather than duty. But does that leniency extend to members of his own guard? Would he truly allow it?

Feeling suddenly flustered, I glare up at Raelan and say, "There's nothing to tell him about us. You kissed me. Twice. That's it."

Raelan tilts his head, eyes narrowing. "No, *you* kissed *me*. I'll take no responsibility for that."

An ember of defiance flares to life inside me. "You weren't complaining about it last night," I mumble with a shrug.

And though I don't think he means to, Raelan lets out a low growl. It sends a shiver across my skin.

"You shouldn't speak to me of last night," he bites out.

"Why?" I challenge.

His jaw feathers again, and he finds my elbow once more. Though it may be my imagination, I think his hand is warmer now through the fabric of my long-sleeved dress. He leads me farther down the alley. It's quieter here, a distance off the main road, and very few people even turn their heads to regard us as they pass by, too absorbed in their own business to care.

"Because," he growls, "I came very close to—" He clamps his jaw closed hard, huffing out a breath. I want so badly for him to finish that sentence, but he's not even looking at me now. "We can't let it happen again."

"Is it because of . . . ?" I nod toward his chain, with the burn visible just beneath the links.

Raelan sighs again. I'm not sure I've ever seen him so annoyed with me. Still, it comes nowhere close to how upset he was about Tristan.

"No. My pain has nothing to do with it."

"Then what are you so afraid of?"

This forces him to meet my gaze. Now his dark eyes burn.

"You are the one who should be afraid. You saw my mother. Do you have no sense of self-preservation?"

"Of course I do." A strand of hair drifts across my face, and I reach up to push it behind my ear, noting Raelan's intake of breath as I do so. "But I . . . I trust you."

Ralean scoffs and turns away, pacing a few steps from me, his back turned. His broad shoulders appear tight. "You shouldn't."

"Why?" I stand up straighter and lift my chin. "Give me one good reason."

He whips around and crosses the alley to me in two wide steps. His chest forces me back, and I let out a small breath as he pushes me against the ivy-clad brick wall, his hands coming up on either side of me so his arms cage me in. Against the whites of his eyes, his pupils are sharp again, having tightened into narrow lines. "Because you have no idea what I want to do to you."

Again, I realize I should be afraid. But instead of wanting to cower back or run from him, I find myself getting warm, heat blossoming in my low belly and between my legs.

And I can't stop myself from grabbing his tunic and pulling him closer, can't resist the desire to press my mouth to his, even if it's foolish—and potentially even dangerous, for *both* of us.

Unlike yesterday in the castle corridor, when Raelan froze beneath my mouth, this time he responds immediately, his lips moving against mine without hesitation. He tastes of chocolate and strawberry, and his body puts off so much heat that it washes over me like a summer breeze, keeping me warm despite the chill in the air.

My fingers work their way down his tunic, to the waistband of his trousers. When they curl around the edge, Raelan lets out a trembling snarl, and he forces his weight against me, pushing me back into the wall and grinding his hardening length against my thigh.

I've kissed boys, have fooled around with them in darkened halls and firelit parlors, but I've never felt a man inside of me. And I know now, with certainty, that I want Raelan to be my first.

I kiss him hard and fast. My mouth finds his jaw, then his neck. Beneath my lips, his muscles strain, every inch of his body coiled tight as my touch trails across his skin. He smells slightly of the café, mixed with a pleasant muskiness that's distinctly *him*. It twines around me in the heat put off by his body, serving only to make me wetter, to make me want to wrap my legs around him and discover what it would feel like to have him buried inside me.

"Tell me," I whisper against his skin, making goose bumps pebble along his throat beneath my breath.

"Tell you," he grunts out, "what?"

I smile slightly against his throat. "What you want to do to me."

Against his skin, the chain starts to glow blue. Raelan is breathing harder now, the trembling of his body intensifying. I pull back to look at him, but he has his eyes squeezed shut, his brow furrowed with pain or concentration—I can't tell which.

His eyes open, finding mine.

And I can see the dragon within him. Flecks of gold have appeared in his eyes, beautiful and otherworldly.

"Alina, I—"

Raelan's head jerks abruptly to the side, his words cutting off as his gaze snaps to the mouth of the alley. His eyes narrow, and I follow his gaze.

Across the road, a few people are walking, drawing their cloaks closer about their bodies against the breeze. Dancing leaves swirl down from the trees lining the cobblestone walkways, coming to rest upon the road, where they will soon be crunched into leaf dust by horses' hooves or carriage wheels. I can see nothing of note.

"What is it?" I whisper. "Did you see something?"

Raelan pushes off the wall, his slitted eyes still turned away from me, but what they're searching for, I've no idea.

"I don't know," he says at long last. The tightness in his trousers lessens, leaving me feeling frustrated. What will it take for him to finally touch me in the way I crave? "But we should get back."

Raelan draws himself up, looking every bit my protector. I just don't see what he thinks he needs to protect me from.

I ease myself off the cold brick wall, feeling chilled now without Raelan's body heat to keep me warm. Disappointment floods through me, twisting my stomach into a knot. But I try not to let it show. "Very well."

CHAPTER 22

RAELAN

IT WAS HARD TO TELL THROUGH THE DESIRE AND heat flooding my body, but I felt a threat, felt eyes roving over us, felt a curious intensity that made me pull back from Alina and scan the cobblestone road. Though I saw nothing, I couldn't shake the feeling that someone had been watching us.

The entire way back to the academy, I was quiet, focusing my full attention on scanning our surroundings and ensuring Alina—and her dizzying scent—didn't distract me. After that moment in the alley, I felt nothing else, but I'm still on high alert even now as I sit with Alina and her roommates in the stands flanking the runeball field.

I've never been interested in sports, and I don't believe Alina is either, but energy thrums through the onlookers, and it seems the students are grateful for time away from their studies. The smells of spun sugar and toasted cinnamon pecans fill the air, making my mouth water. Perhaps I'll go to the nearby cart and purchase some—maybe even try to enjoy myself while I'm here, seeing as Alina doesn't seem eager to leave anytime soon.

"Which one is your brother?" Lyra asks. She's seated on Alina's other side, some sort of apple-scented sticky-pop held in one hand. Her tongue is stained green from sucking on it.

Maeve lifts a hand and points, bracelet jangling on her wrist. "There. The big one."

All our gazes follow her finger, and I home in on a player who towers well above the others. His long hair is pulled back into a messy bun, the sides of his head shaved just above his pointed ears. His skin has a slight green tint to it, and small tusks protrude up from his bottom lip—an orc, then.

Together, we all look back at Maeve. She pushes her glossy hair over her shoulder and says, "We're stepsiblings. My mom married his dad."

That would explain it.

"It's Aric, right?" Lyra asks.

Maeve nods.

In what I've come to know as being typical of the fire witch, Lyra pushes to her feet, waving her hands in the air, and screams, "Go, Aric!"

His gaze shifts in our direction—along with the gazes of everyone else in the vicinity. Between Maeve and Lyra, Poppy sinks down, looking humiliated to have so many pairs of eyes on her. But Lyra just screams again, "Crush them!"

I'm not even sure who the other team is—it looks to me like they're all Coven Crest students of varying ages—but the sentiment makes Aric smile, and he thrusts a burly fist into the air.

"Lyra!" Poppy whispers. "Sit down! Everyone's staring!"

"Oh, it's fine, Pops." Lyra takes her seat on the bench and slips the sticky-pop back into her mouth, waggling her fingers at the other onlookers who're still staring at her.

Beside me, Alina laughs. It's a beautiful sound.

A horn blows, echoing over the stands, and the players arrange themselves on either side of the field, seven per team. With another blast of the horn, the game begins, the players launching into movement. They converge on a glowing sphere—it looks like a ball enchanted with elemental magic—and the team opposing Aric's takes control of it.

"Come on!" Lyra yells, fingers curling into a fist. A little tendril of smoke rises from her clenched fingers.

I've never seen this sport played before, and I have to follow the game closely to understand how it's played. It seems the teams are trying to control the sphere and put it through their opponent's goalposts. As they move through different areas of the field, the colors and characteristics of the sphere change, affecting the players' ability to control it.

"See those runes?" Alina asks, leaning slightly closer to me. I can hear her just fine over the din of the crowd, but I make no move to shift away from her. "They activate when the arcane sphere passes through their zones. That one"— she points to the rune that just flared to life on the grassy field—"is the fire rune."

Sure enough, the sphere bursts into flame, and the players have to change their tactics, using their wind magic to move it rather than kicking it or tossing it.

And I see now why Aric, being as big as he is, doesn't necessarily have an upper hand on the smaller players. Each student has the choice to move the sphere using their magic rather than just throwing or kicking it, and those players with powerful elemental abilities seem to reign.

Aric seizes control of the flaming sphere, and he sends it flying through another rune zone. The flames sizzle out, and the sphere becomes covered in a layer of shimmering ice, making it difficult to catch or hold.

"Come on, come on, come on," Lyra chants, very nearly vibrating out of her seat.

Finally, Aric's team sends the sphere through the opposing team's goalposts, and Lyra leaps to her feet with a victorious scream. Beside her, Poppy shrinks away from the raucous outburst. Alina claps politely. Maeve looks bored.

"You know this game well?" I ask Alina.

She smiles. "I used to go to runeball games with my father when I was young. Though it's been many years now since we last attended one together."

Of all the royals, I probably know Alina's father the least. He's the quiet sort, not given to extroverted activities, and when not holed up in his office or the library, he's often away on royal business. Having never been assigned to his duty, I've not come to know him with any sort of familiarity.

The reminder that my own father left when I was so young makes my stomach squeeze. Sometimes, I wonder where he is, whether he'll ever return. If he did, my mother would undoubtedly take him back. Even all these years later, I know she thinks of him, misses him. I see it in her eyes sometimes, the faraway look she gets as if watching for him to walk through the door like nothing even happened.

I picture my mother's scars, the horrific injury that left her marked and blind in one eye. And when I look at Alina, with her soft brown cheeks and windswept hair, I can't imagine ever doing anything to hurt her.

Her leg touches mine, our thighs brushing on the bench, and though I don't know if she did it on purpose, I still pull away, reminding myself that I'm a danger to her, that despite how badly I want her, I can't ever put her through what my mother experienced.

I'm not sure I could survive it.

And if not for the chain around my neck, warm against my skin even now, I know I would've needed to refuse this post as soon as the king assigned it to me. Because without the magic keeping my beast in check, I fear I would've already taken her, claimed her, perhaps even hurt her.

The thought makes my stomach turn. I shift farther away, putting more distance between us. Alina glances down at the gap between our thighs, the space I occupied beside her now empty, and a complicated emotion flicks across her face.

"Alina!" someone calls, and we both look up.

An instinctual growl rumbles in my chest when my eyes find the man she was talking to in the dining hall—*Tristan*.

Alina glances at me, then back at him, and I'm almost led to believe the flirty smile she gives him is done purposefully to piss me off.

And it fucking works.

She waves him over, then tells me, "Can you make room for Tristan?"

I'm so shocked that I actually snarl at her—good thing her roommates don't hear over the sound of the crowd—but she just smiles back, undeterred, then scoots closer to Lyra, squishing their hips together to make room for Tristan between us.

And I have to use every ounce of my willpower not to take him by the back of the neck and throw him clean into the runeball field. I'd probably like this sport a lot more if he were the one being tossed through the goalposts.

He eases past the other students on this bench, then says, "Pardon me," as he brushes by me to sit next to Alina. On my knees, my fingers curl into fists, and the warmth from my chain ignites against my skin.

What the fuck is she doing?

"Hey, I just wanted to check on you," Tristan says, settling in next to her and ignoring me as if I don't exist, as if I couldn't snap him like the scrawny human boy he is. "Is everything okay? I was worried about you the other day."

Liar, I want to snap. Instead, I narrow my eyes and focus on the field, trying to distract myself from the violent fantasy playing out in my head right now.

"Oh, everything's fine. Just some family stuff," Alina lies smoothly. "But thank you for checking on me."

In my peripheral vision, I see her reach over and place a hand on his. My dragon thrashes against my bones. I fight not to let my struggle show on my face.

"Of course," Tristan says. "I'm glad." He pushes a hand through his mop of brown hair, and his smell makes me want to wrinkle my nose unpleasantly.

There's something about him that sets my teeth on edge. His smell, the sound of his voice, the way he's sitting way too close to the princess . . .

"Oh!" Alina sounds unlike herself, too giddy, her voice pitched slightly higher than usual. "I don't think you've met Raelan, have you?"

"No." Tristan shakes his head, then turns to regard me, as if just noticing I'm sitting right beside him. "I'm Tristan Colbrook." He holds out a hand.

I stare at it coolly. A long-enough moment passes that he glances back at Alina questioningly. But she's looking at me, blue eyes challenging. Is this some sort of game to her? Watching me struggle like this?

I won't let them win.

Shoving my hand into Tristan's, I give it a firm shake. "Sir Raelan Ashvale."

"Good to meet you," he says.

I tighten my grip. Slowly, the expression on his face shifts as he no doubt notices the crushing strength of my hand in his, his bones protesting against my tightening hold.

"Likewise," I say, giving him a pleasant smile. At least, I try to make it pleasant. It might look more like a snarl.

Behind him, Alina narrows her eyes at me.

Tristan keeps a smile on his face as he yanks his hand from mine, attempting to disguise how he rubs it uncomfortably with the other and flexes his fingers as if trying to determine if they still work properly.

Good. I hope it hurts. It'll remind him to—

"Raelan," Alina says, "would you mind getting us some of those toasted pecans? I've been dying to try them."

She's trying to irritate me. It's growing more obvious by the moment.

"My apologies, Your Highness," I say, adopting my cold professional tone. "I'm not permitted to leave your side. But perhaps Mr. Colbrook would be willing." My eyes flash to his.

Alina opens her mouth, probably to argue, but Tristan quickly says, "Sure, I'd be happy to." He pushes to his feet, much too eager for my liking. "I'll be right back."

I deliberately don't move, making it more difficult for him to slink past me. Once he's out of earshot, Alina narrows her eyes at me and hisses, "What's the matter with you?"

I sit up straighter. "I told you before, I don't trust him."

She rolls her eyes at me. "Why? He hasn't done a single thing to draw your suspicion."

I can't argue with her—not without having to tell her that I haven't quite determined why Tristan sets me so on edge. Other male students speak with Alina—walk to class with her, greet her in the hallways—and while that *does* make me seethe, there's still something about Tristan that feels off, and I've yet to determine if my dragon distrusts him because of his interest in Alina or because it has detected something about him that the human part of me has yet to home in on.

We fall into a tense silence. Alina's scent changes slightly, tinged now with her hot anger.

And it makes my dragon coil inside me, pushing against the magic in an attempt to get out. It likes the ferociousness in her ice-blue eyes, likes the sharp set of her jaw as she regards me unflinchingly.

Perhaps for the first time, I feel why she's my mate. Despite having seen me in my true form, despite knowing what I am, she stares back at me fearlessly, meeting me glare for glare.

Fuck, I want her.

The crowd cheers around us, the roar loud against my sensitive ears. But Alina doesn't look away, doesn't turn her eyes from mine to watch the players sprinting across the field. My gaze flicks to her lips, traces the soft shape of them. I know now from experience that they fit mine perfectly, know how they taste after a cup of tea, warm and plush and—

"Toasted pecans!" Tristan announces from behind me.

I turn my eyes up to him, barely restraining the urge to growl. He makes to step around me and reclaim his spot beside Alina, but I shift at the last moment, pressing myself close to her despite the strain it puts on me. She draws a small surprised breath.

"Thanks," I say, reaching out and snagging the paper bag from Tristan's hands. He looks surprised but doesn't voice any complaint as I pop a few of the toasted pecans into my mouth. They're warm and coated in cinnamon sugar. I pass the bag to Alina.

"Thanks, Tristan," she says.

Heat rises inside me at her use of his name.

"You want to watch the rest of the game with us?" she continues.

Tristan hesitates a moment, his eyes flicking between me and Alina. Finally, he smiles and says, "Absolutely."

He sits beside me, and Alina reaches across my chest to offer him the pecans. Her scent drifts around me, and a floaty strand of her hair brushes my chin.

And I know she's doing it all on purpose, driving me crazy like this just because she can.

But at least I'm between them now, in the spot right beside her.

In the spot where I belong, whether it's painful for me or not.

CHAPTER 23
ALINA

SAMHAIN IS QUICKLY APPROACHING, AND it's different and exciting seeing Coven Crest transform in the days leading up to the festival, which is to be held here on the grounds. The air has grown colder and smells of rich soil, decaying leaves, and woodsmoke from the fires burning nonstop in the castle and outbuildings. Even now, as I sit in the library with Maeve, the giant hearth crackles, sending out sparks and red-orange light, bathing us in warmth as we work on our papers.

I dip my quill into my inkwell, then tap off the excess ink. I'm writing a paper for Magical History and Ethics—exploring the morality of communicating with the dead—and it's slow going. Even now, my gaze is drawn up from my parchment and across the library, to the closed double doors. I know Raelan is standing on the other side, my dutiful sentinel.

He's not kissed me again, has not even given me the opportunity to do so. I dream of him most nights, though the types of dreams vary. Last night I dreamt of riding upon his back as he flew through the clouds high over the wilds of Elarwyn, the wind in my hair and sunlight on my skin. It was so thrilling I woke with my heart thundering in my chest. And I wished it were Poppy who'd dreamt it instead—maybe then I could hope it would one day come true, as so many of her dreams seem to.

Across from me at the small two-person table, Maeve tips her head and says, "You're distracted today."

I think to deny it, but I've learned Maeve is much too perceptive to be so easily tricked.

With a sigh, I set down my quill and prop my cheek on a fist. "I can't seem to get Raelan out of my head. He's driving me crazy."

Maeve blinks her beautiful purple eyes and says simply, "I know. Do you wanna talk about it yet?"

One of my shoulders lifts in a shrug. "I'm not sure there's anything to talk about."

"Well . . ." Maeve sets her quill down and focuses in on me. "You could start with what happened that night you went to his room."

My stomach flares with heat at the reminder of that night. I can still feel Raelan's body against mine as he pressed me against the wall, my legs about his waist, our mouths hungering for each other. I haven't told the girls any of this—though I'm not quite sure why. Lyra has certainly begged me enough. Perhaps it's because I grew up without

175

any siblings or even close friends. I learned at a young age to keep things to myself lest my parents and grandfather discover what I was up to and put a swift stop to it.

But maybe Maeve will understand. She won't judge. And it would feel *so* good to finally get this secret off my chest.

I glance around at the other students dotted through the library, but no one is paying us any attention. They're all busy working on their own papers or flipping through heavy school tomes. One boy is asleep in an armchair by the roaring fire, head tipped back and mouth hanging open. The librarian makes quick work of waking him, sending a dribble of water splashing across his face with a flick of her water magic. The students around him laugh as he jerks awake.

With a soft sigh, I look down at the table and whisper, "Raelan and I kissed."

I'm not sure how I expect Maeve to react, but when I look up at her, she's simply smiling that knowing smile. Her long hair is pulled up in a sleek ponytail, and it glistens in the firelight. "I had a feeling. You two have been different since that day."

Of course she noticed.

She arches a dark brow. "But why's that bothering you now?" Her knowing gaze quickly assesses me. "You're on edge. I can feel the static in your energy field."

A sigh slips from my lips. "I don't understand what's going on with him. He kisses me like he wants me, and then he pulls away just as suddenly and acts like nothing happened between us." I shift to rub my temple with my fingers. A headache is starting to bloom behind my ears. "He's driving me mad."

Maeve hums thoughtfully. "I think it makes sense."

My eyes narrow. "How?"

"He's your knight." She shrugs nonchalantly. "I'm sure he can get in a lot of trouble for getting involved with you. He could probably lose his position on the guard, right?"

On second thought, maybe I should've talked to Lyra instead. She'd have at least sided with me—though I know Maeve speaks the truth. Raelan said as much that afternoon after leaving his family's apartment.

"I don't know . . . Maybe. But why kiss me at all if he's only going to pull away? I mean, we've barely even spoken since the runeball game. It's almost like we're strangers again."

The idea that Raelan may never kiss me again, may never trace his hands along my waist or breathe his warm breath over my neck, makes me ache deep in my chest. He's right outside the library, yet I yearn for him as though I've not seen him in years. How is it that he can make me feel so lonely while standing right beside me?

"It's probably a lot harder for him than it is for you. If you get caught, nothing bad will actually happen. But if he gets caught, he could lose everything he's worked for."

I let out a long sigh. Maeve's right. And it makes me feel like a spoiled brat.

"I don't know what to do," I whisper, keeping my voice down as a few students walk past our table, purple-trimmed robes flapping. Fourth-years, then. "It would be best to keep our distance from each other, but . . ." Heat rises in my stomach. "But I want him so bad. I've never felt like this before, about *anyone*."

Maeve's smile slips, transforming into a thoughtful frown. "I don't know. But it's obvious he wants you too, even if you don't see it. From my perspective, it's impossible not to notice." She reaches across the table and puts her hand atop mine. "Maybe you just need to give it time. And if you're meant to be together, things will work out."

My chest grows tight.

"And if we're not?" I whisper.

This time Maeve doesn't reply. She just squeezes my hand a little. And I'm not sure if it makes me feel better or worse.

"Well, I know what'll make you feel better," she says.

I arch a brow at her.

Still holding my hand, she pushes up from the table and tugs me to my feet. "Come on. Get your books and your knight." The smile on her lips is playful. "We're gonna go practice magic."

DESPITE THE WIND AND THE BITE TO THE AIR, I find myself standing on Coven Crest's runeball field—though this time, there aren't any players sprinting across the runes and calling out to one another, no cheers from the crowd in the stands. It's just me, Maeve, and Lyra. Poppy was busy with a special study group and couldn't join us.

Raelan watches us from a distance, leaning on the low metal fence encircling the field. When I glance at him, I find his eyes trained on the cloudy gray sky, and I wonder if he's wishing he could spread his wings and fly away.

Maeve catches me looking his way and gives me one of her knowing eyebrow arches, and after that, I keep my focus on the arcane sphere.

It sits on the damp grass between us, a simple ball made of some sort of firm material, waiting to be sent flying with a burst of magic or someone's well-aimed kick. None of us have touched it yet.

"So, what are we doing here, exactly?" I ask, reaching up to pull my long hair into a ponytail so it'll stay out of my face.

"Practicing our magic," Maeve states simply with a shrug of her shoulders. Then her violet eyes flash. "And having some fun." She flicks her wrist, and a gust of wind whips around the arcane sphere, sending it up into the air. "The goal is to keep the arcane sphere in the air using nothing but our magic."

The three of us tilt our heads up to look at it. And as it starts to plummet back toward the field, a little burst of excitement zips through my veins. This should be fun.

I hold my hand out, intending to strike it to keep it aloft with a burst of frost magic, but Lyra beats me to it. A stream of fire streaks from her palm, setting the sphere alight and knocking it flying.

Maeve's eyes meet mine. "Well?" she says, gesturing across the field. "Aren't you going to get it?"

Without wasting another moment, I break into a run, keeping my eye on the sphere as it slows and starts to fall back toward me. Legs still pumping beneath me, I yell back, "Damn you, Lyra!"

Behind me, Lyra cackles.

As the sphere falls, I hold up my hands and call on my magic. Frost swirls across my palms, cold like the first kiss of winter. I focus, eyes locked on the sphere. Then I send my magic shooting toward the sphere, intending to knock it up into the air and back toward Maeve.

But instead, I hit it much too hard, my magic swirling out of my hands in uncontained bursts, and the arcane sphere zooms into the air and toward the far end of the field.

Slowing my pace and gasping for air, I let out a groan.

"Guess you haven't been listening in Professor Stone's class!" Lyra yells, her voice and laughter carrying across the runeball field. "You're supposed to ground yourself first, Miss Ravenscroft!"

"Yeah, yeah," I mumble, stepping back into a slow jog to go retrieve the sphere from where it landed on the other side of the field.

Lyra and I both have trouble containing our elemental magic, but at least mine doesn't have the potential to set our dorm room aflame. Which she has certainly almost done—on multiple occasions now.

When I finally reach the other end of the field, I find the sphere has already been picked up for me, and the student who fetched it stands alongside the field, tossing it from hand to hand.

"Tristan," I say, mouth pulling into a smile.

"Thought that was you." He laughs and tosses the sphere again, his dark eyes tracking its movement before flicking back to me. "You plan on trying out for a runeball team?"

"Definitely not." I roll my eyes and laugh. "Just fooling around." A few strands of hair have come loose from my ponytail, and I reach up to push them behind my ear. "Do you . . . Do you wanna play?"

Tristan looks down at the sphere, then back up at me. "Nah. Afraid I'm not very good at my magic yet." He holds out a hand, and while it appears he's attempting to bring a flame into his palm, all he's successful at producing is a wisp of smoke.

My lips quirk up on one side.

Tristan notices. "Are you . . . *laughing* at me, Your Highness?" He narrows his eyes and tips his head, but his expression struggles to remain serious.

"No!" I hold out my hands. "I'm not. I swear."

He continues to stare at me. His gaze sharpens.

"Okay, yes, I was. But just a little."

"I had no idea our princess was so cruel," he mumbles, as if to himself. "I'll have to let everyone know what a bully you are."

I groan and cant my head at him. "Please don't. I have a hard-enough time making friends around here as it is."

"Hmm. Can't imagine why that might be . . ." Tristan's gaze flicks over my shoulder.

And suddenly, I feel heat on my back. When I turn, I spot Raelan staring at us from where he still stands beside the fence encircling the field. He's glaring, lips pulled into a severe frown, hands fisted at his sides. When he catches my eye, he arches a brow slowly.

And if I were younger and just slightly less mature than I am now, I might stick my tongue out at him.

"Anyway, I'll let you get back to your game."

I turn back around to face Tristan. "Are you sure? It's all in good fun. Goddess knows I sure need to practice my magic. It listens about as well as a school of prairie fish."

His smile is soft and friendly. A crisp autumn breeze sends his brown hair swaying about his eyes. "I'm sure. Now, whose turn is it?"

"Maeve's. And she's much too good at this game, so don't go easy on her."

"Oh yeah?" With a little smirk, Tristan lifts the sphere over his head and yells, "Maeve, go long!" Then he hurls the arcane sphere across the field with surprising strength and a little bit of air magic, sending Maeve sprinting after it, her long-legged strides chewing up the grassy field.

I watch her for a moment, impressed by her speed and agility, and my eyebrows shoot up when she blasts the sphere with a small burst of electricity—storm witches and their lightning—and sends it right back up into the sky so Lyra has to scurry after it.

"Well, I'm off." Tristan steps back from the fence, his schoolbag thumping against his hip. "But don't worry too much about your frost magic." The look he gives me is warm, comforting. "You'll master it eventually. Just takes time."

I arch an eyebrow at him and smile. "Speaking from experience?"

In answer, he holds out a hand, and this time he's able to bring a small flame into his palm. It sends a bit of light dancing across his skin, shimmying in the breeze. After a few moments, Tristan closes his hand around the flame, extinguishing its heat and light. "Yeah," he says, "something like that . . ."

"Alina!" Lyra yells. "Come on!"

"Ugh," I groan. "Fire witches. Are they always so impatient?"

"In my experience," Tristan calls out as he heads back toward the castle, "yes!"

"What'd he say about fire witches?" Lyra yells.

But I just shake my head and start back across the field. Raelan's gaze follows me, but I don't meet his eyes. Instead, I send out another little blast of frost magic, and this time, it sends the arcane sphere arcing beautifully into the sky, just like I intended for it to.

Just takes time, I think, letting a smile stretch across my face.

I glance back over my shoulder, searching for Tristan, but he's already gone, with nothing but fallen leaves skittering across the cobblestones in his wake.

CHAPTER 24
RAELAN

THE ACADEMY GROUNDS ARE DRIPPING IN decorations for Samhain. Pumpkins of all shapes, colors, and sizes line the walkways and sit stacked in piles; charmed candles float in midair; and the cool breeze smells of cider and caramel apples and spiced mead.

I've not had a drink since the schoolyear began, and I'd be lying if I said I don't feel like downing an entire mug—or two or three—of mead. Anything to take Alina off my mind.

Things haven't gotten any better. Every day is a struggle, every brush of her scent against my senses an assault the likes of which I barely survive.

Tonight she's wearing a dress I've never seen on her before—which is probably a good thing. It's long and black, and the bodice is pulled snug with laces. A necklace hangs about Alina's neck, a silver songbird pendant coming to rest in the slight depression between her breasts, which are pushed up high enough that I'm struggling to keep my eyes away from them. Her blue eyes are lined and smudged with black, her lips are painted crimson, and her hair hangs loose and wild around her shoulders.

When she stepped out of her room this evening and I got my first full look at her, I had to shift my stance in an effort to hide the hard-on she gave me.

If she's trying to kill me tonight, she's doing a fucking phenomenal job of it.

The academy grounds teem with people—students, faculty, and plenty of visitors. Merchants from Wysteria have set up stands throughout the courtyard, from which they sell food and drink, trinkets, and all other manner of wares.

Alina and her roommates talk and laugh easily with one another, sweeping through the stands and picking up snacks and souvenirs as they go. One stand is selling caramel-dipped apples, and Alina purchases one for herself.

Watching her lips glide over the sticky caramel almost has me tossing her over my shoulder and carrying her back to my room.

This is not good. Really not good.

I've done a damn good job recently of keeping my distance from her. After that last kiss in the alleyway, I've not let myself taste her again. But tonight I feel myself slipping, and it's going to take all my willpower to keep my hands off her waist and out of her hair.

Not like she's doing anything to help the situation.

Her eyes keep finding mine, and her crimson lips have a perpetual smirk on them, like she knows quite well what she's doing and isn't afraid of showing it.

After the women have finished meandering through the stands and pop-up shops, Lyra says, "I'm ready for a drink. Anyone else?"

"*Please*," Meave says.

Alina just shrugs. "Sure."

Poppy's cheeks go red. "I-I've never drank before . . ."

In Wysteria, the drinking age is eighteen. Granted, some of us were slipping into taverns and flirting with barmaids at much younger an age than that.

"How about you, Raelan?" Lyra asks. Like Alina and the others, she's dressed in black, and her bright red hair bursts out from her head in a mess of wild curls. Juniper is perched upon her shoulder, and Lyra reaches up to give her a thin slice of green apple.

I try and fail not to look at Alina. As soon as my eyes flick to her, drinking in the shape of her body beneath her black dress and the curve of her soft brown throat, I know I'm going to need something—*anything*—to take this edge off.

"I'm in," I say.

Lyra lights up. "Yes! Let's go."

We get in line at the mead table. Even from way back here, I can see the man who's serving up drinks—a massive minotaur with thick spiraling horns and a golden hoop ring dangling from his nose. Seeing him, I realize that he must be the one I stole the clothing from the night I crept back to the academy in the dark, completely naked. I've heard talk of Coven Crest's minotaur groundskeeper, but this is my first time laying eyes on him.

As we work our way slowly to the front of the line, I realize how big he is. I stand taller than most of the students here, but he stands well over a foot above me. His arms are like tree trunks. Hell, he could probably lift tree trunks and not even break a sweat.

Behind him are casks of mead, and he serves up drinks with a slight frown and an air of general disinterest.

"Five for us," Lyra says when she gets to the front of the line. "What's on tap?"

The minotaur regards her through slightly narrowed eyes. "Mead."

Lyra's brow arches in the corner. "Well, what flavors?"

"Mead," he replies again.

Alina and Maeve chuckle at Lyra's expense.

The minotaur serves us up five mugs of steaming mead and exchanges them for a few eldertokens. When we've walked away, Lyra scoffs, "How unfriendly. Who even is he?"

"The groundskeeper," Poppy says. Her gaze is turned down, and she regards the mead in her mug like it's a concoction from potions class.

"Well, he's rude. It's Samhain. Can't he even *smile*?"

I hang back, walking behind Alina and her roommates. The mead in my mug sends up steam in the cool air. It smells strongly of alcohol, a potent scent that stings my nose despite the light honey undertone.

Suddenly, I'm thinking this might not be such a good idea. I'm Alina's protector, her knight. I'm not supposed to drink on duty.

But all it takes is one more glance at her as she lifts her mug to her lips, her throat bobbing as she swallows, and I'm convinced that I'm going to need something to help me survive tonight.

So, while the women continue to drift through the crowd, watching the fire dancers before stopping to warm themselves before the bonfire, I down everything in my mug.

The alcohol warms my throat and chest, and it only takes a short while for me to start feeling the effects. The sharpened edges of my consciousness feel smoothed out, and I even find myself smiling at some of Lyra's bad jokes. She seems to appreciate it, if the way she eases closer to me and puts her hand on my forearm is any indication.

Alina, on the other hand, doesn't seem pleased. She watches Lyra with thinly veiled anger. Her blue eyes, made more startling by the black makeup smudged around them, narrow as Lyra's fingers drift across my arm. Lyra seems not to notice—or she's pretending not to.

The fire witch is difficult to pin down—she still surprises me, and it's hard to know exactly what's going on behind her sharp crimson eyes.

"You know, Raelan," Lyra says, turning her gaze up to meet mine while the light from the bonfire dances over her hair, "I think you might actually be fun."

I can't stop the sharp laugh that slips out of me—it's the mead talking. "You *think*?"

"Well, you're always so stuffy." She wrinkles her nose at me. I can tell the alcohol is already getting to her too. "You just need to lighten up a bit. Stop being so uptight."

Music drifts through the air, accompanying the crackling of the flames. Something like mischief glows in Lyra's crimson eyes. Then she's wrapping her fingers around my hand and relieving me of my empty mead mug, setting it on a nearby cart laden with pumpkins and gourds. "Come on. I have just the thing for you, sir knight."

I take a step, then pause and glance back at Alina.

Her eyes are narrowed, her lips puckered into a stern frown.

"Alina, can I take your knight for a minute?" Lyra asks, her voice lilting, as if she's completely blind to the look on Alina's beautiful face. "Just one dance, then I promise to bring him back."

Everyone's eyes shift to her.

Alina's cheeks turn a slight shade of red, though I can't tell if it's from the cold, the mead, or the complicated emotions flickering across her face.

The smile that pulls on her mouth looks painfully false. "Of course."

"Yay! Thank you!"

Now Lyra is tugging at me again, pulling me toward the mass of people dancing on the other side of the flickering bonfire. And despite everything, I allow her to yank me into the fray.

I've done plenty of dancing at taverns and festivals and in those stuffy classes taught to squires at the castle, so this reel is familiar to me.

I just wish Alina were the one dancing across from me instead of her roommate.

The music carries us through the dance, guiding our

steps across the leaf-strewn grass while the scents of autumn twine through the air around us. I'm aware of Alina and her roommates drifting closer, watching us from a short distance away. Every time I glance in Alina's direction, she's staring daggers at me.

It makes my dragon squirm.

I reach for Lyra, spin her in a circle, smell the woodsmoke on her curly hair as it bounces around her shoulders. She's smiling, laughing, leaning closer—

"Lyra, *stop*." Alina is suddenly between us, halting our dance mid-step. I steady Lyra when she stumbles. "That's enough."

Lyra blinks, looking between me and Alina with obvious confusion. "What? You said we could—"

Before Lyra can get another word out, Alina snatches my hand in hers and pulls me swiftly aside, dragging me away from the dance and the big flickering bonfire. When I glance back over my shoulder at Alina's roommates, I find Lyra wearing a small sly smile, and I wonder if perhaps she was baiting Alina all along.

If that's the case, it seems to have worked.

Alina leads me around the far side of the bonfire, her thin fingers clasped firmly about mine. She's never held my hand like this, especially in so public a venue, and the touch sends my chain growing warm about my throat.

As we move through the crowd, I feel a tingle go down my spine. When I turn my head, I catch Tristan watching us from a distance away. A few young men and women linger about him, talking and laughing, but his eyes are on us.

When he sees me looking, I expect him to turn away, ashamed at having been caught staring. But he doesn't. He holds my gaze, and something about the way he does it makes my dragon gnash its teeth, though the alcohol has softened its anger.

I send him a sharp glare in return, and eventually, Tristan glances away. I don't believe Alina even noticed him looking.

Even now, she's still holding my hand, though there's no need—I'll follow her wherever she wants to go. Not that I'm complaining.

She leads me back toward the castle, but instead of taking the stairs to the grand double doors, we veer off, following a winding path toward the gardens along the back of the academy. There are fewer students and visitors here, but floating candles still guide our way, drifting along like glowbugs in the dark autumn night.

"Your Highness," I start, trying to get my wits about me enough to stop whatever it is that's happening right now.

"*Stop* calling me that." Her blue eyes burn as she glares at me over her shoulder. And they're sharp enough that I lapse into silent curiosity.

Where is she taking me?

At this time of year, many of the raised beds have already been harvested, with withered stalks left behind to rot and feed the soil over the cold winter. The dry plant matter crinkles in the breeze drifting around us as Alina leads me toward the greenhouses lining the back of the garden.

When she does at last release my hand, I find my fingers longing immediately to take hers up again, to be twined through hers, woven together like threads in a tapestry.

Get a grip, I tell myself.

I really shouldn't have had that mead. It's making my head pleasantly funny—in a way that is certainly not appropriate around the princess.

And yet I can't bring myself to resist when Alina pulls open the door to the greenhouse and beckons for me to step inside after her.

As soon as she closes the door behind us, the autumn sounds—a gentle wind, leaves rustling on branches and across the ground, the far-off din of festivalgoers—fall silent. The greenhouse is bathed in silver moonlight, and it's pleasantly warm, with a humidity to the air that makes me loosen the collar of my high-necked tunic.

The sharp look in Alina's blue eyes softens as she regards me, the tension in her tight shoulders releasing with a sigh.

"What are we doing in here?" I ask. In the silent greenhouse, my voice feels too loud.

"I—" Alina bites her crimson lip and casts her gaze down into her mug of mead. From here, I can see she's barely had anything to drink. "I just wanted to get away."

I tip my head. "Because of Lyra?"

Her eyes meet mine again. She holds my stare for a moment, then turns away from me and sets off into the greenhouse. The plants housed in here are still vibrant and full of life, protected as they are from the bite of autumn's cold. Alina drifts through them slowly, reaching out at times to rub a petal between her forefinger and thumb or to bring her nose close to breathe in the rich floral scents. The skirt of her long black dress drifts along the ground, whispering against the earth as she walks.

"Back home, I spent a lot of time in the garden. It provided a respite, a sanctuary where I could just get away."

My fingers long to reach out and twine through her hair. In an effort to resist doing just that, I slip my hands into the front pockets of my trousers, my boots thudding softly on the dirt as I follow along behind her. "I didn't know that."

"No, I imagine not." She reaches out to touch another petal. I hope she knows what these plants are; some look poisonous. "You didn't know anything about me."

I knew plenty about her, not least of all the fact that she's my mate. But I don't say this, don't even allow it the chance to dance along my tongue. Instead, I glance away.

"I knew of you," I finally bring myself to say. "I saw you around."

Actually, I tried very hard *not* to see her around. The last thing I wanted was to be caught in close quarters with her, to be put into the position I now find myself in daily.

A brief moment of quiet passes. Then, without turning to face me, she asks, "And what did you think?"

My eyes narrow. I'm not following. "About what?"

Now she turns to face me. Her black-rimmed eyes are focused but soft, her crimson lips looking almost black in the cold moonlight. "About me."

The way she looks at me is different from anything I've seen from her before. She's not angry at me, isn't putting on a polite show for those around her, isn't showing me anything except her truth.

And what I see on her face makes me want to pull her close, to wrap her in my arms and never, ever let go. To hoard her like the precious treasure she is.

I draw myself up and take a breath.

"Truthfully?" I whisper.

Alina gives me a firm nod.

"I thought you were beautiful. Almost unnaturally so." The mead helps pull the truth from me. I flex my jaw. "I tried to avoid you, actually."

Alina blinks. "What? Why?"

"Because . . ." *Because I can't control myself around you. Because of the things I want to do to you. Because I want you so badly.* "Because it wasn't my place to find you beautiful. I had no right."

Her lips tug up on one side. "And now? Do you feel the same way?"

That one's easy. "I do."

Regardless of the bond that draws me toward her, regardless of the way my dragon writhes whenever Alina catches my eyes, I'm still just a knight, and she's the princess, the woman who will one day be queen. And I'm just me. I'm certainly no king.

"Then why kiss me?" She takes a step toward me, and my eyes flick toward her breasts. I have to force them back to her face. "Why touch me like you have?"

I take a step back as my beast reacts to her, straining against the magic holding me in my human form. "We've already been through this," I grunt out. "You kissed me—all three times now, if I'm not mistaken."

"But you wanted me to."

194

She moves nearer still, forcing me back. My shoulders connect with the glass wall of the greenhouse, and there's nowhere else for me to go. This is the second time she's cornered me like this. My mentors would be ashamed. But my dragon vibrates with excitement.

"You may not have kissed me first," she continues, voice low, "but you didn't try to stop me either."

"I'm a weak man," I say, trying very hard to focus on her face and not the sinuous movement of her body beneath the tightly laced black dress.

"So, you admit that you wanted to. To kiss me."

My heart pounds harder, and I curl my fingers into fists, pressing my fingernails into my palms, using the slight pinch of pain to keep me grounded in this moment.

"Don't lie," she whispers.

If only she knew how much I've been lying about.

I grind my teeth, then finally say, "Yes."

"And you wanted to do other things too. You told me so yourself." Alina is only a breath away from me now, the toes of her heeled black boots touching mine.

This time I don't respond. I can't. I'm trying too hard to force my dragon down.

"Raelan."

The word is a whisper, a breath. It makes goose bumps rise along my skin despite the warmth in the greenhouse.

"What do you want to do to me?" she asks.

I shake my head firmly. I can't voice my desires out loud. To do so would be to breathe life into them, to allow myself to think they're mine for the taking.

But they're not.

Alina *should* be mine. My dragon is insistent that she already is, and at times it almost has me convinced. But my beast doesn't understand customs, rules, the hierarchy of society. It doesn't understand that my mother and sisters need a roof over their heads, a stable life they can feel comfortable and safe within.

"Alina, I can't," I finally say.

"Why? Tell me." Her words have a sharp edge now, like she ran them over a whetstone before they slipped off her tongue. "Why have you been so cold again? Why are you shutting me out?"

"Because of your grandfather. If he finds out—"

"Are you going to tell him?" she asks, tipping her head slightly to one side so her pale blue hair slips across her shoulder.

"Of course not," I bite out.

"Neither am I. And no one else"—she casts a quick glance around the greenhouse—"is here to see."

Slowly, I start to harden, my tight hold on my carnal desires beginning to slip. I shouldn't have had that mead. It was foolish, juvenile. But perhaps, in a way, I was hoping for this. Maybe I wanted it to give me an excuse to do what I so badly desire to do.

To do with her. To do *to* her.

"Careful," I tell her, my voice dropping low as I try to force my beast into submission. Thus far, I'm failing.

"Of what?" Alina reaches out, placing her warm hands on my chest. I'm certain she can feel my heart galloping against her palms.

That single touch sends my dragon breathing fire through my veins. It snaps the tenuous thread of self-control I was desperately clinging to. And I can almost ignore the pain blossoming along my neck beneath my chain as I wrap my hands around Alina's waist and draw her in.

And this time, for the *first* time, I'm the one who kisses her.

Her mouth tastes of sweet caramel apples and honey-flavored mead. Her lips are soft and warm and a perfect fit for mine.

But it's the sound she makes as I bite her lip that sends me to my edge. It's part whimper, part moan. At the same time, her fingers curl into the fabric of my tunic, grasping at me as if I'm an anchor amidst a violent storm.

What she doesn't know is that I'm not the anchor—I'm the storm. And I've been holding myself back for three years, since she first came of age and I realized who—and what—she is.

I want so badly to have my way with her, to claim her, to make her mine. But I can't. And I remind myself of this fact even as I turn us about and press her against the glass wall of the greenhouse.

"I can't," I grind out after stealing my lips back from hers, "do this."

"Please, Raelan," she whispers, her hands finding my face, drifting along the stubble shadowing my jaw. "I want you. Don't you want me?"

My cock strains against my trousers, growing so hard it makes me wince.

Of course I want her. How can she even ask that? Doesn't she see what she does to me?

Maybe I can do this. Maybe I can control myself.

I imagine spreading her legs, sinking into her, filling her pussy with my heat. Immediately, the chain binding my neck burns hotter, warning me, cautioning me. My dragon lingers just beneath the surface, coiling and uncoiling itself, waiting for its chance to escape.

Jaw flexed so hard it makes my teeth ache, I press my body against hers. "I can't give you what you want," I say, even though it's excruciating to resist her.

She pulls back and looks into my eyes. "Then give me what you *can*."

Taking one of my hands, she guides my fingers to the place between her legs, like she did that first time we kissed in the darkened hallway.

I grunt, squeezing my eyes closed.

Like that first time, I'm overcome with pain, with heat burning along my neck and inside my veins. But this time, I'm prepared. This time, I won't give in. I'll withstand the agony for as long as I can, if only to feel her for one brief moment.

I touch her through the silky fabric of her dress. She gasps as my fingers glide across her folds, and her body trembles delicately, so small and breakable beneath mine.

I open my eyes, searching hers as they sparkle.

"Have you ever been touched here?" I whisper, my breath shifting the thin hairs around her face.

Without saying a word, she bites her lip and shakes her head.

"But you want me to touch you?"

Now she nods fervently.

She's never been touched.

My beast rejoices at this.

Mine, I think. *No one else's.*

I bunch the fabric of her dress in my fist, then guide it up, exposing her smooth legs, her thighs gleaming in the moonlight. I use my knee to press her legs apart. Her eyes, blue as winter ice, watch my fingers as they move up her thigh, then dip between her legs. There's only a thin undergarment between us now, and she's already soaked the fabric.

My cock throbs.

I find Alina's eyes and hold her gaze as I ease my fingers into the waistband of her panties. Her crimson lips open with a gasp as I press the pad of one finger against her swollen clit.

"Oh my—"

Her words cut off as I circle her clit, then slide my fingers lower, pressing through her folds to find her slick entrance. She's soaking.

"Fuck," I grunt, biting back another wave of pain as it crashes over me. "You're so fucking wet."

"Is that," she whispers breathily, "a good thing?"

I push my middle finger against her pussy. It's tight. But slowly, it yields to me. As my finger slides inside her and she draws a sudden breath, I say, "Yeah, it's a good thing."

I push my finger deeper. It sinks into her up to my first joint. She tips her head back against the glass, crimson lips opening with a breath. Then I push deeper, up to my knuckle. She's so tight around me, so wet and ready. Ready for *me*.

But I can't. This is already way over the line. If anyone were to find out about this, I'd be done for.

"Fuck, Alina." I brace my forearm on the glass over her head, working my finger in and out of her as she pants beneath me. Her cum coats my finger, drips down the back of my hand. Seeking some sort of relief, I press my cock against her thigh, wishing so badly I could sheathe it inside her.

"What," Alina gasps, "can I do for you?"

My immediate thought is to tell her she doesn't need to do anything for me. But before I can, her small warm hand finds its way to the straining pressure in my trousers. She rubs me through the fabric, making me clench my teeth. Even my gums ache, my fangs fighting to break through.

That *can't* happen. I'm not so sure I'd be able to resist sinking them into her throat. Though with my magic held at bay with the charmed chain about my neck, I'm not sure if the claiming would even work.

No. I can't. I *won't*.

Sliding my finger out of her, I drag her slick wetness up to her clit, massaging it beneath the pads of my fingers. Her hand stills on my cock, like she can't focus on touching me while being touched like this herself.

I lean back slightly to look at her face. It's bathed in cold moonlight streaming through the glittering glass ceiling. Her eyes are closed, her brow furrowed delicately. Her lips are open as she pants. I lower my head and press my mouth to hers, and she moans against me.

Still kissing her, I adjust to slide my finger inside her again, then use my thumb to rub her clit. Her hands come up to grasp my shirt, clinging and gripping like she's adrift in a turbulent sea. A light layer of ice dances across her fingers and up her wrists—her magic is seeping out, and she doesn't even seem to realize it.

And she's still so fucking wet.

I kiss her harder, finger her faster. Her panted breaths become barely controlled moans.

And I can't believe my hard-on hasn't burst through my trousers yet. I'm going to have to get some sort of release tonight, whether that's by my hand or Alina's. Pain is already wrapping around my balls, squeezing as the pressure builds inside me.

But I continue focusing on her. Her icy fingers are still tangled so tightly in my tunic that I think she might rip straight through the fabric. Her breasts heave in the tight black dress, making me hunger for a taste of them, for the feel of her puckered nipples against my tongue.

Alina's pussy starts to tighten around me. She draws a breath and holds it, her lips going still against mine. Icy fractals dance in the air around her, magical snowflakes coaxed into existence by her pleasure.

I continue fingering her fast, but I slow the pace of my thumb on her clit. And I fucking take her there.

When she cums, it's the single most beautiful thing I've ever seen. It's trembling legs and tangled hair, a whimpering moan that makes me want to drop to my knees to worship her at her feet.

But it's also pain. *My* pain. Because I want her so badly, want to claim her and send my magic spiraling through her veins. The chain burns hot and bright, making me grit my teeth against its onslaught of excruciating heat.

She whimpers and moans as I work my finger inside her, her walls spasming. I try not to imagine what it'd feel like to have her cum around my dick.

As soon as her pussy stops throbbing around my finger, I push away from her, breaking her tight hold on my tunic and leaving her trembling against the glass wall. Her eyes flash open, confusion written across her face.

"R-Raelan," she whispers as I stumble back, bumping into a raised garden bed. "Are you okay?"

No, I'm not okay. But I'm inflicting this pain upon myself. Despite telling myself a thousand times a day that I can't have her, my dragon still bleeds through, still wraps around my consciousness and tempts me into pushing the boundaries with her.

It's foolish. I'm a fucking fool.

And I'm so turned on now that I can barely think straight.

So when Alina walks toward me on trembling legs and sinks to her knees in front of me, I have no power to tell her no.

CHAPTER 25
ALINA

I'M DRUNK ON RAELAN'S TOUCH. I'VE TOUCHED myself before—even recently, with his burning dark eyes in my mind—but to be touched by him is something else altogether. It makes my own fingers feel clumsy in comparison.

And now that he's given me a taste of what he can do, I want more. I want to give him the same in return . . . if he'll let me.

He heaves with strained breaths as I sink to my knees before him. The look on his face is one of agony, though I can't tell if it's from the magic searing his skin or the pressure trying to burst free from his trousers. Perhaps both.

And I can relieve at least one of those.

"Alina," he whispers as I tug the cord on his trousers free. "You don't have to—"

"I want to." I'm still thrumming with pleasure, and I'm going to chase that high for as long as I can. "Just tell me what to do. I've . . . I've never done this before."

At first, I think Raelan may be disappointed that I'm so inexperienced when he is clearly not, but instead, hunger flashes across his face, betraying his thoughts before he can battle the expression into submission.

I take the waistband of his trousers in my hands and slide them down slowly, being careful not to hurt him.

And when he springs free, I'm caught completely by surprise.

I've never seen a man's cock before, and though I had some idea of what to expect, this is . . .

"Fuck," Raelan grinds out, cutting off my train of thought. He drags his hands down his face and across the stubble shadowing his jaw. "What the fuck am I doing?"

Before he can decide against this, I wrap my hand around his shaft, and he flinches at the touch. His skin is silky and hot against mine, and I can feel his heartbeat as I begin to stroke him.

I don't know what I'm doing, but I think it's working, because Raelan closes his eyes and tips his head toward the glass ceiling. The muscles along his neck are pulled taut, and the chain that rests there glows blue white as the magic pours into him.

The head of his cock bobs with each stroke of my hand along his length, and I watch as glistening moisture gathers at the tip. A burst of longing goes through me. I want to taste him, to know what he feels like between my lips, where no other man has been.

So I lick my lips, lean forward on my knees, and take him into my mouth.

His response is a guttural moan. He reaches out to steady himself upon a cart laden with gardening tools, and his other hand comes around to grip my hair. I'm not sure if he means to or if he's becoming lost to his own pleasure, but his fingers tangle in my long blue strands, tugging, begging me to increase my pace.

And I do just that.

His cock fills my mouth, and I do everything I can not to choke on him. The gentle pressure on my head intensifies. In response, I feel my pussy flutter, and I wonder what it would feel like to have him inside me.

The thought makes me suck him harder, my tongue dragging along his cock as I work him in and out of my mouth. I'm moaning now, little sounds that slip out as I lap at him, trying so hard to give him what he just gave me.

I've never cum so hard before. And I want to make him cum for me.

The thought makes me wet again.

At once, his fingers tighten in my hair and his cock goes impossibly hard. I'm not sure what's happening. Then heat spills across my tongue. I'm surprised by it, enough so that some slips out the corner of my mouth, but I swallow the rest down, maintaining my pace as he moans, the sounds of his pleasure filling the quiet greenhouse. My knees dig into the dirt, pebbles biting my skin, but I don't care. I'd have stayed on my knees all night if it meant I could finally taste him like this.

He's still in my mouth, yet I'm already thinking of doing it again, am already yearning for more.

What has he done to me?

When he's left gasping, I lean back, releasing his cock from between my lips. My gaze turns up to him in the cold silver light.

When he meets my eyes, his are flecked with gold, and they fluctuate between narrow slits and dilated pupils. It's like I'm seeing his dragon for brief moments at a time as it fights to break through, but he successfully pushes it down, though not without the chain burning bright around his throat.

As he catches his breath, he reaches down to ease me to my feet, his hands coming around my head to cradle my face. With one thumb, he wipes the moisture from my lips.

"Are you okay?" he asks, voice gravelly. "Did I hurt you?"

I shake my head. "No. I'm fine." I glance down at him. He's still hard but growing softer by the moment. "Was that . . ." My heart is still thrumming, and I swallow hard. "Was it okay?" I ask. "Did I do it right?"

Raelan smiles. And it's a stunning smile. Maybe the most genuine smile he's ever given me. "Is that a joke?"

My cheeks flare with warmth. "What? No. I—"

He cuts me off with a kiss, his lips crushing against mine as if we need each other to breathe.

Maybe I do.

The thought is both terrifying and exhilarating.

I soften against him, and when he pulls away, he's smiling.

"It was fucking amazing," he says, and by the look in his eyes and the light trembling of his hands on either side of my face, I'm inclined to believe him.

Then my gaze goes to his throat. The chain has only a subtle glow now, but I can see clearly the seared skin beneath, and it makes my stomach twist. "You're the one who's hurt."

Raelan seems to notice his injury only after I point it out. He reaches up to touch the metal and winces, expression morphing into one of pain. "I'll be fine," he says. "It'll heal. Just need time."

"I can help. I learned a healing salve in herbology."

"You don't need to. Really. I—"

"Your duty is to me, right?" I ask.

He arches a dark brow at me.

"Then I order you to allow me to help you."

His eyes narrow, still flecked with shimmering shards of gold. Then he lets out a sigh and tugs his trousers back up, securing them around his waist.

"Very well, Your Highness. I'll allow you to heal me."

CHAPTER 26
RAELAN

Somehow, I find myself in Alina's dormitory, seated on one of the couches as the fire sends heat curling through the room. The others haven't returned yet, so for now, Alina and I are alone.

Apart from Yuki, that is. And I imagine Maeve's snake is around here somewhere.

Yuki hops up onto the couch opposite mine, his dark eyes watching me closely. He makes a small sound, like a mixture between a whimper and a whine, and Alina glances over and gives him a quick smile, making me wonder what it is he said to her.

Alina fetches one of her schoolbooks and flips through it, then seems to find what she's looking for. Setting the book down on one of the desks pressed against the wall, she begins to gather her ingredients, though I've no idea what they are. Different smells float through the room as she pours and sprinkles and stirs. The whole time, I watch her face.

Her lips are puckered in concentration, her brow furrowed. She's not yet combed her hair, and seeing how messy it is reminds me of how it felt to tangle my fingers in those soft strands. I had to try so hard not to hurt her, not to thrust myself down her throat. And when she looked up at me, a trail of my cum tracing its way down the corner of her mouth, I felt I would burst free of my chain and carry her away right then and there.

As if to remind me what a fucking idiot I am, the burns on my neck send heat and pain screaming through me. I wince and curl my fingers into tight fists, tearing my gaze away from Alina.

Now that the mead has been burned off and my dick finally had a release, I'm left feeling like I made a huge mistake.

Kissing Alina was one thing, and that alone would've been enough to get me in trouble with the king. But now I've put a finger inside her, have felt her lips on my dick, have done things a knight should never do to the princess he's sworn to protect.

And I'm afraid of what might happen next. I'm afraid I don't have nearly as much self-control as I thought I did.

"Here we go," Alina says, coming to join me in the sitting area. She pulls a plush purple footstool over and takes a seat in front of me, scooting close and settling herself between my legs. She abandoned her heeled boots at the door when we first stepped into the dorm, letting out a sigh as they dropped to the floor, and now she's barefoot, her toenails painted a deep shade of blue.

It's become increasingly clear to me that she doesn't realize how much is at stake here, least of all her own safety. Thus far, the charmed chain hasn't failed me, but I don't know how much longer it'll be able to withstand the beatings I'm putting it through. The witch who created it for the king told us that there may come a time when I need a new one, with fresh magic, and I fear that time may be drawing near.

But mostly, I fear what might happen if I allow myself to keep pushing it to the brink, to the point where it shatters and frees my dragon. That can't ever happen around Alina. I won't let it.

Alina settles her mixing bowl in her lap, then reaches up to tie her hair into a knot at the base of her neck. Her eyes meet mine. "May I see?" she asks, gesturing to my throat.

I swallow hard, hands still clenched on my knees. Then I nod once. "Just be careful not to take it off," I warn her.

The smile she gives me is small and soft. "I'll be careful. I promise."

Tipping my head back slightly, I give her access to my throat. She dips a few fingers into the salve she made, using her other hand to lift the chain delicately, moving it away from the fresh burns it left on my skin.

When she sees them, she winces.

"Raelan, these . . ." There's a moment of hesitation. Her brow furrows, a frown tugging on her lips. "These look bad. They must hurt terribly."

I make a small sound in my throat. Yes, they hurt, but it's nothing compared to the pain of keeping myself from her, the pain of resisting my instincts and the bond that draws me to her time and time again.

But I don't say this.

Alina gets to work, gently applying the salve to my burns. At first, the concoction stings, making me grind my teeth, but after the initial discomfort, it starts to give off a cooling effect, and I feel the bunching of my shoulders start to relax.

While Alina is focused on tending to me, I allow my eyes to flick down to her, and I wonder what she might do if I finally came clean about my secret.

She already learned one, but how would she feel about the other? Would she feel repulsed by the idea that my beast wants to claim her? Would she tell her grandfather at the first opportunity, thereby having me thrown from the guard?

Somehow, I think that last idea implausible. Still, I can't help but to wonder how she'd react to the truth.

I almost want to tell her. It wouldn't take much. All I'd have to do is open my mouth and say it. It would only take four words.

You're my fated mate.

As the idea crosses my mind, my dragon stirs. I hate denying it like this, denying the truth of my being and my blood. Yet I can't bring myself to do it. And as Alina sits back and settles the chain gently into place over the already-drying salve, I feel yet again what a fool I am.

I can't do this, can't allow this to go any further.

211

But I also know that I am weak to resist her. My attempts at keeping my distance from her—both physically and emotionally—have all been futile.

And with a sickening turn of my stomach, I know what I must do.

No matter how much pain it causes us.

ALMOST AS SOON AS ALINA FINISHES TENDING TO my wounds, her roommates return to the dormitory, and I bid them good night swiftly, trying to ignore their curious gazes as I slip from the room and climb the stairs to my own dorm.

Once inside, I close the door and lock it—though I've since learned that Alina must have a way of unlocking it, considering I found her in here the night of my transformation. With the door barred, I press my back against it and slide down until I'm sitting on the cold stone floor.

The night flickers through my mind: Alina's hand on mine, the moonlight cutting through the glass ceiling of the greenhouse, the slick warmth between her thighs as I slid my finger inside her.

Being around her is intoxicating in a way I was not prepared for. And I know this was all a mistake. Not just kissing her and pushing my hands through her hair and allowing her to please me until I poured down her throat—it was a mistake long before then. Now I must make it right, before anything else happens.

Before I hurt her.

I know that this may threaten the agreement I have with

His Majesty, but if I go to him with this information, rather than allowing something to find its way back to him secondhand, I can control the narrative, control what I say and how I say it. And I can only hope that he'll understand and that he'll uphold his part of the bargain: keeping my mother and sisters safe.

Even if he has to send me away, even if I never see Alina again, I have to do this.

For her sake and for mine.

Even though it's the last thing I want to do.

My mind is made up.

I push to my feet and stride across the room to the small desk near the window. I take a seat, light a candle, and unroll a fresh sheet of parchment. It lies there on the desk, staring up at me in the flickering candlelight. Clenching my jaw, I reach for a quill and dip it into a well of ink.

Then I begin to write.

I tell the king the truth: that Alina is my fated mate, that I've known it since she turned fifteen, that I thought I could carry out this duty without faltering in my conviction. But I tell him I can do so no longer. Someone must relieve me of this post, and they must do so swiftly, before Alina and I can grow any closer.

Before I do something I can't take back.

I don't tell him about our stolen kisses, and I certainly don't mention what happened in the greenhouse tonight. But everything else is laid bare on the page. And though every drop of ink is a physical pain pressing against my bones, begging me not to separate myself from her, I don't allow myself to stop.

Because I have to think of Alina as well, have to remember what my father did to my mother. And I have to protect her from danger—namely, me.

I sign my name at the bottom of the page, a rough scratch of the quill against the parchment. Once the ink has dried, I fold it in three and seal it with melted wax.

Letter in hand, I depart my room, pausing only briefly outside Alina's door to ensure all is well, then continue down the spiraling stone stairs, moving through the shafts of colorful moonlight that gleam through the stained glass windows. It is late, but many students still roam the halls—it is Samhain, after all.

Charmed candles float through the entrance hall, and I brush one aside, sending it drifting off in a new direction, before pushing through one of the doors and stepping into the crisp cold of the night. The air smells of mead and woodsmoke, and light from the bonfire casts moving shadows through the courtyard.

I make my way toward the stables, which are situated on the outskirts of the castle's courtyard. Inside, it smells of hay and dust. The horses have already been fed, and the stablemaster is sweeping the aisle, whistling to himself. When he sees me, he jerks upright, then gives me a clumsy bow.

"S-sir," he says, "how can I help you?"

"I need a letter delivered. And I need to ensure utmost caution. Do you have a messenger suited to the task?"

The stablemaster nods quickly. "I do, sir. Very trusted lad. He'll get your letter where it needs to go."

"Good." I reach into my pocket and pull out a few eldertokens. It's significantly more currency than this task requires, but I want to ensure discretion, and coin has a way of achieving this.

I place the letter in the man's outstretched hand, then drop the three coins atop it. "One for you, two for the carrier. No one else learns of this."

"Of course not. And where's the message to be carried, sir?" he asks, closing his fingers around the letter carefully so as not to crumple it.

I draw myself up and take a deep breath. No turning back now.

"Ravenscroft Castle. To His Majesty the king."

CHAPTER 27
ALINA

SOMETHING'S WRONG WITH RAELAN. EVER since our evening together in the greenhouse, he's acted distant, colder now than he was when first we met. His eyes rarely meet mine, his lips remain pulled into a focused frown, and he speaks only when spoken to.

And it's tearing me up inside—to the point where I finally grab hold of Lyra's wrist and drag her up into our loft, where we sit cross-legged on my bed. I pull the drapes closed, then level my gaze on her.

"Okay, what's going on?" Lyra asks, arching a brow at the closed curtains hanging from my bedposts.

Yuki was taking a nap at the foot of the bed when we intruded upon him, and he makes a huff of disapproval before yawning and jumping off the bed, then padding down the stairs, probably to go sit with Poppy in front of the fire while she studies.

"I have to tell you something," I say.

Lyra's brow remains quizzical. "Okay. What is it?"

I turn my words over in my head, trying to figure out how to say what I need to. But Lyra's slept with boys before, has more experience than I can even hold a candle to. She'll understand.

"I . . . kissed Raelan. A few times."

Her brows arch up.

"And then he . . . touched me."

"He *touched* you?" she asks.

Cheeks starting to tingle with warmth, I tell her what we did in the greenhouse and only have to shush her once when she squeals too loudly.

I was so mad at her on Samhain—perhaps unfairly so—and watching her dance with Raelan that night lit a fire beneath my skin, stoked my hunger for him until I had to act. And I know now that she did it all on purpose.

Clever fire witch.

Finally, after she's calmed down, she asks, "Wait, why are you telling me this?"

"Because he's acting strange now," I say, and feel the truth of it in my stomach. Grabbing one of my pillows, I hug it to my chest. "He's not acting like himself. And I don't know what to do."

Lyra purses her lips and leans back onto her hands. "And you think this has to do with that night?"

I shrug. "I don't know. But I can only assume so. What else would cause him to become so cold toward me?"

Twirling a strand of wild red hair, Lyra considers this. "Maybe he's afraid."

My brow arches. "Of what?"

217

"Seriously?" Lyra pushes herself up. "Of *you*. Of your position. You're the princess. What's he supposed to do? Ask the *king* for your hand?" She shakes her head. "I don't know. I mean, I obviously don't know your grandfather, but do you think he'd allow this? You to be with one of his knights?"

I want to say yes, that Grandfather would never attempt to keep me from a man I—

Love?

The word hits me with such force that I have to blink away the surprise.

I don't love Raelan, do I? I may dream of him, and my eyes may seek him out even when I don't mean for them to, and I might wish he were beside me every night when I fall asleep, but that doesn't mean I love him.

My body feels drawn to him, almost like something in my magic calls to his, a connection that simmers just beneath the surface, there but intangible, a mirage or a shadow that just brushes my awareness before vanishing again.

I know I want him. I want him even more now than I did before the greenhouse. His touch was like fire, his mouth the only air I wanted to breathe.

And I thought he wanted me too.

Was I wrong?

"Well," I start, "maybe—"

The curtains around my bed are flung open, and Maeve stands there, Poppy lingering behind her. Isis is coiled around Maeve's throat like a necklace, the top half of her body glistening black, her underbelly more vibrant red than Lyra's hair. It still gives me a shiver to see how casually

Maeve lets the snake slither across her, but I'm trying to warm up to Isis. Yuki is still hesitant around her as well, but Juniper, like Lyra, seems fearless around the snake. Maeve has promised that Isis will do us—and Juniper—no harm, but I'm not yet convinced.

"You just need to talk to him, Alina," Maeve says, voice taking on a firm tone. She crosses her arms and pops a hip, her vibrant purple eyes homing in on me. "Tell him exactly how you feel, and ask if he feels the same way. That's the only way you're going to get the truth out of him."

I blink up at her, lips open in surprise, and she tips her head.

"You two aren't nearly as secretive as you think you are," she says. "Also, don't trust Lyra's opinions. She's in one messy relationship after another."

"Hey!" Lyra says.

Behind Maeve, Poppy giggles and says, "Well, it's true."

"Doesn't mean you have to *say* it." Lyra glares up at Maeve, and Isis hisses in response, making us both jump.

Maeve strokes a finger down Isis's glossy black head, and the snake stops hissing and instead nestles herself into the divot at the base of Maeve's throat. "I'm serious. You'll drive yourself crazy trying to guess at his feelings—and besides, it's *Raelan*. He's like a block of stone. He's good at hiding what he's actually thinking."

I slump my shoulders with a sigh. "I know. You're right. It's just . . ." I nibble on my lower lip, afraid of speaking the truth, of letting it take root in my heart. "What if he doesn't feel the same way?"

"At least then you'll know," Poppy says. Her voice is quiet, and she stands a few steps behind Maeve, but even she has a point.

"And then you can either get with him or move on," Maeve finishes. "It's the waiting and wondering that's the worst. It's better to know."

"I'm with them," Lyra says, jutting a thumb toward Maeve and Poppy. She arches a fiery brow and says, "See? I have good opinions."

Poppy laughs, and Maeve's lips quirk up in one corner.

"Well?" Maeve tips her head at me, glossy purple-black hair tumbling over her shoulder in a sleek waterfall. "You gonna go talk to him or what?"

I TOUCH UP MY HAIR, SWIPE BALM OVER MY LIPS, AND then go to stand before the door. My roommates huddle nearby, out of sight of the door, egging me on with whispers and waving.

Near my feet, Yuki looks up at me and says, "Whatever he says, I'm always here."

I quickly kneel and pull Yuki into a hug, burying my face in his warm fur. He smells like home, like everything I've ever known. "Thank you," I whisper. "You'll always be my favorite, you know."

"I know." He whines softly and nuzzles his cool snout into the crook of my neck, then pulls away.

My heart thunders in my chest as I stand and face the door again, and I have to remind myself that this is Raelan I'm about to confront. I *know* him—or what he's allowed me to know, at least. He's not a stranger. Not anymore. I can do this.

With a steadying breath, I open the door.

The air is much cooler out here than in our room, and goose bumps immediately rise along my arms. But perhaps that's only partly because of the cold. I think the sight of Raelan is partially responsible.

He's standing with his back to me, hands clasped behind him. His face is turned up to the stained glass window, as it often is, and when I step into the corridor, he turns his head slightly. It's early evening, and the sun is setting. Golden light streams through the glass, limning his profile in warm yellow orange. His jaw is sharp, and I remember drawing my fingertips across his face, feeling the roughness of his stubble against my skin.

Raelan takes a visible breath, then turns fully to face me as I pull the door closed. "Your Highness." He dips his head quickly, and it immediately sends a wave of cold anger through me.

Why is he acting like this?

"I want to talk to you," I say, trying to keep my tone light.

Raelan straightens up. He levels his dark gaze on me. "Of course."

When he makes no attempt to move, I gesture up the spiraling stairs toward his room. "Can we go somewhere more . . . private?"

As if to punctuate my point, two students come down the stairs at a quick clip, their boots thumping against the stone stairs.

"Excuse us," one of the girls says as she slips by. Her friend glances at me, then at Raelan, and I don't miss the way her gaze sweeps quickly up and down his sturdy frame, his broad shoulders, the sharp features of his face.

I bristle.

Then they're both gone. And Raelan is still looking at me.

He clears his throat. "I think it's best we stay here."

My eyes narrow as the girls' voices drift away down the stairwell. "Why?"

Now Raelan's eyes slide away from mine, to look at something over my shoulder. His gaze goes faraway. "It's not appropriate for us to be alone together, Your Highness."

My fingers curl into fists. "What's that supposed to mean?"

He doesn't respond. His silence is a dagger pressing slowly into my chest.

"Raelan, *look at me*. That's an order."

Reluctantly, he draws his gaze back to mine. With the sun setting over his shoulder, his features are cast mostly into shadow, but I can see the flicker of his pupils, the way they very briefly pull into narrow slits before returning to normal.

"What's going on? Ever since Samhain, you've been . . . different." The heat in my chest cools for a moment, and I say more softly, "I don't understand. Has something changed?"

Raelan takes another breath, but he doesn't soften. If anything, the look in his dark eyes only hardens. "My behavior on Samhain was unacceptable. I apologize. I assure you, it'll not happen again."

His words hit me so hard I almost double over. The dagger finds its way into my heart.

"Raelan," I whisper, taking a step forward and reaching a hand out for him.

But he takes one crisp step back, out of my reach. His eyes don't soften.

"Why are you being like this?" I ask.

Finally, a look of emotion brushes against his lips, his eyes. Something like heat flickers in his gaze.

"I'm being like this," he says, voice hard, "because I must. Because we can't keep doing the things we've been doing."

"I can't believe we're back to this again." I let out an incredulous laugh and shove my fingers through my hair. "We already talked about this. I thought we agreed."

Raelan shakes his head firmly. "No. And I'll not be talked out of it, Alina."

My name sounds forbidden on his lips.

As I stand there in the sunset light, with Raelan just out of my reach, I'm overcome with a confusing mixture of anger and sadness and pride.

I thought he cared about me. I thought he wanted me.

But if he can pull away from me like this, deny me this way, then he doesn't feel toward me the way I feel toward him.

And I'm just making a fool of myself.

"I-I see."

Straightening up, I take a breath. I remind myself that I'm the princess, granddaughter to the king of Elarwyn. I can't be seen crying in the north tower over my knight, the man whose duty it is to protect me. Especially not when he's looking at me with such an expressionless mask while I crumble before him.

I pull myself together, at least for the moment, for as long as Raelan's eyes are on me.

If he wants to go back to being cold acquaintances, fine. I can play this game too. Even if it rips me apart inside.

"Very well, Sir Ashvale."

The formality in my tone makes him narrow his eyes slightly.

"I'll be ready for dinner shortly. You can escort me to the dining hall then."

Without giving myself another opportunity to beg him, to fall apart at his feet, I turn on my heel, step into my room, and close the door with a quiet click.

The girls—and Yuki—are lounging on the couches in the sitting room, and they all sit up and turn to me as I walk in.

"Well?" Lyra asks. "How'd it go?"

I open my mouth to tell them, thinking I can do so with some shred of dignity.

But all that comes out is a quiet squeak of, "He doesn't want me."

And then my eyes mist with tears, and I'm suddenly enveloped in a swath of arms. And they hold me as I cry.

CHAPTER 28
RAELAN

As I watch Alina from across the crowded dining hall, I repeat a mantra to myself. *I must keep her safe. This is the only way. I must keep her safe. This is the only way.*

I know she cried when she returned to her room—I could hear it despite the stone walls and thick wooden door—and it felt like a sword being driven slowly into my chest, twisting at an excruciatingly slow pace as it inched through the gaps in my armor.

Never do I want to be the cause for her tears again. And that's yet another reason why I must leave. If I stay, I'll only hurt her further.

A scent brushes my awareness, and my gaze shifts slightly. Tristan just entered the dining hall, and he immediately makes note of Alina, then of me. I narrow my eyes at him. But he disregards me, going about heaping food from the buffets upon his plate, then crossing the hall again to approach Alina. They exchange words—I can't hear them over the clamor of so many students eating and talking and laughing—and then he takes a seat beside her.

Alina turns toward him, smiling like she wasn't crying an hour ago. She laughs at something he says. And then she reaches out and touches him.

And I can't help but to feel she's doing this just to get back at me, to hurt me in the way I hurt her. I want to storm across the dining hall and rip him away from her, want to announce to everyone in this room that she's *mine*.

But I do no such thing. Instead, I curl my fingernails into my palms and repeat, *I must keep her safe. This is the only way.*

They're still laughing and talking when footsteps approach from the arched doorway to my left.

"Sir Ashvale," a voice says.

I turn slightly and find a familiar woman standing there, her long silver-blue hair coiled atop her head and stuck through with an emerald-studded hair stick.

"Headmistress." I nod my head to her.

"There's someone here to see you." She beckons, the rings on her fingers flashing in the candlelight. "Come."

My eyes flick back to Alina. My dragon is hesitant to leave her. But she's surrounded by friends and faculty, laughing and smiling as though she has not a care in the world.

With a small sigh, I acquiesce, following the headmistress through the wide corridor. Our boots tap out a staccato rhythm on the stone floor as she leads me into the entrance hall. And I see at once why she fetched me.

Another knight stands in the center of the expansive space, his head tipped back to regard the elaborate artwork oiled across the soaring ceiling.

"I've been told he's here to replace you as Miss Ravenscroft's guard," Headmistress Moonhart says. She tips her head, and her hair catches the moonlight streaming in through the high windows. "Is this true?"

The knight has snapped to attention and is watching us silently, awaiting my answer.

I bite down my feelings, trying to bury them even as my dragon writhes inside me. "Yes. This is correct. As of tonight, he'll be taking my place. I'll ensure he's aware of our agreements and protocols."

The headmistress glances between the two of us, then gives me a curt nod. "Very well. If you need me, sir," she says, directing her attention to my fellow knight, "you can find me in my office."

"Understood, Headmistress." He bows his head, and then the headmistress departs, leaving us standing in the entrance hall.

The knight steps forward and offers me his hand. "Sir Ashvale, I was sent by His Majesty to relieve you of your post. I'm Sir Callahan."

After a brief moment of hesitation, I meet him halfway, shoving my hand into his and giving it a firm shake. "Thank you for coming."

My gaze flicks back the way I came, to where the dining hall is, to where Alina is. I thought I'd get a chance to say goodbye, but perhaps it's better this way. It's better if I go quietly.

I focus on Sir Callahan again, shoving my feelings down as deep as I can. "I'll get you up to speed. We've much to discuss."

CHAPTER 29
ALINA

WHAT ARE YOU TALKING ABOUT?" Lyra says, sitting forward at the dining table and leveling a look at Tristan. "Fire is definitely the strongest element. There's no comparison."

"You're wrong." Tristan braces one arm on the table. "Water far outpowers fire. It can even carve away stone. Can your flames do that?"

Lyra narrows her crimson eyes, gearing up for another rebuttal.

I glance at Maeve, who lost interest in their discussion ten minutes ago and is now flipping through a small book of poetry. Beside her, Poppy has pulled out one of her schoolbooks and is sipping a cup of tea while reading through a chapter. I swear, she reads her textbooks like they're romance novels.

It's taken all my willpower not to glance over at Raelan during dinner. After what he said to me in the hall, I can barely stand the thought of looking at him, of seeing his dark eyes and shadowed jaw and remembering what his hands feel like, all while knowing I can't ever have them again.

Thinking of it sends another ember of embarrassment and anger burning through me. How could he do that to me, especially after I told him I'd never been with anyone else? I can't help but to feel like he led me on, knowing all along he had no intention of taking what we had seriously.

Finally, I can't resist lifting my gaze and glancing toward the doorway, where Raelan typically stands while I eat.

Except, Raelan isn't the one standing there.

Someone else has taken his place, a man I barely recognize save for crossing paths with him at the castle. He's staring right back at me, and when I meet his eyes, he gives me a barely perceptible nod. Cordial. Professional. Cold.

Just like all the guards at home.

But where is Raelan?

My stomach pinches painfully.

I push to my feet, but Maeve is the only one to notice, given Poppy is lost in her book and Lyra and Tristan are still arguing over elemental magic.

"What's wrong?" she asks.

"I . . . don't know," I mumble, not tearing my eyes from the new knight. "I'll be back."

Striding across the dining hall, I walk right up to the knight, who bows his head when I stop before him.

"Who're you?" I ask. "And where's Sir Ashvale?"

"I'm Sir Callahan, Your Highness. I've replaced Ashvale as your personal guard."

A tendril of cold snakes through me, gripping my heart and squeezing. "*What?*"

Sir Callahan's forehead furrows, a curious tilt to his head. "Were you unaware of the change, Your Highness? Sir Ashvale requested immediate replacement. His Majesty sent me as soon as he received word."

Raelan did this? He wrote to Grandfather asking to be replaced?

The cold in my heart turns to heat. My fingers curl into fists, and I feel ice spreading across my knuckles as my anger seeps out. "Where is he?"

"Your Highness, I—"

"Answer me. Where is Sir Ashvale?"

A few students have turned toward us and are watching our exchange with unveiled curiosity. But I can't bring myself to care. All I care about right now is finding Raelan and demanding he explain himself.

How could he do this?

"He is likely in the stables by now, if he hasn't already departed."

I'm walking before the last word has passed his lips. My boots tap out a sharp, angry rhythm on the stone floor as I sweep from the dining hall and into the corridor leading to the academy's grand entrance. Immediately, Sir Callahan follows, his footsteps heavier than mine. He has no trouble catching up and falling into step behind me.

Though I'm not dressed for the crisp autumn weather and didn't think to grab my cloak before leaving for the dining hall, I don't hesitate to push through one of the big entrance doors and step out into the night.

The wind cuts right through my long-sleeved top and tailored vest, and it sends my skirt snapping around my ankles as I descend the stairs and start across the courtyard toward the stables. Braziers have been lit atop the stone wall encircling the academy, and they toss dim light across me as I move through the dancing shadows.

I'm halfway to the stables when two figures emerge—a man and a horse. Though they're swathed in shadow, I can see the man is adjusting the saddle, preparing to swing up onto the horse's back. This makes me pick up my pace. My boots crunch across the gravel, my breathing coming faster as my anger builds, and I'm near enough to see the cut of Raelan's sharp profile when he finally turns and sees me.

"How *dare* you!" I say, storming up to him so quickly his horse shies to one side. I'll apologize to her later, but my rage is bubbling over, incapable of being contained. "You were going to leave just like that? Without even saying *good-bye*? Do I truly mean so little to you?"

Raelan's dark gaze flicks over my shoulder, to where I know Sir Callahan is standing. Let him overhear—I don't care. All I want is to hear Raelan's reasoning, his explanation for fleeing from me in the night.

Like the thief he is. Because he stole from me, stole my affection and my attention, then tossed them away like nothing.

"Sir Callahan," Raelan says, moving to step around me. "Would you hold Penelope for a moment?" He transfers her reins into Sir Callahan's outstretched fingers. Then Raelan turns to me. "Let's speak inside. You're not dressed for the cold."

"What do you care how I'm dressed?" I snap, though I allow him to lead me to the stable. He pulls the big sliding door open just a crack, and we slip inside.

The air smells of horses and hay and sawdust, reminding me of home. It's warmer inside, out of the wind, but I try not to let Raelan see what a comfort it is to me.

"Sir Ashvale," the stablemaster says, popping his head out of one of the open stalls. "Is there something else I can do for you?"

"No." Raelan holds up a hand. "Just need a moment to speak privately."

The stablemaster's gaze slides to me where I stand just behind Raelan, and his bushy silver brows rise with curiosity. "Certainly. You can use the office. It's just through there." He points, and Raelan nods his appreciation, then guides me toward the door and ushers me inside.

The office is small, lit by only a single candle. There's a desk, a worn chair, and a couch that's seen better days. Raelan closes the door, but it takes him a moment before he turns and faces me.

And when he does, his face is a mess of emotions I struggle to understand.

"You're leaving?" I ask.

He nods once. "Yes."

His confirmation nearly knocks the wind out of me. Even having seen him preparing to mount his horse and ride into the night, I was holding out hope that I'd somehow gotten it all wrong, that there'd been some misunderstanding.

"Why?"

His jaw flexes. "Because I need to leave. You'll be better off with Sir Callahan . . . and away from me."

My anger and sadness swirl into a maelstrom, and mist leaks into my eyes as snowflakes start to fall around me, pulled into existence by my magic. "So, what is it? You finally had a taste of me and then decided I'm not the right flavor?"

Another flicker of emotion crosses Raelan's face, this one surprised and perhaps a bit hurt. "Of course not. Alina, that's not what this is. You know why we must stop."

"No," I snap, "I know your *excuse* for why we must stop. But that's not a real reason. I could speak with my grandfather. This is *my* choice. It's my body. I'll do whatever I want with it. I choose the people I care for, no one else."

Raelan takes a breath. His fingers curl into loose fists. "It's not just about you. Have you taken even a moment to consider what this is doing to me? How excruciating it is to want you this way, knowing I can't have you? Knowing I'm a danger to you?"

"You're not a—"

"I *am*!" He steps forward, close enough to me now that I can see his pupils are fluctuating between a thin line and a normal circle. "You saw my mother. And that was *nothing*." His hand comes up to cradle my face, warm despite having just been out in the autumn chill. "I could tear you into ribbons with one swipe of my claws. If this chain is ever to fail me when you're near"—he lifts his chin so I can see the metal around his neck, the wounds that have almost healed just beneath the links—"I won't be able to resist it again."

My heart thumps. His hand is still on my cheek, and I don't want him to pull away. I want to stay right here, in this moment, for just a little while longer.

"Resist what?" I whisper.

A brief silence passes between us. We exchange a breath.

Raelan's fingers curl around my cheek, and then he whispers, "Claiming you."

I hold my breath.

Claiming me?

"What . . ." I whisper, blinking up at him. "What does that mean?"

Now his other hand comes up, and together, his hands cradle my face, tipping my head back so the candlelight hits my eyes. His face looks pained as he says, "It means you're my fated mate, Alina."

Those words, *fated mate*, echo through my mind, thrumming with the beat of my heart.

At the most basic level, I know how shifters work—as a member of the royal family, it's expected that I have an awareness of the many different types of people who live in our kingdom—but I never even considered the possibility that a mate connection could form between us.

A princess and her guard.

A witch and her dragon.

"I'm your . . . mate?" It tastes like a forbidden secret as I whisper the words into the space between my lips and Raelan's.

His pupils fully contract. They pull into dark slits, and for a moment, his fingers tighten about my face, and I'm sure he's going to kiss me.

235

But then he pushes away from me, stepping back until he's against the closed door. His chest rises and falls with rapid breaths, and he nods quickly, the movement sharp. Beneath the collar of his tunic, his chain glows. "Yes."

I'm struggling to understand, to wrap my mind around what this means. "H-how long have you known?"

Raelan swallows hard, his throat bobbing with the movement. His eyes are still inhuman, reptilian. "Since you turned fifteen."

I draw a breath.

Three years, almost four. He's known all this time, yet he's only now telling me.

"Does anyone know?" I ask.

"My mother."

"You never told my grandfather?"

A muscle in his jaw feathers. "Not until recently. I feared he'd have me removed from the castle, sent away from my family. I couldn't risk it."

I open my mouth, wanting to express my anger and frustration at him for having kept such a secret from me—from all of us—for all these years. But Raelan's face is twisted into a mask of hurt, and it steals the heated words right from my tongue.

Instead, I say, "What does this mean? For us?"

Slowly, his expression morphs, a mask rising up to hide what he's truly feeling. I know him well enough now that I can see how it settles into place, as if each day for him is a masquerade ball, yet another waltz to dance through, hoping he doesn't miss any steps.

"Nothing," he says. "We can't allow it to mean anything."

Now that I have a better understanding, an inkling of what's truly going on beneath Raelan's cold exterior, I'm not brought to anger quite so quickly.

"You're afraid," I say. "Is that why you're running away? So you don't have to face this? Don't have to feel this pull between us?" I take a step toward him. "Because I feel it too. My magic *wants* you, Raelan. I don't know if it's the bond, but it's . . . unlike anything I've ever felt."

At my words, more snowflakes fall around us silently, melting as soon as they land on the desk or the floor.

"You're young yet." Raelan's voice is cold and hard. He's trying to push me away. "You'll find someone else. Someone better. Someone who's not a danger to you."

"I refuse to believe you're dangerous," I whisper, then recall how fearsome he is, how absolutely powerful and awe-inspiring his dragon is. "Well, at least to me."

Raelan shakes his head. "I can't do it. Can't endanger you. I won't. It's why I'm leaving." He takes a deep breath. "I'm sorry."

Before I can say another word, he sweeps across the room and presses a kiss against my mouth, his lips hot and hard and trembling against mine.

I can feel his desire, his anguish, his struggle to control himself. I want to wrap him in my arms and tell him everything will be okay, that we'll figure this out together.

But then he's gone, his long black cloak swirling as he pulls open the door and vanishes into the stable, moving so quickly I have to catch my breath before hurrying after him.

"Raelan!" I yell as I squeeze my way through the gap in the sliding barn door and step into the windswept evening. But he's already swinging a leg over his horse and pulling his hood up against the chill.

And he doesn't even glance back at me as his horse gallops from the courtyard, his cloak billowing behind him as he goes.

"Raelan!" I scream again, but my voice is carried away by the wind, and it takes another thirty seconds of staring after him into the dark before I realize that tears are leaving frigid tracks down my cheeks and ice is creeping across my skin.

"Please, Your Highness," Sir Callahan says from behind me. "We should get you inside, where it's warm."

But I'm not sure I'll ever be warm again. Because the man I want—the man I may very well love—just left me behind, and I don't think he's ever coming back again.

CHAPTER 30
RAELAN

I RIDE THROUGH THE DARKNESS, MY DRAGON EYES granting me night vision as we speed away from the academy and onto one of the soft dirt trails that meanders through the Mistwood. The wind rustles the pine trees and sends dead leaves skittering around Penelope's hooves.

Every stride carries me farther from Alina, but the pain in my chest only grows.

At least now she knows the truth. Now she won't ever have to wonder if I want her.

I want her more than anything. But this changes nothing.

Loosening my hold on the reins, I give Penelope her head, allowing her to set her own pace down the wooded path.

And though all I want is to turn around and gallop back, to sweep Alina into my arms and carry her far away, to a place where only the two of us exist, I don't allow it. I keep my gaze forward, my face turned firmly away from the academy as it no doubt disappears in a haze of darkness behind us.

I do what I should have done long ago: I leave Alina behind, where she's safe, where I'll never be a danger to her again.

My dragon weeps angry tears of flame.

And it's the most pain I've ever known.

CHAPTER 31
ALINA

I**T TAKES ME MUCH TOO LONG TO FIND SLEEP, AND** I'm awoken much too quickly.

I'm dreaming of Raelan, of his slitted pupils and gold-flecked gaze, when something stirs me awake.

Around me, all is dark. Yuki sleeps at the end of the bed, curled into a ball with his fluffy tail over his face, snoring gently. Is he what woke me?

There's a distant sound, down on the main floor. A knock.

My skin prickles, my heartbeat spiking.

It's the middle of the night. Who could possibly be at our door?

Deep in my chest, I yearn for it to be Raelan. Perhaps he's returned, having realized the error of his ways.

Maybe . . . Maybe he came back for me.

I slide quietly from bed, careful not to disturb Yuki as he sleeps. The floorboards are cold, and I ease my feet into slippers and slip into a thin robe before making my way slowly down the stairs and into the main living space. The knock sounds again at the door, making my pulse pound. Upstairs, someone sighs and shifts in bed, but no one else is yet awake.

The fire in the hearth has burned low, and the embers barely give me enough light to see by as I turn the lock and pull open the door.

And immediately, all my hopes are dashed.

Because it's not Raelan standing there.

"Tristan," I say, keeping my voice low. I glance up and down the stairwell, but he's alone. "What are you doing here?"

"It's Sir Ashvale," he says, voice breathy with what sounds like barely contained panic. "He's been injured on the road into Wysteria. He's asking for you."

Raelan's hurt?

My muscles constrict, and my heart jumps into my throat. "What? What happened? Where is he?"

"Come, the academy has prepared transportation for you." He steps back and gestures down the staircase with one hand. "Hurry!"

Without pausing to grab my cloak or even my boots, I step into the corridor and begin following Tristan down the spiraling staircase. We move through shafts of dim moonlight as we go around and around. He keeps just ahead of me, though he glances back often as if to check that I'm still here.

Of course I am. If Raelan needs me, I'll go to him.

We finally reach the bottom of the stairs and start through the corridors toward the entrance hall.

"Do you know what happened to him?" I ask, barely feeling the cold of the drafty halls as I trot alongside Tristan, striving to keep up with his long strides.

"An accident with his horse, I believe," he says.

My stomach churns.

How could something like this happen?

I should never have let him leave. I should have tried harder to keep him here.

As we move down a hall lined with portraits of current professors, I think to ask Tristan, "How do you know about this?"

"Couldn't sleep. I was wandering the halls, and Headmistress Moonhart stopped me. She sent me to get you right away."

If the headmistress is involved, the accident must be dire indeed.

I feel like I might be sick.

We hurry into the entrance hall, which is bathed in thin silver moonlight. Tristan pushes one of the heavy doors open for me, and I step out into the cold night to find a carriage prepared and waiting. Their livery is unfamiliar to me, but the carriage is draped in purple and silver: Coven Crest's colors.

One of the footmen opens the door, and he offers me a hand as I climb up and into the padded interior. Immediately, Tristan slides in behind me.

The door closes with a definitive click, and in a few short moments, the carriage is moving. I clutch my thin satin robe around my shoulders. My fingers, trembling now from

243

a mix of adrenaline and the cold, reach to pull the curtain back from the window. Outside, Coven Crest's outbuildings pass by, and then we're moving off of academy grounds and toward the Mistwood.

"Do you know exactly what happ—" I start to ask, turning toward Tristan.

But I don't get a chance to finish.

Tristan holds up a hand, and as soon as I'm facing him, he blows a shimmering purple-pink powder into my face. It makes me sneeze, and my head starts to swim with dizziness. Tristan's face blurs in my vision, an oil painting melting across a canvas.

"Sorry, Alina," he says, but the words sound faraway and distorted, like I'm underwater or in a dream.

"What's going . . ." I whisper, tongue heavy and cumbersome in my mouth. "On?"

I'm encompassed by black.

CHAPTER 32
RAELAN

THE HALLWAYS IN THE CASTLE ARE EXACTLY the same as when I left, yet somehow, everything feels different: the light slanting through the high windows, the polished shine of the floors underfoot, the scents that hang in the air. I've not been gone long—only a couple months—yet I feel like this place has changed in my time away.

But perhaps I'm the one who has changed. All because of her.

I tossed and turned all night once I finally arrived back at the castle. My bed in the barracks isn't near so comfortable as the one in my room at the academy, and even when sleep arrived to tug at the edges of my awareness, Alina's face would come floating in, waking me again, making me question whether anything I've done has been the right thing. I feel like I've made a mess of all of it.

Even now, as I tip my head at two passing maids on my

way to the king's study, I wonder if I've made a terrible mistake.

He knows the truth now, knows that Alina is my mate, knows that I had to separate myself from her lest my beast finally succeed in taking over. The thought of what he could do to me—or more specifically, to my family—has my heart beating fast in my chest.

I'd typically take the three hundred stairs to His Majesty's study, but this time, I opt for the air tunnel. I'm already sick inside with anticipation, and I'd rather get this over with as quickly as possible.

The metal gate closes behind me, and I only have a moment to catch my breath before the air wraps around me and sends me shooting upward through the narrow tunnel. Despite my love of flying, the air tunnel has always made me feel woozy, and when I step out onto the top floor, I have to brace my hand against a wall and catch my breath.

"Look who's back," one of the guards stationed outside the king's study says.

The other gives me a once-over. "Haven't seen you in a while."

I ignore them both as I adjust my uniform and step up to the king's door. After one sharp rap of my knuckles against the wood, he calls, "Enter!"

With a steadying breath, I take hold of the door handle and step into the office.

The space is warm and lit with firelight and the thin gray sunlight that manages to slip through the thick cloud cover outside. It's a drizzly autumn day, with a biting wind that sends you hurrying for the hearth after being outdoors for even a moment.

King Jorvick's pale eyes find me from across the room. My chest squeezes.

"Your Majesty." I bow my head deeply to him.

This is the moment I discover whether or not I made a terrible mistake. Whether my mother and sisters will still have a roof over their heads. Whether—

"How do you take your tea?"

I lift my head slowly. The king sits in one of the armchairs before the fire, stirring cream into his cup of tea.

"Cream?" he asks. "Sugar?"

"No, Your Majesty. Black is fine with me."

He lifts a hand and gestures for me to join him before the fire. When I sit down, he offers me a cup of steaming dark tea, and I take it with a grateful nod.

"Raelan," he says, and the use of my name draws my gaze toward his.

For some reason, I'm hesitant to meet his eyes, afraid of what I'll find there. But he's looking at me with the same gentle contemplation he's had since I was a young boy first brought under his wing, a dragon child with the potential to do both great and terrible things.

"It seems we've much to discuss." He stirs sugar into his tea—he's always had a sweet tooth—then sighs as he leans back into his armchair.

"Yes, Your Majesty." I curl my fingers around the teacup, not flinching away from the heat against my skin. "Please allow me to apologize for keeping the truth from you for so long."

"Why the secrets?" he asks, voice level, no hint of anger in his tone.

This is the moment of truth.

"My mother and sisters," I say simply. "I feared revealing the truth to you would result in me losing my position here and them losing their home."

The king's wrinkled brow furrows. "You truly believe that?"

I nod once, throat tight.

"Son, I don't go back on my promises." He leans forward in his armchair. "Trust and loyalty are of utmost importance to me. I told you when you were eleven that we'd make a deal: You'd serve me as a member of my guard, and in return, I'd ensure your family had a safe place to live and build a life. You've served me faithfully since the moment you shook hands with me that day. But you think I'd so easily go back on my word?"

He sounds upset, but not in the way I feared. He sounds . . . *hurt*.

"I felt I'd failed you, Your Majesty."

"Nonsense." He shakes his head, pale eyes focused as they regard me. "You've failed no one. You even fought against your own instincts in an effort to carry out the duty I'd assigned to you. I can't imagine that was easy . . ." One of his bushy gray eyebrows arches.

Now I shake my head. "No, Your Majesty."

The king makes a thoughtful sound, then takes a sip of tea. His lips twist up on one side, and he immediately adds another sugar cube to his cup. I almost shudder. That's much too sweet for my liking.

"Tell me," he says. "How did Alina take all of this? Did you tell her?"

I recall Alina's face, illuminated by candlelight, when I told her the truth in the stablemaster's office. Her magic sent snowflakes falling all around us, beautiful and silent, and when I pressed my lips to hers . . .

For a moment, I thought I wouldn't be able to let her go.

But I had to.

I clear my throat and sit straighter. "I did." I take a sip of my tea before continuing. "She was upset. She asked me not to leave."

Upset.

I saw the hurt in her eyes, heard the pain in her voice when she screamed my name as I left her behind. It still sends my skin prickling and my stomach twisting.

"But you did anyway," the king says slowly. "You left."

I nod.

"Why?"

The answer to that one is easy. And now that I'm being honest, my words flow freely. "Because I don't wish to harm her, and I feel I'm a danger to her. Telling you the truth was the only way I could keep her safe. This is the best option—for both of us."

In response, the king tips his head. He strokes his long gray beard a few times, his rings catching the firelight, then says, "Are you sure about that, son?"

A short humorless laugh slips past my lips unbidden. "Depends on when you ask me."

King Jorvick's blue eyes narrow. "I'm asking now."

Was leaving the best option? My dragon and heart say no. But my brain, the logical part of me not controlled by my unquenchable thirst for Alina, says yes.

I let out a deep sigh. "Now . . . I believe I made the right choice, even if it doesn't feel that way just yet." Looking down, I find my reflection swimming in my teacup. My brows are pulled low, my eyes pinched and hard. "But in time, I think Alina will come to understand why I needed to do it."

"And what about you? As far as I'm aware, shifters aren't supposed to defy the bond. It goes against nature. How will you carry on?"

"I'll do what I must," I say firmly, though I'm not sure if I'm trying to convince the king or myself. Perhaps both. "And I may need more magic." I lift a hand to touch the chain around my throat. "I worry I may be running low."

The king sits forward again. "That can be arranged."

The look in his eyes softens, and for just a moment, I feel like he's *my* grandfather, sitting with me before a fire, offering me his wisdom. I never knew my parents' parents. He may truly be the closest thing to a grandparent I have.

"But, Raelan—"

A violent pounding on the door startles us both. The king spills some of his tea, then mumbles, "Curses, I'd just gotten it right." He fetches a linen napkin and wipes off his hands, then calls out, none too kindly, "Come in!"

The door immediately bursts open, and three uniformed guards step in. Tension ripples through the air, and my dragon coils in response.

Something's wrong.

"Your Majesty," says Sir Larsen, a weathered knight I've known since I was a boy. He's a firm teacher and a sturdy mentor, and I've always respected him, ever since the early days of me learning how to hold a sword and ride a horse and scrub the floors until every inch of them shined. "We've received urgent correspondence."

"Urgent?" The king arches a brow. "Well, bring it here." King Jorvick holds out a hand. Sir Larsen crosses the study and hands the parchment to him.

I study the king's face as he reads. What starts as mild confusion quickly morphs into anger and concern. When his eyes flick up to meet mine, I see something I've never seen in them before: fear.

What could that letter possibly have to say that would frighten the king?

Suddenly, my skin is crawling, like my dragon knows something I don't. And it's rarely wrong.

"Someone's taken her," he says, his voice a fluttering whisper. "Alina has been abducted."

My heart pounds harder, faster. I can scarcely hear the other knights talking to one another over the rushing of blood through my ears.

Without meaning to, I shatter the teacup held in my hands, sending broken porcelain and hot black tea all over the king's fine rug.

"Who?" I demand. "Who took her?"

The king holds the letter out to me. I push to my feet and take it from him.

To His Majesty, King Jorvick of Elarwyn,

We trust this letter finds you in good health, though we understand your heart must be heavy with the weight of this loss. Princess Alina is in our hands – alive and unharmed, at least for now. We will keep our word as long as you do exactly as we say.

Your Majesty, you have something we desire – something more valuable to us than gold, something we are willing to exchange for your granddaughter's life: your dragon shifter. Do not attempt to deceive us, for we know he is yours. Bring the shifter to the abandoned church on Old Serpent Road. Meet us at midnight beneath the shadow of the broken archway.

You are to come alone with the shifter. We shall ensure that no harm comes to the princess as long as you honor this agreement. Any attempt to deceive us or bring forces beyond the shifter will result in consequences you will regret. The princess's life depends on your compliance.

Do not fail us.

Your granddaughter awaits your arrival.

-The Veiled Hand

"The Veiled Hand," I whisper. My eyes flick up to meet the king's. "Someone has hired them for this?" The paper shakes in my trembling hand. Around my neck, the chain starts to burn. "To kidnap the princess? For *me*?"

The Veiled Hand is a notorious group of mercenaries, assassins, and spies for hire, operating under the guise of anonymity. They take on the dirtiest and most dangerous jobs—regardless of the morality or political ramifications. And their services come at a steep price.

"Sir Larsen, you'll stay. The two of you are dismissed." The king waves his fingers at the two lesser guards flanking Sir Larsen. They immediately bow their heads before striding from the room.

"Give him the letter," the king tells me.

I shove the parchment toward Sir Larsen. He takes it from me and begins to read.

"Your Majesty," I say, voice laced with panic, "we must do as they say."

King Jorvick studies me. "You would sacrifice yourself like this? Take her place? You've no idea what the Hand wants with you, nor who they've been hired by."

"It doesn't matter. There's no other way. We can't risk her life."

"Sir Ashvale is right." Sir Larsen lowers the letter. His eyes meet mine briefly, curiosity swimming in them, before he tears his gaze away to regard the king. "We must give them what they want. But we likewise must ensure forces are present. They could just as easily kill you and take them both."

"They clearly state we are to go alone," King Jorvick says.

"Of course they do. They are assassins and spies; their strength is not in numbers, but in stealth and secrets. We could dispatch them with ease."

"No." King Jorvick stands and paces to the fire, one hand stroking the length of his beard. "They will be watching for us. If we don't comply with their requests, they will disappear with Alina, and retrieving her will be made even more difficult."

"Your Majesty, I insist—" Sir Larsen starts, but I cease listening.

They took Alina. My princess. My mate.

And they will suffer for it. They will perish at the tips of my fangs and beneath the might of my claws.

I know what I must do.

"I don't believe they will harm the king," I say suddenly, stopping whatever Sir Larsen was saying midsentence. "They want me, not him. And they can have me." I curl my fingers into fists, trying to control my breathing as my dragon thrashes inside my chest, causing the chain to burn hot against my still-damaged skin.

"You are certain of this?" the king asks, his brows drawn low over his eyes.

"Yes. I ask only that my mother and sisters are looked after, regardless of what happens to me."

There's a long moment of tense silence. The only sounds in the room are the fire crackling and the wind tapping at the windowpanes.

"It is done," the king says.

I square my shoulders. "Then we will trade me for Alina." I grit my teeth, then say through the tension in my jaw, "And at the first opportunity, I will destroy them."

CHAPTER 33
ALINA

SUNLIGHT WAKES ME SOFTLY. IT CREEPS around the edges of the drapes, sneaking into the room one inch at a time.

My senses turn on slowly. I'm warm, held comfortably in a deep mattress with blankets draped across my body. The air smells of woodsmoke tinged with dust. I'm still wearing my nightdress, if the silky slip of material across my skin as I shift in the bed is any indication.

I go to lift a hand to my head, where a headache has started to blossom, and I'm startled to realize my wrists are bound.

This wakes me immediately.

I shoot up in the bed and wriggle the unfamiliar blankets away to see that I've been put in shackles. They're metal, but the cuffs themselves are wrapped in plush linen, likely to spare my wrists from the bite of the iron.

Why?

When I dig through my hazy memories, I recall being awoken, Tristan at the door telling me Raelan had been injured, the carriage, and then—

The powder.

It knocked me out immediately, before I could even think to fight back.

Tristan did this to me.

My heart stings with betrayal. I thought he was my friend, thought he may even have had an interest in being more than that. Now I'm quite certain he was only trying to get close to me for his own nefarious purposes—whatever those purposes may be.

My heart gallops as fear spikes through my body.

Focusing on the shackles, I attempt to bring ice to my hands, to freeze the metal and hopefully make it brittle enough to snap, but nothing happens. I try again, and though my magic tingles through my veins, it can't manifest outwardly.

The cuffs are stifling my magic, dampening it.

Shit!

Trying very hard not to panic, I kick the blankets away and am relieved to find that I am, indeed, still dressed in my nightclothes. I twist about and set my feet upon the floor, which is chilled despite the fire burning in the hearth. Quietly, in an effort to not alert anyone in this place that I've woken up, I cross from the bed to the window and use my bound hands to shift the drapes aside.

The sun is much higher in the sky that I expected. It seems I slept through the night and a good portion of the day. As if to remind me of this fact, my stomach grumbles pathetically.

But I can't focus on that now. I'm too busy assessing the landscape outside the window, trying to determine where I am.

I'm on the second floor of a building, though I'm not yet sure what type of building. Outside, a crumbling stone wall wraps around the property, and beyond that, all I see are trees. Deep and dark and overgrown, the forest is impossible to see through. And given the derelict state of the outbuildings peppered along the forest line, I'm starting to determine that I'm being held on some abandoned farm, perhaps on the distant outskirts of the farmland surrounding Wysteria. But if I was unconscious all night and part of the day, it's possible I've been carried many, many miles from Coven Crest.

I could be anywhere.

Dread twists in my belly, cold and heavy.

What does he want with me?

Behind me, there's a creaking of floorboards. I whip around just in time to see the door creak open slowly. And Tristan, the *traitor*, is the one who appears.

"Oh." His dark brows rise toward his floppy brown hair. "You're awake."

He's no longer wearing his Coven Crest robe and has since donned unremarkable brown trousers, brown boots, a forest-green tunic, and a cloak that looks warm and sturdy.

If I were to see him in Wysteria, I'd not look twice, and if someone were to ask me if I'd seen him, I probably couldn't even call him to memory.

It's the perfect attire for someone going about the dirty business of kidnapping princesses.

He steps into the room, a tray of food held in his hands, and pushes the door closed with his boot. "You must be hungry. I brought you some soup and bread. It's a bit stale, but it'll do." He smiles.

And it makes my stomach turn.

"How *dare* you," I seethe. "What is the meaning of this?"

Tristan crosses the room to the small table and chairs that stand before the fire. The table wobbles a bit when he sets the tray down, and he takes a moment to pull a square of linen from his pocket and use it to brace the table leg. He seems completely unconcerned, like the situation we find ourselves in is the most normal thing in the world.

Has he done this before? Is he even who I *think* he is? Maybe his name isn't even Tristan.

"This isn't about you," he says as he straightens up and turns to face me. "You're just one piece of the puzzle. But no one's going to hurt you."

"Oh?" I arch a brow and lift my shackled wrists. "Then why am I bound like a prisoner?"

"Can't be too cautious." He smiles at me like he's my friend. The *liar*. "I know what your frost magic can do."

My eyes narrow. "Yes, because you went to class with me. Because I thought you were my friend. That was all a lie, then?"

"No, not all of it." He busies himself with throwing another log on the fire and blowing flames onto it with his fire magic. I strive not to let my expression betray my surprise.

A memory flits through my mind: Tristan alongside the runeball field, trying and failing to bring a flame into his palm.

I was under the impression that he was a beginner warlock, someone only just learning how to control his magic, and he never led me to think otherwise. But I see now even that was a ploy, likely to lull me into a false sense of comfort around him.

Has it all been a lie?

"Is your name even Tristan?" I ask.

He has the audacity to laugh. "No. Sorry."

"What is it, then?"

"Afraid I can't tell you that. Anonymity and all." He dusts off his hands, then gestures to the tray of food. "You really should eat. It's not poisoned, if that's what you're thinking. The king wouldn't be happy about that."

I perk up. "My grandfather knows where I am?"

"No, but he knows what we want. And if he follows our instructions, we'll be taking you to him tonight."

I don't move, though my stomach growls again, making Tristan—or whoever he is—smile.

"Who's *we*? And what is it that you want?"

"Afraid I can't tell you that either. I've probably said too much already." Propping his hands on his hips, he shrugs. "Well, up to you if you want to eat. I'll leave it here. Just holler if you need something. Someone'll hear you."

He gives me a jovial smile—the ass—then leaves, and almost as soon as the door clicks closed behind him, there's the tell-tale thunk of a lock falling into place. His footsteps drift away down what I assume is a hallway, and I'm left with only the flickering fire as company.

Immediately, I start fussing with my shackles again, trying to get them off. But no matter how I twist my wrists or scrunch my fingers up in an effort to slide them off, they won't budge.

I quickly search the room, trying to find something, *anything*, that I can use to free myself. But the bedroom is bare. It feels like no one has been here in years, if the dust built up on the floors and in the corners is any indication.

Once more, I try to call my magic, but it remains trapped just beneath the surface, unable to manifest. It fills me with frustration, like an itch that can't be scratched.

And suddenly, I realize that this must be what Raelan feels like every single day. His chain does the same thing these shackles do: holds his magic at bay, keeps him from manifesting his power, from being truly whole.

I feel I've greatly misunderstood him, have been inconsiderate of how infuriating and uncomfortable it is to be unable to bring forth the magic you were born with. It makes hot shame curl through my stomach, knowing our moments together made it so much more unbearable for him. And yet he persevered. For me.

I've been selfish and foolish. And now I've gotten my grandfather into who knows what kind of situation with my rash decision.

I should've known Headmistress Moonhart would never send a student to fetch me in the middle of the night.

But Tristan was around me often enough to see how I interacted with Raelan—perhaps even to see how I feel about him. And he used that to his advantage, used my feelings as a weapon to manipulate me.

Perhaps the only good thing about this is that Raelan wasn't hurt after all. Where is he now? Back at the castle? Does he know what's happened to me?

Closing my eyes, I draw a deep breath in through my nose. And immediately, Raelan's words from last night come back to me.

It means you're my fated mated, Alina.

His mate. The one chosen by his blood, by destiny.

Something inside of me shifts, starting to simmer.

I'm tired of waiting and hoping and wishing. I want Raelan, and I *know* he wants me. How many times did I have to see it in his eyes? How many times did I have to feel the heat in his touch?

He's been holding himself back, afraid for his family, afraid of my grandfather, afraid for me.

But fear has no place in love. And I'm ready to be fearless.

I can be that for the both of us.

A new sense of determination rises up in me.

When I get out of this mess, I'm going to find Raelan, and I'm going to tell him *exactly* how I feel. I'm going to be the mate and partner that his dragon yearns for—that his dragon deserves. I'm going to rise to whatever challenges that requires.

And I'm not going to let fear control me.

I'm going to control *it*.

And I'm going to make sure Raelan never has to feel powerless and trapped again.

It's time to set him free.

CHAPTER 34
RAELAN

WHEN THE CART DRAWS TO A HALT, I know we've reached Old Serpent Road. It is here that the forces who've accompanied us will fall back, taking defensive positions within the forest to await the king's return. From here onward, it will just be the two of us—like the Veiled Hand demanded.

I'm bound and locked in the back of the enclosed wagon. There are no windows, no moonlight. All is darkness.

And I am fighting with every breath to remain calm.

But all I can think is that I'm the one who left Alina there, who rode away and didn't even bother to turn around as she screamed my name. The kidnappers acted as soon as I was out of the picture, as soon as they could steal her away beneath the cover of night.

They will regret it. I will not falter.

When I was being bound in chains and loaded into the back of the wagon, I paused to tell the king one thing.

"No matter what happens to me," I said as the padlock was secured about my chest, "ensure Alina is safe."

And though his eyes were troubled, he said, "We will. I promise you."

I believed him. He'll keep his promise.

I shift on the hard bench, making the metal around me sway and clink. The chains are not because I plan to fight back—they are another of the Veiled Hand's demands, sent after the original correspondence was received. There's a cloth wrapped around my eyes as well, blinding me to the world.

But I have my hearing, my sense of smell, the instincts that guide me even when my dragon is held at bay.

If the Veiled Hand thinks these chains and a flimsy blindfold will stop me, they're wrong. The only thing that will stop me is the charmed chain about my neck.

The king tried to remove it, saying I'd need my powers, but I refused. My blood is already boiling, and the links burn my skin. If not for this magic, I'd have already torn free of these chains and the wagon I'm being carried in, and I'd be headed for the meeting location with every intention of decimating the people who dared lay a finger on Alina.

But to do so would be to endanger her, and I refuse to do that again. The chain must remain around my neck.

At least until she's safe.

Then I will fight it with everything I have.

OLD SERPENT ROAD IS LONG AND WINDING, AND given how rough the going is, I imagine it is not often traveled. I'm jostled about, but the heavy chains weigh me down, grounding me.

For it is almost time.

I can feel Alina at the edges of my perception. My magic yearns for her, reaches out with stretching fingers, tries with all its might to grasp her and pull her in. It takes every ounce of willpower I possess to banish my thoughts of her.

To think of her now will only make me emotional, and I need to be cold, focused, calculated. I need her *safe*. Apart from that, my desires cannot get in the way.

Despite being locked inside this creaking wooden box, I detect sounds in the nearby trees: arrows being nocked, boots rustling the fallen leaves, low whispers being exchanged. Without my sight, my other dragon senses are heightened.

But no one makes a move toward us. I imagine they're lying in wait, ensuring the king and I came alone, as the first letter demanded.

His Majesty would hear none of it when Sir Larsen argued against the two of us coming alone. With Alina's life on the line, the king was unwilling to budge. And I'm left hoping it was the right decision.

To kidnap the princess is nefarious enough, but to kill the king would drag the Veiled Hand into a battle they would never, ever win. If their reputation and the whispers surrounding their organization are to be believed, they are not unintelligent, and they will not start a war they cannot win.

And besides, they don't want Alina, or even the king.

It's me they want. But for what purpose—and client—I can only guess.

For ten years, I kept my dragon a secret from everyone except my mother and the king. No one knew the truth of what lurked beneath my skin. I was always careful, always hid myself in darkness when I would take those rare delicious flights over the untamed wilderness outside of Wysteria.

But Alina changed all of that. She freed my beast, allowed me to feel the rain on my scales and taste the never-ending expanse of the sky.

A burning realization takes root in my mind.

Someone must've seen me that night. The rain and fog shielded me from many of Coven Crest's windows, but someone had to have been there to see me change.

A student? A faculty member?

Anger and shame rise inside me.

This is *my* fault. If only I'd been able to control myself, no one would've discovered my secret. And Alina would be safe. She's in this situation because of me.

Up on the driver's bench, the king clears his throat. That's the signal to tell me we're approaching the meeting place.

I draw a long breath, fighting the heat burning through my veins. I calm myself, banishing my emotions, focusing only on the task at hand. And when I let out that breath, I'm ready.

The wagon creaks to a halt. Outside, words are exchanged in low voices.

"Hail, traveler," says an unfamiliar man. "What brings you down the Serpent?"

"My mule came this way," the king says, using the code the Hand set out for him in the second letter of correspondence. "You haven't seen her, by chance?"

There are mumbled words and the shifting of boots and cloaks.

"We have. Come with us," the same man says.

Then the wagon is moving again, but this time, footsteps accompany the creaking wheels and the crunching of leaves on the path.

We continue on in this way for five minutes, and then the wagon turns, likely onto another side road.

"Stop here!" the man calls.

The wagon stops.

I'm still calm, still collected. I will not do anything that will put Alina in danger. I will not compromise this exchange.

"Your Majesty," says a new voice, this one female. "It's an honor to meet you."

I can't tell if her tone is derisive or not.

The king doesn't bother with niceties. "Where is my granddaughter?"

The female lets out a low laugh. "She's fine, good king. And you will see her as soon as we see our package."

Package?

Inside, my dragon snarls. I calm it just in time for the wagon door to swing open.

Cold night air rushes in, scented with leaf matter and rich soil and the hint of an approaching rainstorm. Mixed with these smells are the scents of the people who must be standing at the open doors, looking in at me.

"You!" the female voice calls. "Come here."

Boots thump over soft dirt, and then a familiar smell hits me. Immediately, I growl.

Tristan.

It was him. I should've know.

"Is this the shifter?" the female asks.

"Yeah," Tristan says, and just the sound of his voice draws claws down my spine. "That's him."

I knew all along something was off about him, but I let my bond with Alina get in the way of my instincts, which have screamed at me all semester to be wary of Tristan, to keep him well away from her.

Now I know why. And it's yet another thing I'll berate myself for in the quiet hours of the night, assuming I get through this encounter alive.

In centuries past, dragon shifters were hunted almost to extinction. It's why there are so few of us now—and why the king chose to hide my secret, even from his own men, his own *family*. We are both feared and desired, wanted alive just as often as we're wanted dead.

And depending on who hired the Hand to obtain me, I may very well not live to see the light of day.

As long as she's okay.

"His name?"

There's a brief pause. Then Tristan says, "Raelan Ashvale."

"Keep my name off your vile tongue," I snarl.

A ripple of tension moves through the air. The female lets out a low chuckle.

"A dragon shifter. Never thought I'd see one." There's an air of reverence to her voice, even as I sit chained and blindfolded. "Get up, Ashvale. Let's go."

I remind myself, probably for the hundredth time, that all of this is for Alina. I will not endanger her. I will comply.

As I push to my feet, the chains binding my arms to my sides clink heavily. Every step I take is weighed down, and my boots thud across the wagon floorboards. As I step up to the edge of the open doors, someone reaches up to take my elbow, trying to steady me, but I shake them off with a barely restrained growl.

In one smooth movement, I jump from the wagon, vision still obscured, and land with a grunt, the chains trying to drag me down. But I don't let them. I stand tall and square my shoulders. All around me, whispers are exchanged.

"Now I will see my granddaughter," the king says from off to my right.

"Of course, good king. A deal is a deal." The woman lets out a low whistle. "Bring him."

Something prods me in the side, and I'm sent walking through the darkness, using scent and sound to guide my way. I'm in only a tunic and trousers, no cloak, but my anger and my dragon heat me up from the inside, keeping me warm despite the crisp autumn air.

We walk a short distance, then the woman calls, "Stop here. You two, get her."

Her. Alina.

My dragon coils, its magic reaching for her.

Boots hurriedly move away. I can still smell Tristan, and I imagine what I'll do to him once Alina is safe. If I have anything to say about it, he will not live to see another sunrise.

No one betrays her and gets away with it.

On a brush of wind, Alina's scent hits me. I jerk upright, the chains clinking. She smells like herself, delicious and intoxicating, but with a tinge of fear.

If they've hurt her, I—

"As promised," the woman says. "We will exchange her for your dragon."

"*What?*" Alina snaps. "What's going on?"

She's so near, every cell in my body urges me to run to her, to hold her close, to wrap her in my arms and carry her far, far away, to a place where no one will ever find us.

"Give her to the king. But leave her shackles on," the woman says.

"No!" There's the sound of a struggle. "Grandfather, you can't do this!"

"Alina, come," he says, voice low, calm.

"No!" she yells. "Raelan!"

There's such pain in her voice that it makes my chain burn white-hot. I say nothing, focusing all my attention on not losing control of myself and my dragon. I just need her out of here, and then I will do everything in my power to—

Boots scuffle over the dirt, and someone gasps. Then feet thump across the leaves, and a moment later, Alina is throwing herself against me, her head nestled upon my chest despite the chains wrapped around my body.

I would know the feel of her anywhere, even without my sight.

"Raelan," she whispers, her body trembling against mine, "I'm sorry. I didn't know. I'm so sorry."

"Go," I tell her, with no uncertainty in my tone. "Get to safety. I'll be fine."

"But—hey! Let go of me! I said *let go*!"

Alina is dragged away, and by the sounds of it, she's fighting them all the way.

"Go, Your Highness," I say, louder this time. "It's the only way."

Her grandfather mumbles to her, trying to calm her, but I can still hear the struggle he and the others have to get her into the wagon.

I need them to get her out of here. My dragon is roiling now, rising to fight. It wants her. It wants to kill anyone who dared touch her. It wants to thrash and rage and leave destruction in its path.

Not yet. Not yet.

I clench my fists and jaw, fighting my beast, feeling the scald of metal against my throat.

Not yet.

"Raelan!" Alina calls out one final time. But the wagon is already moving, the wheels creaking, and I turn a deaf ear to her cries until they drift away on the wind.

Because this is the only way. Even if it's tearing me apart.

Finally, after what feels like a lifetime, her scent starts

271

to disperse, and I can breathe deeply again without fear of getting drunk on her smell. Now I am in the dark, with midnight wrapped around me and the Veiled Hand at my sides.

"Get him loaded up," the woman says. "And secure him fully. We can't take any chances. We don't know what he's capable of."

Hands grab my arms and force me forward. My dragon snaps and snarls. It wants to take their hands off, to remove their limbs from their bodies and delight in the violence.

But not yet. Alina is still too close. I need to give her time to get away from here.

Time to get away from *me*.

I'm dragged forward and loaded into another enclosed wagon, this time with more chains binding me to the bench I'm seated upon. A set of shackles is clamped tight around my ankles.

The door slams and locks. In the quiet, I take a breath.

Soon. Soon, I will fight back with everything I have.

They wanted a dragon, and they got one.

Now they will feel a dragon's wrath, and they will regret ever having set a finger upon Alina Ravenscroft. I'll make sure of it even if it's the last thing I do.

CHAPTER 35
ALINA

RANDFATHER, NO! WE HAVE TO GO BACK! We can't leave him!"

Grandfather sits beside me on the driver's bench, wrapped in a simple brown cloak. He doesn't wear his crown, and instead, the hood of the cloak is pulled up over his head. If one didn't know better, they'd think him an old merchant just passing through. He guides the horse as it trots down the winding road, lanterns swinging from the wagon, just barely illuminating the wooded path.

Overhead, the clouds are thick, and the dark of night feels almost impenetrable.

I twist around on the bench, staring back the way we came. I can't see anything through the swath of darkness. But somewhere behind us, Raelan is blinded and bound in chains, and my grandfather willingly handed him over.

"Grandfather! Please!"

"He chose this," my grandfather says. His voice is strained. I don't think he derives any joy from this. "He wanted to exchange himself for you, Alina. He would've done it whether I permitted it or not. It was the only way . . . He did it for you." His eyes meet mine, swimming with a concoction of sadness and rage.

My heart thrums in my chest. Then a spark of hope flares to life inside me. "His chain. Did you remove his chain?"

Grandfather gives a small shake of his head. "I tried. He wouldn't allow it. He felt it would endanger you."

I let out a cry of frustration and collapse back in the bench. "Then he's powerless!" I struggle with the shackles around my wrists, trying again to call to my magic, but it's still dormant. If only I were free of them, I could go back, I could try to use my magic to help Raelan get free. "Get me out of these!"

Grandfather gives me a deep frown. "I've got guards stationed at the bottom of this road. Once we're there, they'll have what we need to free you." He gives the shackles a disgusted look, then lets out a heavy sigh. "I'm so sorry, Alina."

I clench my fingers into tight fists. As soon as Grandfather helped me up into the wagon, he wrapped me in a thick woolen cloak. It smells of home as I pull it close, but it brings me very little comfort. I slump forward, eyes filling with tears of frustration.

"He's going to be okay," Grandfather says. His voice has a harder edge now, though it's not unkind. "We both know what he is. And if anyone can escape the Veiled Hand, it's him."

I sniffle and glance up. "They were with the Hand?"

Grandfather gives a single nod in confirmation.

"So, who are they working for? Who *actually* wants Raelan? And what do they want him for?"

The Hand are known to work for whoever has pocketfuls of money, and more often than not, that means they're the shadowy extensions of nobles and monarchs, politicians and lords.

Someone wants Raelan for their own purposes. The realization makes my stomach turn, and I suddenly wish I hadn't eaten the soup and bread the man I once knew as Tristan brought to me. It's no longer sitting right. Add that to the long list of other bad decisions I've made recently.

"We don't know," Grandfather says. Then his pale eyes cut to me in the dark, illuminated by a thin beam of moonlight that manages to slip through a break in the dense cloud cover overhead. "But whoever it is, they'll be dealt with. You don't attack the family of Ravenscroft and get away with it." His lips press into a firm line, and I see the king who wears my grandfather's face, the man he is when he's not enjoying tea with me before the fire or reading the silly stories I used to write for him when I was a girl.

I see King Jorvick Ravenscroft.

My anger with him slowly slips from my shoulders, and I allow my body to slump against his, my head finding his soft shoulder.

"Promise he'll be okay?" I whisper into the dark.

Grandfather turns to press a kiss to the top of my head. "I promise. Whatever happens, we will get him back. We'll bring Raelan home."

IT IS SOME TIME DOWN THE WINDING DIRT ROAD BE-
fore the faint call of a mourning dove drifts through the
trees. I sit up straight, my gaze going to the woods along
either side of the path.

Grandfather lowers the reins and cups his hands over his
mouth, letting out a similar mimicking call.

Immediately, the woods swarm with life. Soldiers of the
King's Royal Army step from the trees, and in moments,
we're surrounded. Torches are lit, illuminating the narrow
section of woods, and one of my grandfather's most loyal
knights, Sir Larsen, reaches up to help me down from the
wagon.

"Your Highness," he says, his eyes sweeping over me in
what appears to be a quick assessment of my well-being, "are
you hurt?"

"No." I shake my head. "But I need these off. They're
dampening my magic." I hold out my hands.

Sir Larsen regards them as my grandfather climbs down
from the wagon. "We should be able to pry these open," he
says, then sends for another knight to fetch him what he
needs.

I pay little attention as he gets to work loosening the
hinges of the shackles, instead searching the bits of dark sky
I can see through the trees overhead. Perhaps Raelan will
escape, perhaps he'll make his way back to me, perhaps—

One of the shackles pops open, freeing my wrist. I shake
it out and try my magic again, but even the single cuff is
enough to keep it held dormant inside me. Grandfather

finishes speaking with a few of his knights, then joins us just as Sir Larsen frees me from the second shackle.

Immediately, my hands tingle with magic, and I test it out. Frost glitters across my palms and up my wrists, then melts as I call a tiny spark of flame into each hand. My elemental magic lessons are paying off.

And finally, I'm free.

The relief I feel is so palpable and overwhelming that it leads me right back to thoughts of Raelan. How can he live like this day in and day out? How can he bear to keep his magic trapped inside when it longs so badly to be unrestrained?

I don't want him to live in shackles any longer. Somehow, I have to free him.

"Let's move out!" Sir Larsen calls, my open shackles hanging from one of his hands. "Take these," he instructs a younger knight passing by. "We'll take them back to the Shadowfall Court, see what they make of them."

The knight takes the shackles and nods quickly before hurrying off into the swarm of soldiers.

Grandfather reaches for me, wrapping an arm around my shoulders.

"He's going to be okay, Alina," he whispers, trying his best to comfort me.

But again, my gaze goes to the sky, searching unceasingly for Raelan.

Searching for my dragon.

CHAPTER 36
RAELAN

I WAIT. I BIDE MY TIME. ALINA NEEDS TO BE FAR, far away. She needs to be safe.

As I'm jostled along in the back of the wagon, each bump rougher than the last, I think about the decisions I've made, the choices that have been laid out before me.

When the king first called me into his study to assign me the duty of being Alina's knight, I could've told him no. I had every opportunity to tell him the truth. But I was terrified of how he'd react—perhaps unnecessarily so. Since picking me up off the streets of Wysteria when I was just a boy, he's shown me nothing but kindness and understanding. My time training in his guard hasn't always been easy, and I had to struggle at first to catch up to the other boys in my group, the ones who'd been training since they were seven, but he was always there, always watching, always encouraging me to do my best.

And I realize now that he was instrumental in molding me into the man I've become.

Maybe part of my secrecy was not wanting to disappoint him. I felt almost ashamed for having discovered my bond with Alina, some voice deep inside telling me I'd never be good enough for her. She's a princess, and I'm just a man who has to fight day in and day out to keep a beast locked inside.

My dragon snarls at that thought. It wants to be free. It yearns for it, like any caged thing. And rightly so. We all want freedom.

In my lap, my fingers curl into tight fists.

When first presented with the Veiled Hand's letter, the king seemed hesitant to acquiesce to their demand, though I could see the pain in his eyes. At the end of the day, Alina will always be more important to him, *should* always be more important to him, yet I knew it pained him to think he'd have to trade me for her.

And seeing that, I knew that I'd misunderstood him all along.

I recall what he said in the study just before the letter arrived.

Son, I don't go back on my promises.

He ensured me my family will be safe. And with that final chain having been snapped, I feel I am finally free to do what I must.

And I must fight back.

We have been traveling for some time now. And with Alina traveling in the opposite direction, putting twice the amount of distance between us, I am no longer in danger of hurting her.

Which means it's time.

All the rage I've been fighting to keep locked inside, all the yearning and heartbreak and terrible anger, is finally allowed to flood through my body.

Immediately, my skin warms, my heart starting to pound. The chain about my neck burns.

But this time, I don't try to clamp down on my magic, don't attempt to force it into submission. This time, I will fight to break free. It's my only chance.

My dragon coils. I call to it, trying to pull it through my bones. It snarls and writhes. It wants to tear through me, to shatter these chains into a million pieces, to deliver justice upon those who dared touch my princess.

My mate.

The chain burns hotter. It scalds me, sending the scent of charred flesh up my nostrils, undoing all the careful work Alina did in trying to heal me.

Still, I draw on my magic. I imagine bursting free, unfurling my wings, screaming my anger into the sky.

Faster, faster. My heart is galloping now.

The sizzle of magic against my throat makes me scream. It's excruciating.

Somewhere outside the enclosed wagon, someone asks, "What was that?"

"Should we check on him?" another voice says.

"No!" It's the woman this time, their leader. "Don't open that door. Keep walking."

Her voice is like a thorn in my boot, a finger pressing into a wound.

They took Alina from me. They dared threaten her. And now they'll pay.

I scream again, the pain mounting until I'm slumped forward, the chains the only thing holding me upright as agony rips through my body.

And then, all at once, it's over.

The chain around my neck snaps, its magic having finally given way. The broken links fall into my lap and around my boots, clinking against the wooden floorboards. Behind my blindfold, my eyes flash open. A smile curls across my lips.

The transformation is quick; my dragon is ready.

My bones shift, my skin pulls. Scales form across my arms and legs. My gums split to make way for my fangs.

As my body writhes, the chains attempting to hold me put up a final protest. Then they, too, succumb to me, snapping and snaking into heavy piles upon the floorboards. The shackles they clasped around my ankles break free, the blindfold tears.

Then the wagon is suddenly too small. It can no longer hold me. The wood creaks as my scaled spine presses against it. With a cacophony of snapping, the wood splinters.

And those standing closest to me scream.

My body tears free of the wagon, leaving it a crumpled mess of wood and metal. My weight crushes it down, breaking the yoke holding the horses to the wagon. Immediately, they flee, leaving the humans stranded and entirely at my mercy.

As the transformation completes, I unfurl my inky wings and stretch them toward the night sky. It feels like a breath of clean air, a glass of water after a long hard journey. For a brief moment, the relief distracts me.

Until an arrow attempts to puncture my scaled hide.

My gaze snaps to the stupid human who thought it wise to attempt such a thing. I surge forward, and he has but a second to scream before he's nothing more than a mess beneath my clawed paw, flattened into the earth.

The others level their weapons at me and loose their arrows all at once. Each sharpened arrowhead glances harmlessly off my scales, doing nothing but angering me further.

But this anger feels *good*. It feels *right*.

These men and women are kidnappers, assassins, spies. They threatened my king. They threatened my mate. And they won't ever do it again. Not to me, and not to anyone I love.

I scream my rage to the sky, a burst of blue flames burning through my chest before shooting toward the clouds overhead, lighting up the blackness stretching across the land. Then I turn my slitted gaze toward the mass of panicking humans.

And the justice I dole out is swift.

The unbridled power coiling though my body is why they killed my ancestors, hunted us until we were very nearly a thing only of legend. But they don't understand that they *made* us this way. They gave us a reason to fight, to defend ourselves and our loved ones.

It didn't have to be this way. But humans rarely learn from their mistakes.

Instead, they lean on pride and arrogance, wrapping themselves in it as though it will protect them.

Tonight, the Veiled Hand learns. And I will be their teacher.

WHEN THE SCREAMING STOPS AND THE FOREST FALLS silent, I take a moment to assess the damage. A few trees fell victim to my rage, and they lie about the forest floor, their pine needles blanketing the rich earth. The animals all fled, leaving the night quiet and still save for the far-off rumble of thunder. The humans are dead. All except for one. I search the trees for him. And my gaze homes in on his familiar face.

Tristan.

He's attempting to hide behind a tree I felled with a single swoop of my tail. His hair is matted and tangled with leaves and pine needles, his eyes wide, blood dripping from a cut on his temple. He at least has the good sense to look terrified.

Aware he's been spotted, he pushes to his feet and attempts to flee into the dark woods.

Stupid human.

I surge forward, and with one swipe of my claws, I scoop him up, relishing the scent of his fear as he writhes and struggles to escape my hold. I lift him to my eye level.

"No!" he screams, trying to kick his feet. "I'm sorry! Please! Don't hurt me! *Please!*"

A growl rumbles through my chest, fire building in my throat.

I could scorch him, leave him as nothing but ash to feed the forest floor.

But when I look into his tearstained eyes, I think of Alina.

Would she want me to do this?

My dragon screams *yes*, but the tiny human part of my brain says *no*. And apart from the connection Alina once had with this pathetic excuse for a human, Tristan also has information the king needs—information regarding the Hand and who hired them to try to obtain me. I've not left any of the others alive; he is our last chance to learn of the shady workings behind the organization.

And therefore, he must live—even if every scale on my body tingles with the desire to crush him in my paw.

"Please!" he screams again. "I have a family."

I tighten my claws around him, and he finally ceases his useless struggling, as if only now realizing how fucked he really is.

I swallow down the flames burning in my throat.

Without sparing a last look at the humans left to be claimed by the earth, I spread my wings and turn my gaze to the sky. It opens its arms to me, beckoning for me to come home.

And I wait no longer.

I fly.

CHAPTER 37
ALINA

A BURST OF BLUE FLAMES TEARS ACROSS the sky, illuminating the forest and causing the horse pulling our wagon to spook. Grandfather deftly calms her down, shushing her gently as she prances in place, harness jingling.

The entire company whirls around, searching the darkness for the source of the fire.

On the front bench seat, I twist about, casting my gaze to the sky. And as I do, a reptilian scream cuts through the night.

My heart leaps.

Raelan.

He is free.

While the others pick up their pace, trying to hurry us along the narrow dirt road back toward Wysteria, I wait with a mixture of excitement and apprehension curling through my veins.

"What the hell was that?" one of the knights asks.

Another says, "It sounded like a—"

"Keep moving!" Sir Larsen calls, cutting them off swiftly.

I wonder if he knows. Grandfather most certainly does. But what of all the others? How many of them are aware of what Raelan truly is?

Another scream rends the night, this one long and echoing. It sends goose bumps dancing across my skin despite the thick cloak draped over my shoulders. The knights move faster, their armor clinking in tandem with one another as their boots strike the soft ground. They're moving at a slow jog now, the horse pulling our wagon clipping along at a trot. No one speaks, but I can feel their fear.

It has been a century since the Dragon Wars, since most of the dragon shifters were killed or went into hiding. I was taught all about this as I grew up, but the words on the pages of my history books were only that: words. Now I feel them in my bones, have finally come to understand what the books meant when they described the awe-inspiring power of the dragons.

"Grandfather," I say, whipping around to face him. "We should go back. We—"

A tremor shakes the ground, jostling the wagon so violently I very nearly fly from the bench. Some of the knights lose their footing and hit the ground hard. The trees around us sway and creak.

My gaze flicks up to the path ahead.

But it is obscured.

By a dragon. *My* dragon.

"Raelan," I whisper. And before Grandfather can stop me, I leap from the wagon, the heavy cloak billowing around me as my feet hit the dirt.

"Your Highness!" Sir Larsen calls. He reaches for me as I sprint by, but I twist from his grasp at the last moment.

And then I'm running toward the beast that everyone else is backing away from. I break through the front line of knights, and now all that stands between me and Raelan is a stretch of wooded path sprinkled with crinkly autumn leaves.

Like the first time I saw his true form, I am filled with a mixture of reverence and terror. But I don't let the fear stay my feet. I push myself forward, closing the distance between us one stride at a time.

Raelan rises up, his sharp head reaching the tops of the trees. His eyes glitter with flecks of gold despite the thin moonlight. And when he looks down at me, I feel he sees right into me, like his gaze is tugging at the threads of my heart.

"Your Highness!" someone calls from behind me.

Then Sir Larsen yells, "Don't!"

I think he's speaking to me. But then a whistle sounds, the tell-tale sound of an arrow cutting through the night.

My magic reacts before I can think to call upon it. I throw my hands out, and a burst of ice strikes the arrow midair, sending it flying into the woods rather than into its intended target.

Finally, my magic does what I want it to.

Raelan blinks slowly, and a rumbling growl vibrates from his massive chest.

"Let me go!" a familiar voice yells. My gaze is drawn immediately to Raelan's clawed paw, which is wrapped tightly about a struggling figure.

With little fanfare, Raelan opens his claws and drops the figure onto the cold dirt. I wince as the person hits the ground.

"Shit," the man says, gasping for air as he pushes himself to his hands and knees and shakes pine needles from his messy hair. When he looks up, my stomach turns.

Tristan.

Raelan brought him back to us. He could easily have ended him with a tightening of his claws, and yet he stayed his paw.

And I wonder, somehow, if he did it for me.

I turn my back to Raelan, putting myself between the company of knights and my dragon. Their hands are on their swords, and some have bowstrings already drawn, arrows pointing either at Raelan or at Tristan, who sits back onto his heels with a defeated sigh.

In the wagon, Grandfather stands. Pushing back the hood of his cloak, he looks upon Raelan with eyes wide and lips parted.

There's movement behind me. Then Raelan's head is beside me, his slitted eye easily as large as my hand. More bowstrings are drawn as he breathes warm air over me, like a summer breeze on the warmest of days. My hair flutters away from my face, and my cloak billows softly.

"Raelan," I whisper, lifting a hand to place it upon the end of his scaled nose. He blinks slowly, like a cat, then casts his gaze to the night sky.

He wants to fly. Of course he does.

And I'm going with him.

"Alina!" my grandfather calls, but I don't heed him as I turn fully to face the dragon towering above me. There's a murmuring of dissent amongst the ranks as I walk closer to Raelan, so close I have to tip my head all the way back to look up at him.

With trembling fingers, I reach out to trail my hand across his scales. They're warm and glossy, soft like silk against my skin. And at the gentle touch, Raelan lets out what sounds like a low purr.

He lowers a wing for me, and with my feet bare, I climb upon it, then gasp as he lifts me into the air. I wobble but don't fall. Then I'm walking carefully across his wing and settling myself into the spot just between his neck and mighty shoulders.

"Lower your weapons!" Sir Larsen shouts at his knights. "That's the princess you're aiming at!"

But I'm not paying attention to the army anymore. Because Raelan is stretching out his glorious wings, turning his head toward the sky. I lean forward, taking hold of his glistening scales in my hands.

And I don't even scream as his wings come down in a mighty gust and he lifts off the ground, buffeting everyone below and rising into the night.

CHAPTER 38
ALINA

EVERYONE ON THE GROUND—MY GRANDFATHER, Sir Larsen, Tristan, all the assembled knights in their polished armor—shrinks as Raelan's heavy wingbeats lift us higher and higher into the chill air. Even the tops of the tallest trees become but pinpricks below us, and the forest becomes a swath of dark across the land.

I should be afraid. I should be *very* afraid. I'm on the back of a dragon, for goodness' sake.

And yet I can't bring myself to fear anything except the dizzying drop to the earth below.

This is just like that dream I had, the one I wished would come true. But I never thought it would. Even now, I almost wonder if I'm imagining this, imagining the kiss of cold air on my face, the roll of thunder in the distance.

I cease looking down, trying to quell the nausea twirling through my stomach from the sheer height. And as soon as

I'm able to peel my eyes away from the ground and cast my gaze upon the sky, everything changes.

Up here, flying just beneath the clouds, I can see for miles. The distant Emberstone Mountains look smaller from so high up, rather than the towering giants they are when I look at them with my feet planted on the earth. It's like I could reach out and drag my fingertips across their peaks, scoop a handful of their glittering snow into my palm and watch it melt across my skin.

Raelan's wings beat the air again, sending the wind curling and cutting around us. I lean forward, gripping the edges of his glossy scales to hold myself tight to his back. Up he arcs, climbing higher, and I take a breath just before we cut through the cloud cover.

It feels like moving through a dense wet fog. Droplets of moisture cling to my hair, and I risk removing one hand from Raelan's scales to adjust my cloak and pull it tight, warding off the cold in the air. For a moment, all I see is gray.

But as soon as we break through the clouds and into the air just above, I lose my breath.

With no fluffy gray clouds to impede my view, I'm bathed in silver light. It washes over me, twinkling and cold, and a shiver of awe goes through me.

I've never seen so many stars. They are a blanket above me, and they feel so close that I'm sure if I were to reach for one, I could pluck its glittering brilliance straight from the night sky and cradle it in my hand like a precious jewel.

This is . . . breathtaking.

Yet at the same time, I'm filled with deep sadness.

Because *this* is where Raelan belongs. His wings, glossy black with a subtle shimmer in the starlight, hold us aloft as we glide through the air, shifting ever so slightly as air currents wrap around and over us.

Now that he's not pumping his wings anymore, the ride has become significantly smoother, and though my heart thrums and my hands shake, I challenge myself to sit up fully rather than leaning forward with a death grip on him.

Thin air caresses my cheeks and sends my hair flying out behind me. I shiver, though I imagine it's more from adrenaline and awe than it is from the chill.

Slowly, *slowly*, with hands and fingers trembling, I dare to spread my arms out wide. And for a moment, I can almost pretend I'm the one with the wings, flying high over the earth, going where humans can only dream of.

Raelan shifts slightly, his long neck twisting so he can level one slitted black-gold eye at me. And somehow, I believe he's smiling.

A few tears trickle from my eyes, but the wind whisks them away, leaving but a trail of cold down my cheeks. Then I laugh. The sound is stolen away, but I keep laughing. Then I let out a long scream, yelling into the sky for all the air beings to hear.

This freedom is . . . intoxicating. I don't know how Raelan resists it, how he lives with that chain around his neck, weighing him down in more ways than one.

And I know I must not allow this part of him to continue to remain stifled and caged.

Raelan looks forward, then begins a gentle, steady dive

back toward the clouds. The shift, though subtle, makes me gasp and grip his glossy scales once more.

And yet I know he'd never let me fall. I know this deep in my bones, a knowing that is both instinctual and magical.

I keep my eyes open as we dive back through the clouds, feeling the droplets of water gather upon my cheeks and along my eyelashes. Then we're in the darkness again, flying through the sky with the moonlight veiled by the clouds above.

And in the distance, thunder rolls.

The air smells of an incoming storm, and I can feel an electric current starting to build upon my skin. Raelan must feel it too, for he dives even closer to the ground. We're flying over the wildlands now, the places outside of Wysteria that have yet to be fully settled. Much of this land still firmly belongs to nature—the way it should be—but as such, I've not explored it, have not become at all familiar with the movement of the land or the whispers of the trees.

I believe Raelan must know this place, for he flies surely, no hesitation in his movements.

Our speed decreases gradually, and then Raelan banks to one side, though not enough to send me tumbling toward the ground below. I tighten my legs and hold firm to his scales, then catch my breath as he tilts his wings to slow our speed. The air created by his powerful thrusts sends my hair and cloak whipping wildly about me, obscuring my vision and forcing me to lean forward and press myself against his neck. Then there's a rumble, a rustling of trees, and the wind goes still.

Tentatively, I sit up and open my eyes.

We've landed.

And we're in a small clearing surrounded by trees. Though it's difficult to see with clarity through the dark, I notice there's a ramshackle cottage standing in the center of the clearing, as if it's been here waiting for us all along. Plants crawl up the weathered exterior, slowly reclaiming the structure as their own. It appears to have been forgotten long ago, like many things in the wildlands.

Another roll of thunder sends me looking up at the clouds we were just flying through. Far off, a bolt of lightning cuts through the sky, making me blink against its sudden brightness.

Raelan holds out his wing, and I ease myself onto it, my legs shaking so fiercely I have to kneel and use my hands for balance. He lowers his wing slowly to the ground, and I'm able to get my feet under me and stumble into the cold autumn grass.

Then I turn to face the beautiful beast towering over me.

And I try to save this moment, this image, in my mind for safekeeping.

For Raelan is truly magnificent. He gleams even in the inky dark, his scales glistening like midnight oil. His eyes have a gentle otherworldly luminescence, the flakes of gold putting off a subtle glow.

I wonder if all the dragons were this beautiful.

My heart squeezes.

Learning about the Dragon Wars, I felt compassion and empathy for the creatures, the shifters who were hunted or taken captive, both prized and feared for their power. But now, looking up at a *real* dragon, at *my* dragon, I'm overcome with grief.

How can humans be so cruel? Why do we allow our fears to drive us to such terrible lengths?

The skies should be filled with dragons. Instead, those few rare shifters who still live, their ancestors having escaped the violence, have to hide themselves, have to fear being found or taken or killed.

Because of me, Tristan discovered Raelan's secret, and the Veiled Hand came for him, tried to take him from me. All because of me.

Grief crashes over my shoulders, so wild and overwhelming that, when paired with my still-trembling legs, it knocks me to my knees.

There's a rustling of wings, a rumble of earth as Raelan takes a step. And then he's lowering his head to my height, his nostrils sending hot air billowing over my cold body.

Tears streak down my cheeks, but this time, there's no sharp wind to whisk them away.

"I'm sorry, Raelan," I whisper as I gaze up at him. "I'm so, so sorry."

Another burst of warm air dances across me, making my skin prickle. Then Raelan steps back, and I turn my eyes away as he begins the transformation—I'm still not quite accustomed to the way his body moves, the stretching of skin and rearranging of bones.

A moment later, bare arms are wrapping around me, pulling me into a naked chest.

Raelan's chest.

"Alina," he whispers, and his voice just makes me cry harder. He pulls back and tips my head up so I'm forced to meet his glittering black-gold eyes. "Are you hurt?"

I shake my head, trying to stop my bottom lip from trembling.

"Then what's the matter?"

"It's . . . It's . . ." Another sob shakes my chest. "I'm just so sorry about everything. About what my people did to yours. About what I did. Because of me, they almost . . . almost . . ." My throat closes up, my tears threatening to choke me.

I don't know what I would've done had they succeeded in taking Raelan from me. The very thought makes me cry even harder, nausea twisting my stomach into sickening knots.

Raelan's eyes soften, his lips pulling into a frown.

Overhead, lightning cuts through the clouds again, accompanied by another roll of thunder, closer now than it was before. Raelan looks up, searches the starless sky above us. His jaw goes hard.

"Come on. The storm is near."

I'm still trembling. I try to push to my feet, but my knees shake, struggling to hold my weight.

But Raelan's arms are there, one under my knees and one cradling my back, and I twist into his chest, relishing his warmth and the firmness of his body. And it makes me feel safe, secure. Like there's nowhere else I'd rather be.

He carries me across the dark clearing, the dried autumn grasses whispering around his legs. The cottage is encircled by a low garden fence, but the gate is standing open, and he walks right through, like he knows this place.

At the door, he shifts my weight so he can use one hand to grasp the door handle. The door swings open with a small squeak of complaint. Raelan steps through, then pushes the door closed with one foot.

And as soon as we're inside, the rain starts. It's not one of those slow autumn storms; it's as if a dam has opened, and all the water comes rushing out at once.

"Can you stand?" Raelan asks. Inside, it's even darker, and I can only barely trace the shape of his face in the blackness.

"I . . ." I sniffle. "I think so."

He lowers me slowly to the floor, and I let out a small breath when the cold wood under my bare feet sends a tingle up my legs. But my knees hold steady. I release my hold on Raelan with some hesitance, already feeling colder without him against me.

"This way," he says, his fingers sliding down my arm until his hand grasps mine. "Watch your step." He leads me through the dark. I can't make out what the shapes are in the room we enter, but he helps guide me onto a couch, and I immediately relax into its embrace, my cloak still wrapped about me. "I'll be back. Just a moment."

His feet pad across the room, then up a set of stairs I didn't even see. I stare into the darkness, listening to the rain on the roof and Raelan's subtle movements upstairs.

Yes, he must know this place. It seems he's familiar with it, even in the deep dark.

He returns to me a minute later, and I'm still sitting on the couch when he lights a fire in the hearth. The sudden brightness makes me squint. It takes a moment for my eyes to adjust. And when they do, my gaze goes to Raelan.

He pushes to his feet, then turns to face me. He's wearing a baggy tunic and trousers—certainly fetched from upstairs—and his feet and throat are bare.

No chain.

For a moment, we regard each other. Something like timidity curls through my veins.

"Are you okay?" Raelan asks, his voice barely audible over the pounding of rain and the low hiss and crackle of the fire in the hearth as it climbs hungrily across the split logs Raelan stacked there.

I nod once, reaching up to swipe any remaining tears from my cheeks. "Sorry," I whisper. "I just ..." Brow furrowing, I shift my gaze to the flames. "I think I finally understand you. At least better than I did before. And I'm sorry for all of it."

Raelan lets out a gentle sigh. Slowly, he crosses the room toward me, and my heart thrums as he sinks onto the couch beside me. "You have nothing to be sorry for."

"But I *do*," I say, voice finally finding some strength. "That"—I gesture vaguely toward the sky—"was *amazing*, Raelan. It was ... the most exhilarating thing I've ever felt." My skin prickles with the memory of the star-filled sky, the quiet to be found so far above the earth. "That's where you belong. You deserve to be free."

Raelan is searching my face, and he lets out a gentle chuckle before glancing away. "You don't think I'm free?"

I shake my head vehemently. "No. That chain, the magic that binds you . . ." I recall the shackles that were placed about my wrists, the frustration and anger that arose when I realized I couldn't access my magic. "It's not fair. It's not *right*."

Raelan lifts his shoulders in a small shrug. "It's what I must do."

"To keep from hurting others, you mean?"

He nods once, the firelight illuminating his face as he stares into the flames.

"I want to help you. I don't want you to have to live in chains anymore." The thought of having to wear those magic-dampening shackles day in and day out makes me queasy.

His eyes cut to me. "How? I know of no such magic."

Biting my lip, I shake my head. "I don't know yet. But that's my promise to you. I'll figure something out. We'll figure it out . . . together."

Raelan regards me through dark eyes. A bolt of lightning offers brief bright illumination. But I don't look about the room; I look only at Raelan.

"I was so worried," he says at long last. "When I learned you'd been taken, I—" He flexes his jaw and shakes his head. "I wanted to kill them all."

Recalling the moment Raelan was handed over to them, bound in chains with his eyes covered in a blindfold, I whisper, "I know just how you felt . . ."

Slowly, I reach out from beneath my cloak, allowing my fingers to inch across the dusty couch cushion until they touch Raelan's. And his skin is as warm as the flames. He spreads his fingers, allowing me to twine mine through them.

"I don't ever want to be parted from you," I say into the darkness. I'm not quite brave enough to look upon Raelan's face as I speak; instead, I stare down at our fingers—his light bronze, mine a soft brown. "Please don't push me away anymore. I don't . . . I don't think I can go through that again."

Raelan turns our hands over, his thumb tracing my palm delicately. A shiver dances down my spine, and a light layer of frost forms on my skin, but it melts immediately beneath Raelan's warm touch. "I thought I was doing the right thing," he says. "For both of us."

I finally look up at him. His brows are drawn low over his eyes, his lips pulled into a slight frown. A tremble returns to my hands as I reach out to touch his face. His eyes lift to mine as my fingers trace his jaw.

"And now?" I whisper.

His gold-flecked eyes search mine, trail across my face, my lips. They leave heat in their wake. "Now . . ." His jaw flexes beneath my fingers. He lets out a short sigh. "I'm tired, Alina. I don't think I can fight it anymore, even if I should." His gaze burns.

The emotion in his eyes reaches right into my chest, filling my heart until I feel it might burst.

"Then don't." I start to lean toward him, but he goes rigid.

"I don't have my chain," he says, starting to pull away. "I . . . I won't be able to control myself."

Despite his effort to keep space between us, I scoot closer, pressing my thigh to his on the couch. "I trust you. And I want you. All of you."

He turns his face away, the muscles in his neck and jaw straining. "Alina, I—"

A sudden realization burns through me like a star shooting across the summer sky. I don't question it, don't try to hold it in. Instead, I allow it to fill me with a truth I know deep in my bones, in my blood.

I open my mouth and whisper, "I want you to claim me."

Now Raelan's head whips toward me. In the golden light of the fire, his pupils contract, and a few scales shimmer into existence across his neck and collarbones. But this time, there's no chain around his throat, nothing to attempt to force him into submission. There's only us, this quiet abandoned cottage, the deluge of an autumn rainstorm upon the roof.

"What?"

"I'm your fated mate." I reach for him again, finding his cheekbone, cupping his face so he can't turn away. "My magic wants you. Your magic wants me. I think we've both resisted long enough."

His breathing is turning heavy, like the very thought of it already has his heart racing in his chest. "Do you understand what this means?" He lifts his hands to mine, trying to pry them away, but I hold fast, forcing him to look me in the eye. "Once I claim you, there's no going back. We mate for life. It . . . It'll change everything."

I scoot closer. This time, Raelan doesn't attempt to move

away. "I understand." Slowly, I inch my fingers around the back of his head, pulling him toward me. He allows me to press my forehead to his. "Claim me. I want to be yours."

He squeezes his eyes shut. His body starts to shake. I lean away, catching my breath.

And when he opens his eyes again, they're those of his dragon.

CHAPTER 39
RAELAN

"CLAIM ME," ALINA WHISPERS, THE WORDS like an incantation spoken just for me. "I want to be yours."

Even if I wanted to, I couldn't resist.

I've spent months—*years*—trying to restrain myself, relying on the magic chain around my throat to control me around Alina. But it's gone now, shattered under the weight of my anger, fractured into a hundred pieces. There's nothing to hold me back.

A storm of thoughts rampages through my head: My mother and sisters. The king. My place in the guard. Every heated moment I've had with Alina. The nights I've lain awake, touching myself and wishing it were her. My dragon's anger and grief at not having claimed her yet.

Claim me. Claim me.

I can't unhear those words. She's stirred my dragon into a frenzy. It thrashes inside, hungering for her. My body shakes, heat building just beneath my skin.

My eyesight sharpens further as my pupils change. Despite the low light in the room, I can see everything clearly, as though the moon is right overhead, casting everything into brilliant clarity. My fingernails are next. They grow claws, their points so sharp I could pierce right through Alina's soft brown skin if I'm not careful.

I don't want to be careful. Yet I *must* be careful.

"Raelan," she whispers. Her breath is a kiss upon my face, a trembling thing that makes my cock leap to attention.

"Are you . . . sure?" I grate out, heat continuing to build as I try to hold my beast at bay. "If I do this, there's no going back."

The soft look on Alina's face shifts. Her blue eyes narrow, lips pressing into a firm line.

In one smooth movement, she slides into my lap, her legs on either side of my hips. The thin nightdress she's wearing—likely from when she was abducted—rides up, revealing her bare thighs. Slowly, she reaches to unclasp the cloak she's wearing, and the heavy fabric falls to the floor with a thump, revealing her bare shoulders, the slope of her throat.

"Raelan Ashvale," she says, voice taking on a hard edge. Her fingers come up to wrap around the back of my neck, cradling my head, holding me captive, forcing me to look her in the eye. "Stop resisting. Fucking claim me."

My mouth captures hers as soon as the last word leaves her lips.

I'm done. I can't do it anymore.

I'm hers. Wholly and completely.

No more running. No more fighting.

I submit to her.

Now my hands are on her thighs, her hips, exploring the feel of her body through the satiny texture of the thin nightdress clinging to her skin. When my cock jumps, yearning to be buried inside her, I tighten my grip about her hips and grind her into my lap, feeling her heat through the baggy borrowed trousers I found upstairs. Her response is a breathy moan.

More of my dragon bleeds through. Its hunger twirls through me, and my gums ache as my canines shift into fangs. Alina breaks our kiss and sits back.

I growl, displeased to have been parted from her.

But she doesn't care. With one hand, she reaches for my mouth, and her thumb glides along my upper lip, pulling it back to reveal my fangs.

"How does it work?" she asks. "The claiming."

Again, my cock jumps. She must feel it between her legs, for she lets out another small breath, color dancing in her cheeks.

"I'll bite you," I say. My voice is gravelly, strained. "And then I'll fuck you." I push my hips up into hers, and she gasps. "And then you'll be mine. And I'll be yours."

Her smooth sandy-brown throat bobs as she swallows. A heavy scent curls through the air: desire mixed with fear—*her* fear. The smell is intoxicating. My dragon writhes.

"Are you sure about this?" I whisper, though my dragon rages at the implication that she might say no.

Alina regards me for a long moment—such a long moment that I think she's changed her mind. But then she leans forward, lips a hairsbreadth from mine, and whispers, "I'm sure. Make me yours."

Her words send me to my feet, my hands wrapping around her ass. Then I'm turning us over, pressing her back into the couch cushion. I loom over her, gazing down at the pink in her cheeks, the soft blue hair tangled in a halo around her head.

She's so gorgeous, it makes me ache.

I want her. I need her. I *must* have her.

I peel off my tunic and drop it to the floor beside the couch. Then I stand, and she watches me with wide blue eyes as I pull the trousers from my hips.

My cock stands at attention, hard and throbbing. Her lips part, reminding me of the night in the greenhouse, the feel of her mouth wrapped around my shaft. It makes more scales form across my bare skin.

Then I'm crawling back onto the couch, taking her wrists in one hand and pinning them above her head. Immediately, her breathing accelerates, her chest rising and falling with heavy breaths. Her nipples harden, poking through the thin fabric of her nightdress, tempting me to take them into my mouth the way I've dreamed of doing.

With my other hand, I drag a single razor-sharp claw through the material of her dress, and it splits without a whisper of resistance, parting like water. Alina gasps as the nightdress falls away, revealing her naked body beneath mine.

Her small breasts tremble as she shakes, her muscles tense and coiled with anticipation. The firelight illuminates the contours of her ribs, her stomach, her hips. And finally, I get to see what stays hidden between her legs—a small mound of sky-blue hair, glistening lips hidden right beneath.

A growl rumbles in my chest. My mouth waters.

"You must stay still," I bite out.

I shift on the couch so I'm kneeling between her thighs, my hips holding her legs open. The head of my cock throbs, begging to be buried inside her, and my heart thunders so hard in my chest that it makes me drag heavy breaths into my lungs, like I'm sprinting uphill in my full metal armor.

I hold her stare. "Are you ready?"

Alina bites her lower lip. Her eyes and scent betray her fear. But still, she nods. "I'm ready."

My lips peel back over my fangs. I take her chin with my free hand, turning her face to one side. The firelight dances over her skin. Leaning forward, I trace my nose along her neck, drinking in her scent. It makes my head spin, makes me feel like I'm flying through a storm.

I tighten my other hand around her wrists, pinning her body with mine.

"Don't move," I remind her again.

"I won't," she whispers.

And then I sink my fangs into her perfect throat.

They slip through her skin, sharp points finding her veins, running hot with Ravenscroft blood. Her breath hitches with a caught breath. I expect her to scream, to cry.

But she doesn't. Even as my magic mingles with hers, my claiming bite sending heat and power flooding through her, she does little more than whimper and moan, body trembling more fiercely beneath mine.

And my dragon rejoices. It sends more glittering black scales across my arms and chest, my senses heightening further as Alina's blood absorbs the magic I'm pumping into her.

Then something else happens. Something I never expected, never thought possible.

My beast *stops fighting me.*

For the first time since boyhood, I feel it breathe a heavy sigh, then settle as if it can finally, after all these years, find the rest it so badly needs.

I was young when my father left, barely old enough to understand the weight of power I carried in my veins, the great and terrible things I'd one day be able to do. He never had a chance to teach me about the bond, left it to me to scour libraries and old scrolls in an effort to understand.

Now I realize I didn't need those books at all. My instincts were all I needed to rely upon. I *know* what I need to do. I've known all along what I need to do. And the relief at finally having done it, at having claimed the woman who was always meant to be mine, calms me in a way I've never experienced.

She is the only thing I truly needed. I've needed her all along. To calm me. To control me. To own me.

My beast has found its match. And like a contented cat, it's happy to lie down at her feet, to cease its writhing and snarling and fighting and instead seek the comfort of her flames.

Because of her, I'm free.

Still holding her wrists in one hand, I reach down with the other, trailing my fingers across her skin and along her body until I find the spot between her legs.

And like last time we touched each other, she's soaking wet, ready to take me.

But she's never had a man inside her before, hasn't ever taken a cock. And I need to be careful with her, gentle.

I peel my fangs from Alina's throat. Her brow furrows in pain as my canines slip from her skin. Then I drag my tongue across the wounds, lapping the blood from her skin, where the wounds will soon heal over, leaving a fresh pink scar—my claiming mark—on the side of her neck for everyone to see.

Slowly, I release her wrists from my grasp, and she turns her head to regard me. Her eyes are narrowed, lips parted, her knees still resting on either side of my hips.

I see her as if for the first time, through eyes not fogged with my dragon's needs and demands and relentless, *exhausting* fighting.

My partner. My mate. Alina Ravenscroft.

She reaches up to touch the wound on her throat, wincing as her fingers glide across it.

Now there's only one thing left to do.

I'll bite you. And then I'll fuck you.

Alina bites her lip as her gaze slides down the length of my body, to my cock positioned right at her entrance. I wait until she meets my eyes. Her hands come up to wrap around my neck, and she spreads her legs wider, draping one over the back of the couch.

"Fuck me," she whispers, fingertips tickling the nape of my neck. She's still breathing hard, words just a whisper beneath the sound of the rain and the fire crackling in the hearth. "Please."

She doesn't have to beg. I'll give her anything she wants.

Being careful with her, I shift my hips forward, and a groan leaves my lips as soon as the head of my cock finds the wetness pooled between her legs. There's a bit of resistance, and she bites her lip harder, closing her eyes.

With one hand, I reach beneath her hips, lifting them slightly. Immediately, the change of angle makes her pussy open up to me, and I sink slowly inside her.

She gasps.

Fuck. I've wanted this for *so* long.

As I slide out of her and then push myself back in, her fingers tighten around the back of my neck, her body going taut.

"Breathe," I tell her. "Relax."

She nods once, blue eyes wide.

Leaning down, I begin pressing kisses along her jaw, her throat, her collarbones. I want this to feel good for her. I want her first time to be something she looks back on with joy, for it to become a memory she holds on to fondly. And as I brush my lips across her skin, she softens and relaxes, and her pussy gets wetter around me.

Like she's finally ready to truly be fucked.

CHAPTER 40
ALINA

I'VE NEVER FELT SO FULL.

Back in the greenhouse on the night of Samhain, when Raelan slipped his hand into my panties and pressed his finger inside me, I thought I couldn't stretch any farther. But now he's on top of me on the couch, in this firelit little cottage, and his cock has me filled to the point of breathlessness.

At first, I tensed up, but as his lips skate across my skin, his breath caressing me as he breathes, I soften to him, and the pain that first blossomed as he pushed into me begins to dim.

And soon, it's gone altogether.

Raelan pulls out, then sinks back in slowly. His mouth finds my breast, and his tongue works its own kind of magic, rolling along my nipple, teasing it and flicking it as his cock still moves in slow delicious thrusts.

As my nervousness fades away, the hunger inside me builds.

I've wanted this man for so long, have dreamt of him kneeling between my knees. And finally, I have him right where I want him. Finally, he's mine.

"More," I whisper.

This draws his gaze up, and he ceases heaping attention upon my breasts for long enough to say, "Are you sure?"

A breathy laugh slips out of me. "Why do you keep asking me that?"

His eyes soften. "Because you're precious to me. The last thing I want is to hurt you."

I choose not to tell him how excruciating his claiming bite was, how my body burned as if I were facing trial by fire, how at one point I thought I'd never be free of the torment of his magic searing my veins. Instead, I say, "I'm not as breakable as you think."

His lips pull back into a fang-filled smile, his eyes still slitted and flecked with gold. His arms and chest glimmer with partially shifted black scales, and his fingernails have transformed into long sharp claws.

Slowly, he sits up, leaving his dick buried inside me. Then, with what looks like some effort, he banishes the long talons. When his hands are human once again, he presses the pad of his thumb against my clit, making me jump.

"I never said you were breakable," he whispers as his thumb works circles against me. At the same time, he presses his hips into mine, fucking me slowly, tenderly. "I said you're precious. That's different." His thumb dips down, to where he's buried inside me, and he drags my wetness back up my slit, making me shiver. "If anything," he continues, the words rumbling low in his chest, "you're the one who can break me."

I can't bring myself to respond. I'm too lost in the pleasure of his touch, the heat and trembling building in my low belly and between my legs. My hands slip down Raelan's body, over his glossy scales. Beneath my touch, his muscles are firm, and they flex with each thrust of his cock into my pussy. The couch cushions dip beneath us, cradling us, absorbing each movement as Raelan grits his teeth and fucks me faster.

My body accepts him, draws him in. His balls slap against me, and the sound makes me moan. I want more of him, all of him. I want him to take me and claim me in every way he can.

"I'm almost there," I whisper, closing my eyes.

His groan is a rumble in the firelit darkness. Then his mouth is on mine. His kiss burns like flame, and the mark on my throat, where his fangs pierced my skin only minutes ago, flares with heat. I thread my fingers around his neck, as if I can hold him here, keep him with me forever.

We're bonded now, I realize. *Forever.*

My breath catches. Raelan presses his forehead to mine.

His thumb massages my swollen clit as his cock works inside me.

"Raelan," I whisper.

And he sends me into a deliciously warm spiraling bliss. My magic causes snowflakes to fall around us, and they melt as soon as they make contact with our naked bodies. I throb and clench around him, tipping my head back on the couch cushion, exposing my throat. He presses kisses along my flesh, still working me through my orgasm. His tongue darts out to drag along my heated skin.

Inside me, he gets harder, *bigger*.

My pussy feels stretched to its fullest. I cry out as he pumps in and out of me.

At the last moment, he pulls out and releases his cum across my belly, spilling everything he has onto my still-trembling body. His hand goes to his cock, stroking it, working it until his body ceases spasming. We both gasp for breath, and when his eyes meet mine, a lazy smile curls across his lips.

He's so damn beautiful, it almost hurts to look at him.

But he's mine now. *Mine.*

Forever.

I pull him back down, pressing my mouth to his, though with less fervor this time, my body fully spent after the pain and pleasure he gave me.

And I feel something then, a twirl of emotion through my brain, one that feels like mine yet is not. I stop kissing Raelan, caught off-guard.

"What is it?" he asks. He braces himself on his forearms, hovering over me. His scales are disappearing slowly, leaving bronze skin in their wake.

"I feel . . ." I blink at him, and he cants his head slightly. "I think I feel . . . *you*. Your emotions."

He softens, lifting one hand to push a sweaty strand of hair off my cheek. "It's the bond. I can feel yours as well."

Catching his hand, I flip it over and press a kiss to his palm, then his wrist. His pulse beats against my lips. And in a moment of abandon, I whisper, "So, you know how I feel . . . about you?"

My eyes flick up to his cautiously. The lazy smile is gone from his mouth. He regards me seriously, though with a tenderness I've never seen on his face before. Our bond thrums with pleasure.

This will take some getting used to.

Raelan leans down, his chest pressing to mine, and kisses my forehead softly. As he pulls away, he whispers, "I do. And I love you too, Alina Ravenscroft." His eyes glitter with gold flecks. "More than all the stars in the sky. More than the feeling of wind over my wings." He traces my face with his thumb, brushing my cheekbone, my jaw, the dip at the top of my upper lip. "More than you may ever know."

And in that moment, with him atop me and the fire burning in the hearth, I feel more *whole* than I ever have.

Between one breath and the next, I wrap my hands about the back of Raelan's strong neck, and I pull him in again, feeling his heat curl through the bond as I wrap my legs around him, intent on never letting go.

CHAPTER 41
RAELAN

WE STAY THE NIGHT AT THE LITTLE COTtage, curled up together on the couch as the fire burns low and the rain becomes a gentle patter on the roof. Somewhere in the cottage, I can hear a slow drip, rainwater leaking through in some weak point.

When we awaken the next morning and realize Alina's nightdress is shredded and unwearable, I wrap my hand around hers and lead her upstairs, to the small room with a closet full of old abandoned clothes.

"What is this place, anyway?" Alina asks me, her pale eyes scanning the dusty bedroom.

I flick through the clothing in the closet, pulling a tunic free that I *think* won't completely swallow her. "I'm not sure. I found it years ago when I was flying. I come here every so often, and it's never any different. I might be the only one who knows about it. Well . . . and now you do too."

I like that idea—sharing a secret with Alina, having something all to ourselves.

Alina goes to the window and pushes the drapes aside. Beams of sunlight streak through the dirty glass, illuminating the particles of dust swirling through the air. "I think it's nice." Her lips pull up on one side. "If it's abandoned, maybe we could . . ."

I pause my search through the wardrobe and regard her. "We could what?"

Pink colors her cheeks, and she shrugs, drawing the cloak she's wearing tighter. "I don't know . . . Make it ours?"

A curl of nervousness goes through me, but it's not mine.

It's hers. The bond allows me to feel everything she does, like we can speak a language all our own.

After pulling the smallest pair of trousers I can find from the drawer of the wardrobe, I walk over to join her beside the window. The sun warms the side of my face as I turn to her.

"Maybe it's silly," Alina says.

Another burst of nervousness, this time tinged with embarrassment.

"No," I say. "Not silly at all." I cast my gaze around the small room, covered in dust and left here to fall into the earth, forgotten and alone. I imagine Alina with a mop and bucket, her hair pulled back, sunbeams dancing through the room as she sweeps and scrubs, Yuki padding around at her feet. And the image makes my chest warm.

It's so simple, so . . . mundane. And yet it's even more beautiful for it.

"You don't think so?" Alina asks, her voice lilting with a twinge of excitement. "I mean, I'll be at Coven Crest for the next three years, and I imagine the castle will always be at least partially my home, especially if Grandfather allows me to join the Shadowfall Court, but . . ." Her lips pull up into a shy smile. "Maybe we could have a place too. A place of our own."

I lift a hand to cup her warm cheek, then tip her head back so the sunlight hits her eyes, turning them a shade of icy blue. "I'd like that."

I lean forward and take her lips in mine, and she sighs against me. Pulling away, I wrap my arms around Alina, cradling her to my chest. As her arms come around me, I feel a peace that has only ever been a fantasy.

My dragon doesn't writhe. It doesn't roar or fight or rage, trying to break my bones. It curls comfortably inside me, eased by our new mate connection, completely at peace.

Alina has no idea how much comfort she's brought to me.

Tightening my arms around her, I press a kiss to her head and whisper, "I'd like that a lot."

IT'S A CRISP AUTUMN MORNING, BUT THE SUN IS SHIN-ing, and it slowly disperses the raindrops that still cling to the fallen leaves and dark green pine needles. Alina and I stand in the clearing in front of the cottage. She's wearing the tunic and trousers I found for her, and though she had to cinch the waistband of the pants with a roll of twine I found in one of the kitchen drawers, she seems completely at ease.

"All right," she says, wiggling her fingers at me. "Hand them over."

With a snort and a small chuckle, I strip out of my clothes. Alina's cheeks go a slightly brighter shade of pink as I stand naked before her, and I flash her a smile as I hand her my clothing. "You all right? You look a bit red."

Snatching my clothes and shoving them into a bag she found in the bedroom, she says, "I'm perfectly fine."

"Mm-hmm." I stretch my arms, feeling the cool breeze on my exposed skin. "Step back."

With a nod, she takes a few steps away from me, ensuring I have plenty of space to shift.

I take a deep breath of the autumn air, and then I call on my dragon. It greets me pleasantly, with no rush of anger or prisoned desire. And this time, the transition is smooth, gentle—not the violent twisting and writhing I usually experience.

Alina's awe trickles through our bond as she watches me. And when I open my dragon eyes and peer down at her, she's smiling.

No fear. Just joy.

My mate.

I'm glad I didn't know before what I was missing out on. Now that I know this feeling of connection, of absolute peace, I'm certain there's no way I could ever go back.

We have mate bonds for a *reason*. And mine certainly got it right with Alina.

I lower one of my glittering black wings, and though a twirl of nervousness goes through our bond, Alina doesn't hesitate to step onto my outstretched limb and allow me to lift her onto my back.

She settles into the space between my wing joints and the base of my spine. Her weight is nothing atop me, as light as a summer breeze or a downy feather, and yet it is comforting all the same.

"Okay," she says, her fingers wrapping around my scales. "I'm ready."

Excitement churns through me, and if her small breath is any indication, she feels it too.

I stretch my wings out wide, very nearly filling the clearing, and with one mighty downstroke, I lift into the air, then above the trees, then into the sky.

Then we're soaring through the clouds, heading back toward Ravenscroft Castle, and I feel absolute, unwavering freedom.

And I know Alina is the one who gifted it to me.

CHAPTER 42
ALINA

WHEN RAELAN LANDS IN THE CASTLE'S sprawling courtyard, shaking the earth and sending the gardens thrashing, everyone goes running, screams piercing the autumn air. They don't seem to even notice me upon his back.

Knights stream into the courtyard moments later, weapons drawn. But as soon as Sir Larsen appears atop the stairs leading into the castle, he yells out, "Weapons down! That's the princess, you fools!"

The knights lower their swords and crossbows as I glide gracefully to the ground on Raelan's wing. My knees are trembling, like they did last night when I climbed down from his back, but this time, I don't fall. Raelan's pride curls through me, and I look back at him—at his glossy black scales and slitted black-gold eyes—and smile.

"Calm yourselves!" Sir Larsen yells to the people still

rushing to escape. "It's fine." His eyes flick back to Raelan. "He's one of ours."

I meet Sir Larsen's eyes from across the courtyard, and he gives me a small nod.

"All right." I turn back to Raelan, then reach into the bag I packed and pull out his clothes. "You'd better hurry up, before they all come back."

Raelan lets out a heavy sigh, and smoke curls from his fluttering nostrils. The knights who flooded into the court-yard take a few steps back. I just stand there, holding up Raelan's tunic and trousers, as he lets out a growl and begins the transformation into his human body. A few moments later, he pushes to his feet, naked in the autumn sunlight.

My eyes scan his toned chest, strong abs, narrow hips . . .

I bite my lip as my gaze sweeps lower, and my cheeks go warm as I remember what we did on the couch last night. I wonder if Raelan feels it through our bond, for a sideways smile pulls on his mouth as he steps forward to accept the clothes I'm holding out for him.

"Don't taunt me," he whispers, voice low and edged in humor.

"I'd never."

Just as Raelan is pulling the tunic on over his head, boots and graves sound behind us, and I turn to find Sir Larsen, Grandfather, and—

"Alina!"

My mother pushes past Grandfather and Sir Larsen, and her arms are around me a breath later. She strokes a hand down my hair and pins me against her chest as if she'll never let me out of her sight again.

"I'm okay," I whisper, wrapping my arms around her and holding her tight. "I promise."

When she finally pulls back from me, her eyes go immediately to the fresh scar along the side of my throat. Her blue eyes widen, brow creasing. She glances at Raelan, then back at me. "Is that . . . ?"

Heat creeps into my cheeks, and I give her a small nod.

Grandfather joins us, and his arms loop around me, crushing me into a hug. He smells of woodsmoke and chamomile tea, like his study and old books. He smells like home. "I told Rowena you were fine," he says, a jovial tone to his voice as I give him a loving squeeze, "but you know how mothers are."

"Oh, hush." Mother shakes her head, hands planted on her hips. "You were no better." Her eyes flash to mine. "He very nearly wore a hole through the floor what with all his pacing. And your father is on his way home now. He'll be so relieved to see you."

"Father's coming?" My chest warms. It's been months since I last saw him; between me leaving for Coven Crest and him being away on political business, we seem always to miss each other.

"Of course he is. We sent word to him as soon as we learned you . . . you'd been . . ." Mother's eyes mist over with tears, and her bottom lip trembles. "I'm just so glad you're safe."

I give them a small smile, then step back. Grandfather and Sir Larsen seem to notice the scar on my neck at the same time.

My claiming mark. Raelan's claiming mark.

A burst of nervousness goes through me, but I'm not sure if it's mine or Raelan's. I turn to look at him over my shoulder. His muscles look tight with apprehension. I reach out a hand. It hangs there in the space between us, beckoning him forward, into the circle of people who care for me, who love me.

He belongs here too. Right beside me.

Finally, muscles in his jaw flexing, Raelan puts his hand in mine. I guide him to my side, holding his hand firmly.

"Mother, Grandfather . . ." I look into Raelan's eyes, which are still flecked with gold, then turn to face them. "I . . ." I reach up with my free hand and push my hair fully away from my neck, ensuring the scar is clearly visible in the morning light. "I'm his now." My gaze flicks to Raelan's. "And he's mine."

A moment of tense silence passes between us. Mother and Sir Larsen both cast sideways glances at my grandfather.

But Grandfather is looking at me and Raelan. His blue eyes are soft, and as each second passes, his lips pull up a little more in one corner.

"I figured," he says. Then he holds up his hands. "But please, spare your grandfather the details, hmm?"

Immediately, my mouth stretches into a wide grin.

I should've known he would understand. Of all the kings who've ruled these lands, I think he must have the biggest and most compassionate heart.

Grandfather reaches out a hand for Raelan. Slowly, Raelan's fingers slip from mine, and he steps forward to give Grandfather's hand a firm shake.

"Your Majesty," he says.

"Sir Ashvale." Grandfather pumps his hand once, twice. Then a mischievous glint comes over his eyes. "Tell me, did you ever think you'd be king one day?"

Behind my grandfather, Sir Larsen crosses his arms and shakes his head. Mother hides her smile behind a hand.

But Raelan's face goes completely white, all the blood draining from his cheeks.

"K-king, Your Majesty?"

Grandfather reaches for me, and he pulls us both in, crushing us in a warm bear hug. "Well, what do you think happens when you marry the princess, son?"

"*Marry?*"

A wave of dizziness comes through the bond. Raelan looks more out-of-sorts than I've ever seen him, like he just took one too many falls from his horse.

"Well, you do intend to marry her, don't you?" Grandfather continues, one of his bushy brows arching up sharply.

Now Raelan looks down at me, his mouth frozen open in surprise.

"Don't let him bully you," Mother says, loosening Grandfather's hold on us and starting to pull him away. "There's plenty of time for *that* in the future." She gives me a look, her lips lifting into a smile. "Now come on, both of you. You're a mess. And Headmistress Moonhart will be waiting to hear from us. Not to mention Yuki and your roommates, Alina. They're all worried sick."

Warmth tingles through my veins as Mother and Grandfather start back toward the castle. Sir Larsen waves an armored arm for us to follow.

And right there in front of everyone, in front of all the knights and the people who've slowly trickled back into the courtyard, I push onto my toes and press a kiss to Raelan's mouth. He softens against me, and his chest relaxes with a sigh.

"King Raelan, hmm?" I whisper, then delight in the fear that flashes in his eyes.

"Please, I couldn't."

Taking his hand, I tug him after my family, pausing only to say, "I think your sisters would quite enjoy living here. Don't you?"

CHAPTER 43
RAELAN

NOW FALLS LAZILY FROM THE WHITE-GRAY sky, the flakes fat and silent as they drift to blanket the crinkly brown grass in the castle courtyard. I stand atop the steps, collar turned up against the chill breeze, my gaze trained on the winding road leading from the castle courtyard and through the barbican, upon which knights in full regalia stand, monitoring the movement below.

The grounds have been bustling all day, mostly with merchants coming in from Wysteria to serve their food and drink at tonight's Yule ball. Layla Waverly, Poppy's mother and the owner of the Wandering Cup, arrived just an hour ago, her tiny cart weighed down with pastries and scones and buns in every flavor imaginable. And I *almost* convinced her to part with one before the pages and squires rushed out to help her carry everything into the castle, where I'm certain they're now setting up in the ballroom. If only I'd had another thirty seconds, I would've been successful. My mouth waters at the very thought of a chocolate-strawberry croissant.

I nod to three fellow knights as they pass by. Their gazes linger on me, heavy with curiosity, their conversation halting as they march past the stairs, patrolling the grounds.

Ever since I landed in the courtyard and Alina took my hand in hers, proudly displaying her claiming mark to the world, nothing has been the same.

But I wouldn't change one moment of it. Not for anything.

The others can stare and whisper all they want. In the end, I got my mate.

My princess.

My future queen.

There's movement in the distance, a wagon trundling beneath the barbican and into the snow-frosted courtyard. And with my sharp vision, I can tell immediately that my mother and sisters are the bundled-up forms sitting in the back.

Excitement tap-dances through my stomach, and I can't stop the smile that spreads across my lips as I descend the snowy steps to wait for them.

"Raelan!" Gilda yells, standing in the wagon and then having to whirl her arms to find her balance as it jostles beneath her. Clarice grabs hold of her cloak and tugs her down. But that doesn't dim Gilda's smile. "Raelan, hi!" she calls again.

My smile grows as the wagon pulls to a creaking stop at the base of the stairs.

Gilda and Clarice scramble down first, and they crush me in their small arms.

"I can't believe it!" Gilda says, pulling away from me to stare up at the castle with wide brown eyes. "You actually get to *live* here now?"

My first instinct is to reach down and muss her hair, but it's done up so nicely for the ball that I opt to stay my hand. "Well, no. When not at the academy, I still live in the barracks, with the rest of the guard. But . . ." I turn my gaze up to the castle, with its soaring towers and billowing flags. "I get to spend more time here than most."

"*And* you get to attend the ball!" Gilda says. She holds her hands to her mouth and shuffles her boots in the snow like she wants to explode with excitement. "And now we do too!"

Clarice rolls her eyes, but it's in good nature. "Don't get us kicked out, Gild. Act like we belong here."

"We do belong here." Gilda sounds certain. "Our brother is going to be the prince." She gasps, eyes sparkling. "Will that make *us* princesses?"

My stomach pinches.

If that happens, it's a long way off. Hopefully I'll have some time to come to terms with what that might *actually* mean for me.

Before claiming Alina, all I could think about was having her—I didn't even consider what might happen *after* the claiming, what it might mean to be bonded to the princess of our kingdom. I would've wanted her regardless of her station.

My dragon's urges did a pretty great job of clouding my mind. Thankfully, it's receded into peaceful contentment now.

Mama reaches into her cloak to pull out an eldertoken for the driver, but I swiftly step forward and press a coin into his palm.

"Thank you, sir. Yuletide blessings."

He tips his cap to me.

Mama looks like she wants to argue—she's got her pride, after all—but I soften her with a smile while reaching up to help her down from the wagon. Her hand slips into mine, and I grasp her fingers as she climbs down. As soon as her boots hit the snow, she tips her head back, regarding the soaring towers and turrets of Ravenscroft Castle with something like awe in her eyes.

Her long dark hair is pulled half up, and it falls around her face and shoulders like an inky shroud against the soft white snow. She's even wearing a necklace and earrings—something I haven't seen her do since the day I was sworn in as a knight, kneeling in the throne room at King Jorvick's feet.

"You look beautiful, Mama," I say softly, my breath puffing out around my mouth in a gray cloud.

She flicks her gaze to me, lips curling into a pleasant smile. Then her focus goes to my neck, and she reaches up to pull my collar aside, her fingertips finding the scars that wrap around my throat.

"Your chain . . . ?" A mixture of curiosity and concern dances across her face.

"Don't need it anymore." I reach up and wrap her fingers in mine, then press a kiss to her knuckles. "Alina changed everything, Mama. I'm free."

Her one good eye goes a bit misty, and she pulls me in for a hug. "I'm so proud of you, Raelan. And so happy for you *both*."

"Will we get to see the princess?" Clarice asks, finally turning away from staring at the castle. Her hazel eyes—light like my father's—are made more vivid by the snow, and her long dark brown hair catches in the chill breeze.

She's growing up so fast, I realize. *Both* my sisters are. Soon I'll have to worry about boys chasing them around. The very thought makes me slightly nauseated.

"Can we, please?" Gilda adds.

I pull away from Mama and once again have to resist the urge to tousle Gilda's hair. "You will. She's looking forward to seeing you. She would've been here to greet you, but she had to get ready for the ball. So, in the meantime . . ." I give them all a smile. "How about we get some pastries and cocoa? I might be able to sneak a few."

Gilda's face brightens into a grin, but Clarice says, "You won't get us kicked out, will you, Rae?"

"I'll try not to," I say, tucking Mama's hand into the crook of my arm and starting up the castle stairs. Then I toss a mischievous look back at my sisters. "But no promises."

CHAPTER 44
ALINA

HERE. TAKE A LOOK, YOUR HIGHNESS."

Ms. Fairhaven lowers her fluffy makeup brush and takes a step back, allowing me my first glimpse into the vanity mirror.

I catch my breath.

Ms. Fairhaven has been doing my hair and makeup for these events for years. Typically, we opt for soft, subtle colors: a bit of rouge on the cheeks, a subtle gloss on the lips. But tonight, she's turned me into a masterpiece of blues and grays and twinkling silvers. My eyelids are painted in shades of charcoal and smoke, my lashes bold and dark. My cheeks are tinted pink, and my lips are a glossy crimson.

She's pulled my hair back into a half-up, half-down style, and I tingle with anticipation as I turn my head slightly to admire the claiming mark adorning the side of my throat. Ms. Fairhaven didn't try to hide it. She knows how much this mark—my bond—means to me.

Behind me, Yuki jumps off the bed and pads across the floor on quiet paws. He takes a seat at my feet and tips his head. "You look . . ." He tips his head the other way, gaze considering. "Like a woman."

I can't help but to let out a sudden laugh. "Ugh, why do you have to say it like that?" Reaching down, I trail a hand over his head, then scratch him gently behind one ear. "But thank you." My gaze flicks to Ms. Fairhaven, and I reach out to place a hand on her arm. "And thank you too." I take a deep breath and glance into the mirror. "You really think this is okay? It'll certainly make a statement."

My lady-in-waiting finishes putting her brushes and palettes away, then turns to regard me. Her smile is soft, her cheeks pink from the warmth in my bedchamber. "I think it's lovely." Her gaze flicks to the scar on my neck. "You're not the same girl who left here. You're a woman now, Your Highness." She tips her head, her smile turning playful. "And women get to have all the fun."

"See?" Yuki says. "I told you."

With a roll of my eyes, I look at myself in the mirror once more, my fingers inching up to touch the mark on my throat. It's in the shape of Raelan's jaws, a perfect oval where his fangs pierced me. Even now, when I recall that night, the scar tingles with warmth. I wonder if he can feel it, wherever he is on the grounds right now.

I know his mother and sisters are coming today; he was so excited to see them. It's precious how much love he has for them.

"One more thing," Ms. Fairhaven says. She walks away, disappearing into my closet, then returns a moment later with a jewelry box clasped in her hands. "I've been waiting for the perfect opportunity for you to wear this. And I think tonight is the night."

She opens the jewelry box with a click, then pulls out a gleaming silver necklace. Stepping behind me, she says, "Lift your hair," then proceeds to clasp the necklace about my throat.

It's tight, a choker more than anything else, and the glittering blue and silver gemstones draw even more attention to my new scar. I lift my fingers to trace them along the metal, a surge of excitement rising inside me.

"Well?" Ms. Fairhaven regards me in the mirror. "What do you think?"

I meet my smoky-eyed gaze in the mirror and get a tremble of anticipation at the thought of Raelan seeing me like this. "It's perfect."

There's a gentle knock on the door in the sitting room, and Ms. Fairhaven goes to answer it. After a short conversation, she returns to me and says, "It seems some young ladies are here to see you. Shall I—"

"Yes!" I push to my feet and hurriedly pad across my bedchamber and through the doorway into the sitting room, Yuki right behind me. I haven't seen the girls since our first semester ended, but they all accepted my invitation to the ball, and I've been waiting anxiously for them to arrive.

Grasping the door handle, I pull it open to find a maid standing there, my three roommates gathered behind her.

As soon as Lyra sees me, she announces, "Goddess, Alina! You look . . ." Her crimson eyes sweep up and down the length of my body, and she arches a brow. "Well, I was

going to say sexy, but"—she points at my hastily tied robe—
"what's that?"

I laugh and wave them in after me. "I was just about to
get dressed." They trail into the sitting room, dresses swishing about their legs, and I call back to the maid, "Could we
please have some tea? And some cakes if the kitchen can
spare them?"

The young woman curtsies, then gives me a smile. "Of
course, Your Highness."

I quickly introduce my roommates to Ms. Fairhaven,
who then waves for me to return to my bedchamber.

"Time to get dressed," she says, and I swear there's a
twinkle in her eye as she leads me into the room and closes
the door behind me.

WHEN I STEP BACK INTO THE SITTING ROOM TWENTY
minutes later, I find Lyra, Maeve, and Poppy sipping tea
from hand-painted teacups and trying not to get crumbs
on their beautiful Yule dresses. I have a shawl draped over
my shoulders and hold it tight over my dress. Their eyes all
turn to me.

"Ready to see it?" I ask, a twinge of nervousness going
through me. From far off, somewhere on the castle grounds,
Raelan sends a hint of curiosity through our bond. Knowing he's always with me like this, always connected to me,
brings me deep comfort.

With our bond, I'm never truly alone. He's here with
me, whenever I need him.

Lyra groans. "Gods, yes. Let us see."

Maeve and Poppy stand from the couch, and they all look at me expectantly.

"Okay. Here goes."

Slipping the shawl from my shoulders, I let the light material ripple to the floor. And three pairs of eyes go wide.

The dress Ms. Fairhaven picked for the occasion is unlike anything I've worn before. It clings to me like a second skin, the material so soft I feel I could tear it simply by taking too deep a breath. But when Ms. Fairhaven was helping me into it, tugging it up over my hips, it held firm, much stronger than it appears—like perhaps its enchanted with magic. It's the color of smoky quartz, bejeweled along the plunging neckline with little shimmering crystals, and the skirt is gauzy and soft, with a slit up one side that reveals my leg and the heels my lady-in-waiting selected for me.

My roommates are momentarily speechless.

They blink. Then blink again.

Yuki lets out a soft whine.

I bite my lip and ask, "Well? Is it too much?"

Maeve's lips, which are painted dark purple to match her hair and eyes, quirk up on one side. "I mean, is your goal to *actually* kill Raelan tonight?"

"Of course not," Poppy says from beside her. She reaches up to tuck a short strand of lavender hair behind her ear. "She just means to give him a little death."

Lyra, Maeve, and I exchange surprised glances, then stare at Poppy.

Then Lyra cants her head and says, "Poppy Waverly, did you just make a *sex joke*?"

Poppy's light brown cheeks flare bright pink, and we all burst into laughter—along with Ms. Fairhaven. Yuki shakes his head like he wishes he could unhear that.

"I mean, she's not wrong," Maeve says as she dabs a tear from her kohl-lined eyed.

"I have to be there to see his reaction when he first sees you." Lyra glances at Poppy and Maeve. "I think we all do."

I cross the firelit room to stand with them, pausing along the way to pour myself a cup of dragon-fruit tea. "Well, the ball starts in"—I glance at the clock above the mantel—"about an hour. Think you can wait until then?"

"Hmm. Depends." Lyra holds up a tiny plate dotted in crumbs. "Think we can get any more of those cakes while we wait?"

My lips tug into a smile, and I roll my eyes. "Yes, dear Lyra. I think that can be arranged."

CHAPTER 45
RAELAN

THE BALLROOM TWINKLES WITH CANDLE-light cast from the chandeliers overhead, and bodies move across the dance floor, accompanied by a string orchestra. Tables hug the edges of the wide room, and food and drink are in no short supply. From across the room, I watch my mother laughing at something a man seated beside her is saying. Meanwhile, my sisters scurry across the room with a handful of other children, giggling and high on sugar and Yuletide cheer.

I could join my family—I'm not on duty tonight, after all. Rather than armor, I wear my formal regalia: fitted trousers, polished boots, and a crisp long-sleeve shirt and jacket with gleaming buttons and a sharp collar. A pin shines on my chest, a single emerald embedded in a silver housing in the shape of an eye.

His Majesty awarded it to me the week after Alina's abduction. The Emerald Eye is an honor bestowed upon those who go above and beyond in their duty to the kingdom. There was a ceremony and everything. And yet somehow, I feel I don't deserve it. Because there is no world in which I would've let anyone take Alina from me. I would've given my last scale to save her.

And I need no recognition for that—not now, not ever.

I'd have preferred not to even wear the pin tonight, but the king seemed delighted to present it to me, and I will undoubtedly speak with him tonight. And besides, there's very little I can do these days to avoid the curious eyes and stares of the court.

I used to blend in with the shadows, but they all know who I am now. The knight. The shifter. The princess's dragon. I can't say I'm quite used to it, but in time, I hope for their stares to not cause me to wish to crawl from my skin and fly until all I hear is the wind over my wings.

"Sir Ashvale," says a voice, and I turn to find Princess Rowena standing beside me. Her hair is pulled up and away from her face, and the dark blue gem nestled at the base of her throat makes her blue eyes—the very same shade as Alina's—sparkle in the flickering candlelight.

A man stands beside her. He's tall and light skinned, with the same eyes as the king.

Alina's father.

He's still mostly a stranger to me, but I have a feeling we're going to have more opportunities to get to know each other now.

"Your Highnesses." I bow my head to them both.

"What are you doing over here?" Princess Rowena asks. "You're much too young and handsome to be lurking about on your own. Don't you care to dance?" She uses her wine-glass to gesture to the couples twirling across the floor. "Or do you have two left feet, like my husband here?"

Prince Jorin smiles, and his eyeglasses glint in the candlelight as he tips his head to regard his wife. "We all have our weaknesses, dear. Remember when you tried to make Alina a cake for her third birthday?" His gaze cuts to me, blue eyes twinkling. "It was a *disaster*. Remind me to tell you all about it."

I'm starting to learn that the Ravenscrofts like to tease, and as of late, I'm usually their main target. Even His Majesty's behavior toward me has changed slightly. But I suppose that's what happens when you're suddenly included in family dinner and given invitations to parties instead of having to work them.

I'm still not used to it yet. At least my sisters are enjoying it though.

I draw myself up and smile down at Alina's mother. "I've not yet found a dance partner." I tip my head. "Unless you'd like to do me the honor? Perhaps you can tell me about that cake."

Her blue-eyed gaze flicks to something over my shoulder just as the orchestra finishes their waltz. A smile tugs on her mouth. "Hmm, I don't think so. But perhaps *she* would."

Heads turn, the chatter dims, and when I finally shift to look at what has caught everyone's attention, I find my breath suddenly trapped within my chest.

Up on the second floor, the doors to the ballroom have just opened, and Alina steps onto the balcony looking down at the room below. Her roommates file out behind her, regarding the ballroom with smiles and whispers, but my eyes never leave Alina.

She is . . . beyond radiant. She's a gem the likes of which human eyes have never beheld, something worth more than all the gold and silver the kingdoms have to offer.

She's everything.

And now she's looking right at me.

Princess Rowena lets out a low laugh and nudges me with her elbow. "Well? You'd best go get her, sir knight."

She doesn't have to tell me twice.

My feet move across the ballroom floor as though they're moving through clouds. People part around me with whispers and stares.

But it's Alina they should be staring at. She's the candle, and I'm but her shadow, completely content to go unnoticed so long as I can be near her, can bask in her heat and light.

I arrive at the foot of the stairs just as she's approaching. Her dress hugs her frame, inviting my gaze to appreciate the curve of her waist, the dip of her low back, the column of her—

Her throat.

The dress leaves her neck on full display, and the glittering necklace she wears fastened snugly about her throat only serves to draw more attention to the pink scar in the shape of my jaws.

Tonight, she wears my claiming mark like the finest jewels, an adornment she's proud to let others see.

Something stirs in my chest—it makes me want to smile *and* cry. I opt for the former.

I lift my hand to her and feel the weight of one hundred pairs of eyes as her palm slips into mine.

"Your Highness." I bow my head. "You are . . . exquisite."

I'm not so convinced that word does her justice. I'd have to scour the books in the king's study in search of a word befitting Alina Ravenscroft, though I'm not so sure it even exists.

"You look quite handsome yourself." Her eyes, brushed with a dark twinkling shadow, assess me from my head to my polished boots. Then she sees the pin on my chest and reaches to touch it with a small smile. "You wore it."

"Yes, well, I think your grandfather would nettle me otherwise."

She slips her hand into the crook of my arm, bringing her body close to mine. "He most certainly would've."

I try not to let my gaze linger on the low cut of her dress, the curve of her breasts beneath the thin fabric. But she must feel my interest through our bond, for her smile turns coy.

"Are you quite all right, Sir Ashvale? Your cheeks have taken on a sudden pink hue."

Immediately, I turn my gaze away. "Quite all right, Your Highness."

She hums as her friends come up beside her.

"This is *crazy*," Lyra says. Her red hair bursts out around her head in a halo of bouncy curls. She's wearing a green dress, and I wonder briefly if her rat is hidden in there somewhere. I wouldn't put it past her. "Are all your parties like this?"

Alina shrugs one shoulder, and the movement sends her skin shimmering, as though it's been dusted with glitter. Perhaps it has. Hopefully it's edible.

My dragon curls inside me, and I try to focus on anything besides Alina. As she speaks with her friends, I count the candles in the chandeliers and then take to tracing the patterns in the marble floor. I've only just calmed the heated racing of my heart when Alina says, "Well?"

Flicking my eyes to her, I say, "Well what?"

One of her eyebrows gets pointy in the corner. "Well, do you want to *dance with me*?"

Oh, of course. The orchestra is preparing for another waltz, and new couples are taking to the floor.

Thankfully, dance lessons *are* part of our formal training—I believe the royal family doesn't wish for us to make a mess of things if ever we find ourselves in a position like this one.

Though I never thought I'd be asked to dance with the princess.

"I'd love to," I say, then guide her toward the dance floor while her friends drift off toward one of the buffet tables.

Gilda and Clarice stand nearby, vibrating with excitement, their dresses glittering softly in the candlelight. Alina lifts a hand in a wave.

"I'm dancing with you next," she says to Gilda as we pass by.

My sister's cheeks go bright pink, and I have to strive not to chuckle at her expense.

Gazes follow us, and when we take our place amongst the other couples, I feel a shift of focus and attention, like the whole room is suddenly looking at us. And maybe they are.

But I just look at her.

Her blue eyes. The curl of her mouth. My scar hugging the side of her throat.

Radiant.

There's a swell of strings, a moment to catch my breath as Alina loops the train of her dress about her right wrist.

And then we're gliding across the floor, my hand at her low back, her steps flawless and precise. Her gown swishes and whispers as I twirl her across the marble underfoot. In my periphery, I see the stares, the unveiled curiosity in the many pairs of eyes.

Alina pays them no mind. What she does is smile.

She smiles at me like I'm the only thing she sees, like everyone else could disappear and it would not dim her joy in the slightest. I know this, because it's exactly how I feel.

She's the frost to my fire, the earth to my sky. She's my mate. And destiny got it just right.

The waltz swells and dips, demanding my focus as I lead Alina through the dance. And at the very end, as the strings fade away in a trill of vibrato, she wraps both hands around my neck, pushes onto her toes, and presses her lips to mine as if no one is watching.

And I'm certain that this moment, with her in my arms and the candlelight glittering down across us, will be engraved into my memory for as long as I live.

My first dance with her. And hopefully one of many, many to come.

EPILOGUE
ALINA

Eight Months Later

"IS THAT ALL YOU'VE GOT?" RAELAN ARCHES A dark brow at me, his lips quirked into a challenging smirk. "Really?"

Thin morning sunlight slips through the big windows in my bedchamber, though it shifts with the movement of clouds across the sky.

It's been raining for three days, and the fires have been burning nonstop, trying to chase the unseasonably cool chill away.

But I've got my own personal fire, one that never burns out.

And right now, I've got him pinned beneath me, my legs on either side of his chest, his wrists trapped in my hands. I struggle to hold him down, gritting my teeth as he pushes back against me, as though I weigh no more than a loaf of bread.

With a smirk of my own, I call my magic to my hands, shackling his wrists to the bed with ice. He blinks at me, then turns his head to regard his glimmering manacles. I sit up and cross my arms, victorious.

Seems my first year of magical studies paid off.

But then, with what appears to be very little effort, he shatters right through the ice, sending the glittering chunks skittering across my hardwood floor, where the fire in the hearth quickly turns them to water.

"Silly witch." Raelan wraps an arm around my waist and flips me onto my back. The mattress catches me in a soft embrace. "Don't you know better than to try to best a dragon?"

I sigh and roll my eyes at him. "I've got three more years at the academy. By then, I think you'll have met your match."

Raelan gives me a smile. "We'll see."

His gaze goes to my throat. Softly, he pushes my braid aside, revealing the scar that marks my skin. Even now, all these months after his claiming of me, the scar tissue still tingles whenever he touches it, as if the magic he gave me recognizes when he's near, calls out to him, yearns for him.

I wiggle an arm out from under him and trace his stubbled jaw—he'll most certainly shave before we return to Coven Crest today—then allow my fingers to drift down his throat. He has his own scars, those left behind from the magic in the chain that bound him for so many years. Since his claiming of me, he's not needed that magic once. It's as if his dragon has willingly allowed itself to be comforted, softened.

Though never tamed.

I want him to remain wild, to keep that hunger for freedom alive in his bones. Because I feel it too. And I want to be free with him.

He's my dragon, my mate. My equal in every way.

Except when it comes to chess. Then he's hopeless, and I'll best him every time.

My fingers wrap about his jaw, and I pull him close. His lips meet mine, and I tug him down atop me, wanting to feel his weight against my chest, between my thighs. I ease my legs around him, feel the slip of my satin nightdress as the fabric inches up my thighs.

His groan is a rumble in his chest. Against mine, his skin grows hot.

Then there's a sharp knock upon my door.

"Your Highness? Are you awake?"

It's Ms. Fairhaven. And I know her well enough to know that I've got about ten seconds before she opens the door.

Breaking our kiss, I shove Raelan under the covers, then pull them over his head and arrange my face into a mask of sleepiness right as Ms. Fairhaven opens the door.

When she sees me still in bed, she arches a brow at me. "Your Highness, you know you're leaving today to return to school. The carriage is already packed, yet you dawdle."

"Sorry, Ms. Fairhaven." I give her my most innocent smile. "I'll get up right away. And I'll take breakfast downstairs today. Would you please inform the kitchen staff?"

She huffs out a sigh and puts her fingers to her temple like I'm already causing her a headache. "Very well. But make haste. Even a princess should not cause others to wait!" she calls over her shoulder as she leaves my room, closing the door behind her.

I can just barely hear her footsteps as they cross my sitting room, then the click of the door as she leaves my chambers. And as soon as she's gone, I feel the tickle of fingertips along the inside of my leg, creeping from my knee up.

Then kisses follow. My breath hitches in my chest.

Raelan's mouth trails up my thigh, each kiss lingering longer than the last. And when he presses a kiss to my clit through my thin panties, I gasp, clutching the comforter in my grasp.

"R-Raelan," I whisper. "You know we have to go. We don't have time."

"I can be quick," he mumbles, sending pleasant vibrations through me, causing me to open my lips with a silent moan. "I promise."

Then one of his sharp claws slices right through my panties, and I've only a moment to catch my breath before he's spreading my thighs and burying his head between my legs. He laps at my slit, licking me like I'm sweetened ice at a summer festival. And when he pushes his tongue inside me, I let out such a loud gasp that I'm certain anyone walking by in the hallway outside would be able to hear it.

"Shh, princess," Raelan whispers after pulling his tongue from me, his words muffled by the comforters still tossed over his head. "You know I'm not supposed to be here. You're being very bad, allowing a man into your bed like this . . ."

I don't have a chance to respond, because then his lips are around my clit, and one of his fingers is sliding inside me. His tongue works magic. He alternates between sucking and flicking and licking, to the point where I'm trembling, speechless, unable to think of anything but cumming for him.

My body goes rigid, my pleasure about to peak. In one movement, Raelan is on top of me, tossing the comforter aside, his length sliding inside me. Once he's buried in my warmth, his cock grows bigger—his dragon slipping through. I groan at the stretch of my pussy, and his lips lift into a lazy smile. No matter how many times he fucks me, it still feels like the first time, like that autumn evening on the couch while rain battered the cottage roof.

Raelan lowers himself onto his forearms and begins pressing kisses to my claiming mark, making the skin tingle. I'm still on the edge from his ravishment of my clit, ready to tumble into bliss only he can give me. So it only takes a few thrusts of his hips, with Raelan's weight grinding against my clit, and I'm grasping the bedsheet, crying out with a moan he muffles with his mouth.

I taste myself on his lips, feel his desire in every thrust as I throb around him, soaking us both. And just when I know he's nearing his peak, I break our kiss and lock my ankles around his low back, trapping him inside me. He pulls back, a concerned wrinkle in his brow.

"Alina, what are you—"

"It's okay," I whisper, flicking my gaze to a purple potion bottle sitting on my bedside table. One of Grandfather's witches made it for me, a tonic to ensure I don't get pregnant—at least until I decide to. But it's our little secret. For now, everyone else thinks it's for stress headaches brought on by my studies at the academy.

"Are you sure?" Raelan whispers. His pupils are slits, gold flecks starting to appear in his eyes. His shoulders are already glimmering with black scales.

With a nod, I capture his mouth once more, then tighten my ankles around his low back, driving him into me.

One of his hands fists in my hair, the other crushing the sheet in a white-knuckled grasp. He pounds himself into me, making the sturdy bed frame groan beneath us. And when his body goes rigid and his breath catches, I tighten my pussy around him.

And for the first time, he spills his pleasure inside me, filling me with heat as I smother his moans with my mouth. His body shakes, his chest heaving with every breath.

Our bond burns, licking my insides with fire. It makes my veins twirl with delight, with a hunger fully and completely satisfied.

I unlock my ankles from around Raelan's back, then pull him down onto the pillow beside me. Slowly, his pupils return to normal, though the gold flecks remain—those are always the slowest to leave.

The light in the room shifts, illuminating the scars around his throat. With the most delicate touch I can muster, I lean in and press my lips to his skin, to every spot where once he burned.

Beneath my lips, his pulse flutters, and he lets out a contented sigh.

"Raelan?" I whisper.

"Hmm?"

I press myself to him, threading my arms around his chest and nestling my head beneath his chin. Our bond flares with heat again as I whisper, "I'm glad I'm yours. I don't want to be anyone else's."

His arms come around me, holding me so firm I know he'll never, ever let go. There's a long moment of silence—so long, in fact, that I wonder if he just fell back asleep. Then, atop my head, his whisper a brush of heat, he says, "Does that mean you'll marry me?"

I jerk up so fast that the entire mattress bounces. Beneath me, sprawled on the pillow, Raelan smiles.

"Are you serious?" I ask. My heart is pounding now. "Or is this a joke?"

Mother and Grandfather have been teasing Raelan about marriage since the day we returned from the little cottage in the woods. At first, he seemed petrified by the idea, and their jokes are always quick to make him flush. But right now, all I feel through our bond is warmth and joy—no fear to be found.

"Not a joke." Raelan's smile falters, giving way to a seriousness that smolders like embers in his eyes. His fingers find my cheek, and he twirls a strand of my hair around his finger. "Not now. Not right away. But after you graduate, when you're ready . . . Will you marry me?"

Without meaning to, I let out a squeal and dive at Raelan, making him grunt as I tackle him into the bedding.

His laughter is a rumble beneath my ear. "Is that a yes?"

I squeeze him as tight as I can, heart racing inside my rib cage. "Yes," I whisper. Then I sit up and press a kiss to his mouth. When I pull away, we're both smiling. "Of course I'll marry you, Raelan Ashvale."

His smile is dazzling. Our bond sings.

And I know that no matter what happens in this life, no matter the challenges that come my way, I'll always be okay.

Because I'll always have my dragon.

THE END

THANK YOU FOR READING!

Thank you so much for reading *A Witch and Her Dragon*, the first book in the Coven Crest Academy series.

If you'd like to leave a review of this book (which would be *amazing!*), you can do so by scanning the QR code below. Every review helps, and I truly appreciate it! Thank you.

If you're looking for more cozy spicy romance, make sure to pick up the next book in this fantasy academia series, *A Witch and Her Minotaur*. You can scan the code below to grab your copy!

Other Books by
Emberly Wyndham

Coven Crest Academy
A Witch and Her Dragon
A Witch and Her Minotaur

Season of the Witch
The Witch's Cottage
The Witch's Rite
The Witch's Shifter
The Witch's Spell

The Pureblood Daughter
The Pureblood Daughter
The Pureblood Princess
The Pureblood Queen

What Happens in the Hills
Little Monster

EMBERLY WYNDHAM is a writer based out of the snowy mountains of Colorado, where she lives with her husband and their many rescued animals.

To learn more and keep up-to-date with her new and upcoming releases, you can follow her on Instagram @emberlywyndham or sign up for her newsletter by scanning the QR code below.